FOREIGN AFFAIRS

FOREIGN AFFAIRS

A collection of twenty erotic stories

Edited by Antonia Adams

Published by Xcite Books Ltd – 2012
ISBN 9781908086587

Printed and bound in the UK

Cover design by Madamadari
Full cover by Sarah Ann Davies

Contents

No Running, No Petting
by Janine Ashbless

'I've got one,' says Vittor as I pause at the breakfast bar to collect the glasses he's polishing. 'Room 406. Over there – the blue shirt, by the window.'

I look across the hotel dining room, which is mostly empty now that the second sitting have finished their breakfasts. The man Vittor has indicated is drinking coffee. He's tall, and a bit older than our usual type. Late forties maybe, with swept-back silvery hair and gold-rimmed glasses. Older, but really handsome and trim. He's with a blond woman of a similar age.

'Are you sure?' I ask.

'Swedish. He's here with his wife, but she goes out all day on the coach tours while he sits and reads. I spoke with him yesterday. Gave him the old wink-and-grin. He was jumpy, but flattered.'

So he should be. Vittor is simply gorgeous: tall and broad and *built*, with big dark fuck-me eyes you could just fall into. His immaculately mowed stubble starts at his neck and ends at the crown of his head. He's mostly gay, and I'm mostly not, and we both go for straight guys.

Which is why I'm the bait.

I nod. 'He's cute.'

I check our man out later on, lingering near Room 406 with my trolley full of sugar sachets and coffee cups and tiny bottles of shampoo. As he comes out of the lift and

1

heads my way I bend over to root around in the bottom tray, my arse in the air. The hotel uniform has a tight skirt, at least the way I wear mine, with a split up the back that shows a surprising amount of thigh if you get it right. A glance over my shoulder tells me that he's looking. Staring, actually. I give him a cheeky smile and a bit of a wiggle, and he nearly collides with his doorframe.

But Vittor plans that we make our real move on the hotel roof garden. The hunter has been studying his prey. Room 406 goes up there every day after his wife's left on the coach to see another bit of Malta. He swims twenty lengths of the pool, then sits under the vine trellis and looks through papers. He makes a lot of notes and corrections. I've seen the books in his room: they look like engineering texts to me. Every couple of hours he gets up, swims some more, orders a light beer or a juice at the bar, then does some more work. That's his day until his wife gets back.

The really great thing about the roof garden is that there's almost no one there. The pool dates from before the hotel expanded and there's a much bigger one now, with whirlpools and slides, down on the terrace. And we're on the beachfront anyway: plenty of golden sand and blue Mediterranean. Who'd want to hang out by that small pool up top, all alone?

The other great thing about the roof is that no one can see in.

When I go up that day, Room 406 is already on his sun-lounger, tapping a pencil against his upper lip as he reads his papers. Vittor is waiting behind the bar, ready to lock the stair door as I put on a distraction. I do my best: I'm wearing only a tiny bikini of brilliant yellow lycra. I know how it draws the eye. I'm short, but there are deep curves to my hips and arse and waist. I shake out my long dark hair and stride over to the pool, my breasts jiggling enticingly with every step.

I can feel his eyes on me. But at first I ignore him. I slip

2

into the aquamarine water and do some lazy widths on my back, rolling every so often to show off my bum in its yellow thong. Whenever I put a hand on the pool edge and look covertly in his direction, pretending to catch my breath, Room 406 is watching me.

Then Vittor comes out and joins in, stripped down to his red trunks. We make a helluva contrast; him so big and me so little, but both of us bronzed and glistening, both young and beautiful. We giggle and play together, splashing and kissing. Maybe you remember those old signs they used to have around public poolsides – *No running, no petting, no ducking* –? Well, we break all those rules. I wriggle out of Vittor's arms and haul myself out of the pool, squealing as he chases me to try and swat my arse.

Ever seen a dog chase something past another dog? Dog number two can't help but join in. I run in a little too close to our engineer and then stumble, tripping into him: he puts out his arms to catch me. Part of him thinks he's saving me from a fall, but I know what his underlying instinct is.

'Sorry!' I gasp, landing in his lap. I've been told his English is good. 'Oh, I'm sorry! I've got you all wet!'

I've got him all hard too. It's not subtle, I know, but what man likes subtle? He's got shorts on and his legs are tanned and muscular – I just bet he cycles and skis to work at his factory or his university or whatever it is back home. But he's got a stiffy under those shorts and it's poking me.

Vittor stands a few metres back, grinning.

'That's OK,' Room 406 says hoarsely, his hands still on my waist.

'What's your name?'

'Rolf.'

'Hi, Rolf. I'm Lena. And that's Vittor.'

'He is your boyfriend?' Rolf is a bit confused, and a bit nervous.

I giggle and shrug, which is about as accurate as it gets. 'Want to join us in the pool?'

3

He hesitates, then nods. He can't stop looking at the pool water beaded on my breasts, and my nipples poking up through the yellow bikini fabric. I give him a good flash of my arse as I stand, though, and lead the way to the water's edge, barely giving him time to shed his shirt and glasses. 'First one to catch me ...' I call, and dive.

They're both in the water seconds after me: I hear the twin *whumphs* underwater as they strike. Then the chase begins. We're all three good swimmers and it's fast and fun; I twist and plunge, skimming past their fingertips and scooting between their legs. Vittor hardly has to hold back to make sure Rolf wins. But our man catches me at last and grabs me about the waist. I'm gasping and giggling. He's suddenly self-conscious all over again, not sure what prize to claim, so I plant a kiss warmly upon his lips.

Vittor steps up behind me. They're both tall enough to stand on the bottom of the pool. As Rolf and I grin at each other, Vittor puts a hand to the nape of my neck. Lycra strings tug and my bikini top falls loose, baring my breasts. I shriek, trying in vain to cover myself: it's all part of the fun.

At once, Vittor's hands circle in from behind to cup my breasts, lifting my upper torso clear of the water to present me, like a gift. He's got big hands but my tits are bigger, lush and dark-nippled. Rolf's jaw drops.

'You win,' says Vittor. 'Go on.'

Rolf puts both hands on my breasts, rubbing his palms over my nipples, testing their resilience and firmness as a good engineer should. I squeak and coo in appreciation. Then he rolls them deliciously between his fingers and pinches them until he ascertains the point at which I cry out and wrap my thighs about his, underwater, sliding my skin over his.

'Oh,' he says in that cute Swedish accent. 'You have very beautiful tits.'

'Come over to the steps,' I whisper, and as Vittor releases me I slip out from between the two of them and scull

4

backward to the shallow end of the pool where broad tiled steps ascend. I sit on one that's barely lapped by the water and pat it invitingly, shaking out my wet hair. They've followed me eagerly. Rolf sits himself down at my side; at once Vittor flanks him, grinning. To distract Rolf from feeling too nervous, I tug the bow at my hip and my bikini bottom falls away to reveal my perfectly shaved split.

'Wow,' he says, which makes me giggle. I kiss him and lay my hand on the front of his swimming shorts. His erection makes a big lump under the khaki fabric, and as I find and grasp it Vittor undoes the knot of the drawstring holding those pants up. We've gone much quieter all of a sudden: less laughing and more hungry, anticipatory glances. Rolf's breath is coming short and shallow. I work his cock out into the open.

Now that is a *fine* engineering erection. 'Wow yourself,' I say, impressed, and kneel up, stroking his length. 'Do you want to touch my pussy, Rolf?'

'I think you will get into trouble,' he says, but he slips a hand between my legs. He's a gentleman: he doesn't plunge in but strokes gently instead, and I purr.

'No trouble,' Vittor laughs. 'My father owns this hotel.' Which is why we've been getting away with this all summer, of course. Vittor is supposed to be learning the hotel trade. I'm not sure that was supposed to include fondling the guests' ball-sacs, but Rolf only quivers and makes no protest.

'Oh, I see,' he says.

'You want to see?' Vittor pulls down the front of his own trunks, manhandling his cock and balls into view. They're as beautifully built and groomed as the rest of his body. Biting his upper lip, Rolf gamely takes that thick length in his palm. I'm guessing it's the first time he's groped another man's cock. Or had a guy and a girl stroke him together – my hand is on his shaft and Vittor is caressing his balls.

'Oh this is nice.' I kiss Rolf again, squirming my tongue

into his mouth. He's so well-mannered and submissive that I want to bite him, but I hold back. 'Now kiss Vittor.'

'Oh but I don't kiss–' he protests weakly. But I feel the surge in his cock.

'Kiss him and I'll suck your dick.'

He practically lunges at Vittor's mouth.

I don't want to lose Rolf's hand on my pussy, which is warming up nicely now and getting no drier despite being out of the pool. So I back my arse up the stairs and crouch down with my head low. The guys are chasing each other's tongues very nicely as I drop to take Rolf's lovely stiff cock between my lips. He tastes of chlorine at first, then precome. I can see Vittor's hand rolling his balls just beyond my nose. I'm starting to ache with lust. My bum is pointed at the beautiful blue sky and Rolf is patting and spreading my pussy lips. Out of the corner of my eye I can see his other hand squeezing Vittor's swollen shaft.

Then Vittor comes down, grinning, to join me. Our tongues chase each other all over Rolf's cock, up and down, kissing and sucking, and he makes a noise like he's just discovered paradise. His fingers slip inside me.

I lift my head, breathless, allowing Vittor to grab the bouncing shaft all for himself. 'Will you lick my pussy for me, Rolf?' I ask.

'Yes!'

I shift astride him as he lies back on the steps. It's not comfortable for any of us, but who the hell cares? I'm still facing down his body as I settle my pussy over his mouth, so I get the best possible view: Rolf's legs splayed in the turquoise pool water and Vittor's mouth working hard on his cock.

This is what Vittor wants. He loves to suck other guys. He's better than me, I have to admit, and judging by the muffled noises Rolf is making, our engineer is likely to blow his head gasket very soon. I wriggle harder onto his face, mashing my pussy onto his lips and his thrusting tongue. I pinch my own nipples. Pleasure is building inside me. My arse-cheeks shake. Rolf eats me with great skill and I'm glad now we've picked a man of experience because he's so good that suddenly I've stopped worrying about suffocating the poor guy and I'm just grinding down on his face and squealing and coming and coming and coming …

And he's coming too because I see his hips buck and his cock ram right up into Vittor's open throat and I hear the big man choking it all down.

As soon as my legs work I get off Rolf's face and move down to meet Vittor. His lips are swollen and I kiss him greedily, searching out the flavour of the other man's semen. Vittor's cock is nearly purple with need. I wrap my fingers round his girth and stroke him off, slow and hard. He looks down at Rolf with his smouldering dark eyes as he comes, though, spraying my belly and thighs with his lovely jizz.

Rolf has gone into shock. He just lies there staring. I'm not finished, not by a long way. I want to fuck him, and watch Vittor fucking him too, but we've found it's best to leave them wanting more, first time. I lean over to brush Rolf's lips with my own.

'Tomorrow, Rolf, same time. Not here, though. Tomorrow we give you room service.'

Comrades on a Train
by Z Ferguson

We called each other Comrade Geek, an encapsulation of our mutual interest, no, passion, for Russia. We've been friends since junior high school and it was one night while watching old newsreels of the May Day Parade that we became smitten with Mother Russia. Not the thing you can pass along to fellow classmates, especially during those touchy periods of the 50s 60s and 70s, so we nursed it between ourselves, until college where we "came out" in true Geekistroika, taking language classes and making plans to visit this place that held us so.

Our real names were Nick and Donny. Nick had Russian pen pals in Bratsk since high school, and it was his letters that got me excited about joining him, actually visiting. His friends lived on a farm just outside of the city near the Kuta River. They wrote, "Come on, bring Nick with you, too Donny. Beautiful here."

We saved money like fiends. Like two AA members keeping each other steady, we constantly reminded each other not to buy too many cheeseburgers, don't buy too many T-shirts, ease off the magazines and comic books. When we went to the movies, it was always matinees. We saved a bundle. Our folks eased us across the line with surprise loving contributions.

I packed like a Marx Brother trying to leave a hotel without paying. Kept my suitcase at the door. Nick lay across my bed thumbing through an old comic, taking in my glee. His suitcase was downstairs.

Nick waited for a moment of descending emotion to wedge in a reminder.

'No practical jokes, OK? Remember. This is serious. We'll be on a commuter train. We'll be in the *country* and a country, far from the US embassy. We'll be Americans. We'll be watched. Especially no jokes about *I-Spy* or Boris Badenov.'

There went my best material. *I-Spy* was the TV show with Robert Culp and Bill Cosby that we latched on to via TV's, *Nick At Night*. We immediately saw ourselves as the Kelly and Alexander of our high school, palling around, playing jokes on each other, and doing quasi-spy like stuff. Being black, I was the Bill Cosby figure (Alexander), and Nick, was Robert Culp (Kelly).

Our pranks were private and relatively harmless.

My favourite was the Playboy Pinup I affixed to the class map early, that unrolled with the map of Russia, when Nick gave his world report in class. My favourite prank he played on me was when he hid my jock just before gym, on the day the guys played the girls in softball. Well-developed girl athletes in tight white blouses, and tight blue shorts, and me with no jock, was a volatile combination. Especially when I batted, and my crush, Becky Brame, was in full squat, her shorts retreating between her thighs. Well, that did it. I responded in full. Linda was pitching away from me, anyway, throwing wild with one hand on her mouth. I had to take my base. The guys hooted and the girls gave appreciative applause. Bonnie on first base who looked like a young Penny Marshall with the wit to match, stood next to me saying nothing, then in perfect comedic timing whispered, 'You're supposed to leave the bat at home plate.'

We kept at each other in stitches and on the lookout for each other all the time. Which was why Nick was insistent, 'I swear we won't be able to phone the US embassy for days or anything ...'

I held a boy Scout pledge posture. 'No jokes, no pranks. I promise.' I even showed him both hands, fingers uncrossed.

The train was, as I had envisioned, a huge, bellowing, lumbering giant with red barrel-sized, pistons on either side. Nick smiled looking her over. 'This is the last of her breed. They're going high-speed soon.'

We entered and found seats in a compartment with sliding doors, the seats facing each other. 'Cool,' I said, 'just like *Dr No.*' I opened and closed the doors.

'We won't be alone in here,' Nick said as he sat next to me, 'this is a commuter train. We'll be packed in after two stops.' He leaned back. 'Prepare to embrace the citizenry of Mother Russia.'

Other people got on board, chattering in deep Russian, far beyond my remedial knowledge. I relied on Nick as I watched him listen and occasionally smile. Russian always sounded like voice tapes played backwards to me. I picked out different people as they took their seats.

'What's he saying?'

Nick smiled. 'He's complaining to his friend about the government.'

'Ah.'

I noticed two attractive women talking as they were glancing at us. One was holding what looked like an intense conversation. The other girl giggled.

'What about them?'

Nick grinned and leaned into me. 'She is telling her girlfriend, her new boyfriend is almost too big for her. She says he stretched her like a leg in a stocking.' Then Nick blushed. The two women, wide-eyed, continued their talks holding newspapers over their lips. I chuckled.

'I think you just got made.'

At the next stop a woman got on with two kids. They could've been five and six. A boy and a girl, both with brown, almost black hair and wide unblinking eyes stared at us as they entered the cabin. The woman was blonde with straight shoulder-length hair, and a pleasant oval face that seemed to await a smile. Large eyes like the kids. She clutched her coat together and sat, crossing her ankles. The pale skin of her ample calves showed just above her white socks and sensible black shoes.

She was pretty. Young. A face still maturing. Petite nose. Lips without lipstick, but full. Her hair was in wispy blonde bangs cut along her eyebrows which were brown and I bet pretty expressive, under the right circumstances. Apple cheeks.

I smiled at her. She smiled back quickly, as her kids leaned on her, not taking their eyes off us. I noticed how her pale hands clutched that cloth coat. I wondered what lay beneath.

As the train lurched, the boy asked her something in Russian, and she nodded. They rose from their seats and ran to the door, sliding it open. Nick talked to her in Russian. Her face exploded with discovery. She shot back to him a multitude of phrases that I caught in gleanings, about our trip, friendship and Russia.

'Nick,' said Nick and encircled my shoulder. 'He is Donny.'

She said, 'Donny,' then nodded. The kids returned and she told them about us. Then they seemed to be OK with roughhousing, now that Mom's OK with the strangers. I watched as they romped and figured they must make this trip often. Nick tapped me on the shoulder. 'Her name is Natasha.'

I smiled wide.

Nick punched my shoulder. *'Don't start.'*

I grinned and watched the scenery as it zipped by. We were getting out into the country. I thought about Natasha and the kids and wondered how often they made this trip. I mean commuting is one thing, but ...

The kids were really wrestling. The girl was holding her own. Then Mom, spat some Russian at them. They stopped, stood and looked up at her, hands crossed in front. I smiled. Yeah, don't mess with Mom, I thought remembering my own encounters, she'll put you off this train in a minute. They looked back at us and took their seats, while Natasha kept talking to them.

'She said if they're good, she'll let them have ice cream,' Nick said.

I nodded. 'Bribery. Even here in Russia. I'm shocked.'

I watched cattle and workers and farmhouses and realized that I was thousands of miles away. Over five thousand. And in another country. And not even its capital. The scenery and the trip started to hit me. I knew no one except for Nick and whoever I was going to meet when we got to the farm.

The farm. I imagined I'd be sleeping on a mattress stuffed with hay, then in the morning, naked, in a field, pumping water for a bath. What have I done?

'You OK?' asked Nick, 'you look a little worried. You can't be homesick. This is our trip. Here we are.'

I slapped the seat. 'You're right. Log in memories.'

I looked at Natasha who was reading quietly to the kids. Her coat was open and revealed a flowered dress that looked to have had quite a few washings, but fit her well. I noticed her impressive breasts that served as the kids' pillows. They listened, eyes opening wide at certain passages. We were no longer the centre of attention. I nudged Nick.

'What's she reading to them?'

'Harry Potter.'

Nick stood. 'I'm gonna check the dining car. Want a Coke or something?'

'Bring me something Russian,' I replied.

Nick smiled, 'How about Opecka?'

I smiled. 'That sounds pretty local. What is it?'

'It's this lemon-lime drink they have over here. Kinda

cloudy looking, but they drink it by the gallon, cold.'

'I'll go for that.'

The next stop practically emptied the train, but Natasha and brood stayed put. I was glad. I was used to them and apparently, they to us. I wasn't ready to ride the rest of the way with say, a scowling old woman, retired KGB or a member of the Red Guard. I watched the departed passengers on the platform greeting their friends, business associates and loved ones. One couple seemed really glad to see each other. Her hand reached around him and got a handful of his butt. Nice, I thought.

The kids broke from Harry Potter's spell and got restless. Mom called them together and like a basketball coach laying out a last-minute game plan, she talked to them. They nodded vigorously, then ran to the door, slid it open, then closed it, and barrelled down the aisle. Ice cream time, I guessed.

Natasha smiled at me and crossed her leg. Nice full leg. She shook her hair and blew her bangs up from her face and giggled. I raised my eyebrows. What is going on here? She brought out a *People* magazine. I laughed. Even in Russian, I recognized the typeface and the layout. Not to mention comrade Drew Barrymore on the cover. I decided to read, too, rummaging through my bag, when she said, 'Denzel.' I looked up and she was smiling wide and laughing. 'Denzel, yes?' She held up the magazine.

I looked at the picture. Yes, it was Denzel Washington, but I couldn't believe she thought I was him, though the likeness was mentioned at my school.

This is too easy, but I decided to play it honest. Whatever kind of mischief that could evolve from me pretending to be a movie star probably wasn't worth a month in the Gulag or worse. I shook my head, 'No.' But she patted the seat next to her.

'Denzel,' she said, again.

I sighed and sat next to her. She was scented nicely in

13

lavender and peppermint, and I detected a hint of Ivory soap. She touched my cheek, and I touched her hand. Then she turned back and flipped the pages.

'Jackson? Noo.' she said, then frowned making me frown, turned the pages again to Morgan Freeman. 'Morgan ... uhhh ... no ...' Then she laughed.

I got it. She was comparing my face to stars, and Denzel was the closest match. I touched her thigh and she nodded, handing me the magazine. I turned the pages, until I found Madonna (easily done in *People*). I held the magazine next to her face.

'Madonna? Hmmm ...' I touched her forehead, and hair. She smiled, barely containing her amusement. 'Ohh ... no ...' She frowned.

I turned the pages until I got to Naomi Campbell and held up the picture. She shrieked in gales of laughter, waving her hands, gesticulating like Naomi in one of her hissy fits. I laughed and said, 'no ...'

We turned the pages together, laughing and snuggling closer. I loved watching her full mouth, and her breasts that bounced and shook cradled by her large bra. She watched me, radiating a warm smile that I felt surround my body. I liked her, I thought as I turned the page. There was Anna Kournikova, Tennis star. I smiled. 'Anna?' I said, and nodded. 'Yes.'

She looked at the picture, then at me with a startling gaze of appreciation. I thought I'd misstepped, but she kissed my cheek, looked at the picture, then kissed me again, full on the mouth. I must've done good.

I put my hand on her thigh and felt her soft skin. She purred – I had never heard a woman purr before – then giggled as we kissed again. This time, our tongues touched and danced slowly with each other. My hand moved up her thigh pulling the light fabric of her dress with it. I looked into her eyes and she grabbed my cock and squeezed, drawing a moan from me I thought I didn't have the will to expel. She stopped and patted my thigh, got up and closed the window blinds.

Oh man, it was my turn to sigh as she kissed my neck, and I moved my hand farther, as she draped one leg over mine, and opening her thighs for my advancing fingers. I touched the crotch of her panties. She shook as I stroked the fabric feeling her moisture ooze through. She shifted so I could slide her panty aside and ease my fingers into her. She breathed hard into my face, her breasts bouncing as I stroked her. She grabbed my face for a hard kiss then leaned back, as I fingered her to a rousing come, while she held my prick.

Then, she pulled me up and to her, unbuckling my belt, unsnapping my jeans and pulling them down. She sank her mouth onto my hard cock and I saw flashes as she ran her skilled tongue along the ridge, and flicked the slit of the head. I crumbled like a building in an earthquake, as she sucked and pulled my ass closer to her with her free hand, her finger sliding deep inside my rectum. 'Jesus,' I cried as she sucked, then pushed me back and raised her legs, to slip off her panties.

I moved between them and slid my cock into her deep, feeling our pubic hairs mingle and our hips grind in deep coupling. She nodded sharply and I pumped her in long, hard thrusts. She raised her head and watched in a lustful gaze, as my cock slid in and out of her pussy. She grabbed my head and let her hips fly into me in uncontrolled fury, while drumming my back. She expelled and in my ear, whispered things in Russian that sounded vivid, guttural, dirty and wanton. I responded with a come that felt like it was flooding her inside and deflating my balls. We thrust into each other until my cock fell limp and swung dripping, to her amusement. She kissed me and touched my dick.

'James Bond,' she said and laughed.

We reassembled ourselves smiling, and touching as much of each other as we could before we were fully dressed. She put her panties in her purse, which aroused me, knowing the rest of the trip, regardless of how far, she'd be naked underneath that dress. We sat next to each other and kissed before she directed me back to my seat across from her. I chuckled as we sat looking at each other. She crossed her legs and read her magazine.

The kids returned. Nick returned with a couple of sandwiches and two bottles of Opecka. They looked at us. The kids got back on the seat with Natasha, each holding a cone.

'You know the kids attend an advanced school. They told me about it. Interesting. You and Natasha get along?'

'Kinda. I don't think she speaks English at all, but we managed.'

'Good.'

The train came to a stop, Natasha and the kids got up and gathered their stuff to leave. I watched Natasha's face as she rose. She gave me a small, sly smile. I smiled back, and she pushed the kids out of the compartment, off the train to the station. I watched her on the platform rustling the kids up the walkway. Nick watched me. 'What was that about?'

'She thought I was Denzel Washington,' I said, 'but it didn't last.'

'Well I'm sure she didn't expect Denzel Washington to be riding a commuter train to a farm in Russia. Hungry?'

'Yeah.' I took a bite of sandwich and a swig of Opecka. 'Hey this is good. This Opecka.

Nick smiled. Opecka is Fresca in Russian.'

'Asshole.'

Nick said our destination was just a few miles away. I sat. If I said I was watching the scenery, I'd be lying. I was replaying and replaying my dalliance with Natasha. I decided not to tell Nick. He'd be worried about pregnancy and international relations the rest of the trip. I wondered what Natasha's rest of the day was like. Would she think of me, is she thinking about me, now, like I'm thinking about her? I was an idiot. I didn't even get her phone number or mailing address, even when things were just getting cosy. Was it the single mother thing? Would I have done different had she been single?

The train made a couple more stops. A few folks got on but no one of note. An older couple watched us and smiled as they moved past our seat. I looked at Nick then back out the glass as the train slowly continued.

Nick gave me a shove. 'Hey. What's up? Ground control to Major Don.'

'Just thinking about dating and stuff.'

'Oh, Natasha, huh? The one that got away? Well, don't worry. My friends promise we won't be latched to the farm. We'll hit a couple of clubs in the nearby city. Most of the kids speak English, too, and love Americans. You might even meet someone.' I looked at Nick, then back out the window.

The train arrived at Kuta River Station. Nick signalled this was our stop. We gathered our backpacks. I followed Nick down the aisle to the exit, onto the platform, where stood his pen pals, Ivan and Ingrid.

'Hello, my friend,' said Ivan, giving Nick a big hug. Ingrid gave him a kiss. I thought about the *People* magazine game with Natasha. A nice couple. Ivan looking like a Russian version of a young Tom Hanks and his wife Ingrid, tall and willowy with short, spiked blonde hair. A face like Uma Thurman's.

Ivan shook my hand. 'You must be Donny. Lots I heard about you. Good friend.' Ivan looked around. 'Ah here she is. Someone you to meet.'

Over walked Natasha, minus the kids. I recoiled from the shock, rendered speechless. Nick wore a huge grin.

'Dude, aren't you going to introduce yourself?'

I stepped to her and outstretched my hand, while inside my jeans, further outstretching was taking place. Natasha

17

smiled, and took my hand.

'Hello again, Donny. Nice to meet you. Nick told me all about you.'

'Waitaminute. You speak English?' I looked over her shoulder. 'Where are the kids?'

'My *niece and nephew* are with their parents, my dear. You have me all to yourself.'

I looked at Nick. He said, 'gotcha.'

Ivan stepped in and encircled us both.

'We have limited rooms, but I understand no inconvenience if you two together …'

I smiled. 'No. No inconvenience at all.'

Lucky Lucy
by Jenna Bright

The warm sun soothed the tense muscles in my back from the moment I stepped out of the car from the airport. Miles from home, in the sultry Tuscan air; away from London, away from real life. Away from Tony.

And staring at the most beautiful villa I'd ever seen outside the movies.

'Lucy!' Maria hurried down the villa's stone steps, looking every inch the Italian film star, from the bright red scarf wrapped in her midnight hair to the oversized sunglasses that hid her eyes. 'You're here!'

I submitted to the inevitable European kisses on both cheeks, then stepped back. 'Of course I'm here. It's your wedding weekend. Where on earth else would I be?' Even though I hated weddings, right then. Maria gave me a sympathetic smile, and I rolled my eyes. 'Don't look at me like that. I'm fine.'

'No you're not,' Maria said, blunt as ever. 'But you will be. Come on. There's someone waiting to see you.'

She tucked her hand through my arm, motioning to the driver to follow with my case, and led me up the steps into the incredible opulence of her father's villa.

I'd known at university that Maria's family were rich. It had just taken a while to sink in exactly *how* rich. And by then it didn't matter. She was just Maria. My best friend. The one who put up with me all through our drunken, promiscuous university days. Maria was the one I could curl

19

up with, glass of wine in hand, and confess my most embarrassing escapades, most wild excesses. The one who gave me my nickname, Lucky Lucy, laughing over a bottle of red with Jamie, our third housemate, and saying, 'Because you always have the best men after you, whenever we go out. You always get lucky!'

Jamie had just winked, I remembered, and run his hand up my thigh. 'Feeling lucky?' he'd whispered when Maria went to open another bottle.

But then we left university. Jamie went travelling, I met Tony, and Maria met John. We grew up.

And now Maria was marrying John, and I would be there, sober and well behaved, to hold her veil and make sure her lipstick hadn't smudged. Because I loved Maria. And even John was ... well, he was lovely, actually. And he adored Maria. Which put him far above Tony, swanning around London with his intern – diamond on her finger not mine – after I spent three years trying to please him.

I followed Maria through the imposing front door into the shady cool of the hallway. It was about the same size as my flat in Hendon.

But magnificent as the villa surely was, my attention was quickly drawn away from the majesty and pomp of Maria's wedding venue, to the man descending the sweeping staircase.

Jamie.

'Told you you'd be OK,' Maria murmured in my ear, before taking a step back.

Jamie took the last few steps at a jog, his smile wide and wicked, his dark eyes every bit as seductive as I remembered. I drew in a deep breath, feeling my nipples tighten under my sundress, as an image flashed across my mind. A memory; the last time I saw Jamie, just before graduation. Sprawled across my bed, tangled in the white sheets, afternoon sunlight playing on his golden skin as he ran his sure, certain hands up my sides, from my hips, over

20

the curve of my waist, up to my breasts …

But it was just a memory. I wasn't that person any more. Was I?

As if he could hear my thoughts, Jamie grinned at me, crossing the hallway to wrap his arms too tightly around my middle, hauling me tight against his chest.

'Hello Lucky Lucy,' he whispered in my ear, and I felt my knickers soak through at the desire in his voice.

God, I was in so much trouble. But I couldn't help but grin back.

Maria had planned a rehearsal dinner for that evening. I thought for a moment that Jamie planned to follow me up to my room to help me get changed, but instead he let me go, squeezed my hip, and promised to be waiting for me downstairs.

'But don't be long,' he said. 'We've got catching up to do.'

Maria showed me my room with a knowing grin, which I ignored, and left me to shower and change in peace. As I rifled through my suitcase, relief filled me. Thank God I was such a compulsive over-packer. My planned, sedate sundress would never do for tonight's dinner now I knew Jamie was here.

Instead, I pulled out a tissue-thin, azure blue and cream skirt. Perfectly respectable, unless you looked close enough to realise that it was almost see through.

I picked up some clean underwear, the boring, sensible, white cotton stuff Tony had always liked. Then I looked again at the skirt.

A skirt like that didn't deserve boring underwear.

I shoved the knickers back in my case.

Pulling on a matching azure halter-neck, I fluffed my wavy blonde hair over my shoulders, applied just enough make-up to make me glow, and strapped my feet into high, shiny silver sandals. A spritz of perfume and I felt irresistible. I felt Lucky again.

'Now, there's a sight for sore eyes,' Jamie said as I made my way down the stairs, his gaze running across my body, lingering at the point where my skirt pulled across the top of my thighs before flaring out.

My heart thumped time with my steps as I made my way down the rest of the stairs. 'You were waiting for me?'

Jamie wrapped his arms around my waist again, tight and wonderful. 'All my life.' One hand wandered a little lower than might have been considered appropriate for public, but this was Jamie. It was just who he was.

I smiled at him, happy to be with my friend again. 'So, have you sussed out where we can get a drink yet?'

Jamie raised an eyebrow, as if to say, "have you forgotten who you're dealing with here?" 'Follow me, my lady.'

Maria had set one of the front reception areas up as a bar, complete with bartender. She gave me a knowing smile as Jamie and I grabbed drinks and curled up on a window seat, looking out over the beautifully manicured gardens, but she had too many relatives to entertain to interrupt us. The window seat was tiny, and my legs were crammed right up against the thin, black fabric of Jamie's dress trousers. It was strange to see him out of jeans and T-shirts, but he sure did scrub up well.

'So,' he said, resting one hand on my leg, his fingers warm through the thin material. 'Tell me what happened.'

I blinked at him. 'What happened with me? What happened with you? I thought you were off travelling the world for the foreseeable future.'

Jamie shrugged, and the action made his fingers curl slightly into the flesh of my thigh. I bit my lip at the pressure, and crossed my legs.

'There's only so much world to see,' he said, his thumb stroking my inner thigh. 'Besides, Maria called and asked me to come back for the wedding. Said she needed her best man.'

I tilted my head and gave him the look that always used to make him give up his secrets, when we were students. Apparently it still worked, because he laughed lightly and said, 'Oh, all right then. She told me that Tony was an idiot, you were single, and I should come home and cheer you up.'

Just hearing that cheered particular parts of my body up immensely. Jamie had only ever had one way of improving my mood.

Maybe I *could* be Lucky Lucy again. Just for one night.

'So basically, you came all the way to Italy because of me.'

A smile started to spread across his lips, and his thumb inched further up. 'Maybe.'

'All the way from … New Zealand, was it?' He nodded, and my smile grew. 'Just to get me naked.'

'Perhaps.' His thumb stroked a little higher, almost to the point where my thighs met at the top. I glanced out across the room, but no one was paying us any attention; they were all too taken with Maria, and John, and the free bar.

'Halfway across the world, just to sleep with me again.' I met his eyes as I spoke, and watched them go dark as he answered, '*God*, yes.' Finally, finally, he shifted his thumb down between my legs and the pressure on my clit through the fabric was intensified by my crossed legs, keeping everything tight and tense. I shuddered involuntarily at the feeling. It had been far, far too long since any fingers other than my own had touched me there.

But before I could revel in the experience properly, Maria clapped her hands in the doorway, and summoned us all in to dinner. Jamie gave me a regretful smile, and pulled his hand away, grabbing mine and tugging me to my feet.

'Better get a good meal in you,' he whispered as he led me into the dining room. 'You're going to need your energy for tonight.'

I don't know who was in charge of the seating arrangements that night, but it clearly wasn't Maria, as

23

Jamie and I were seated at opposite ends of the table. I itched, under my skin, all through the meal, just waiting to get him alone and inside me again.

It had been years, and right then it felt like forever. Jamie was, hands down, the best fuck I'd ever had. He knew what I liked, had taken the time to learn, to ask, to question, through long summer afternoons in my bedroom, or cold winter nights in front of the fire in the lounge of our little shared house, long after Maria had gone to bed. I could remember, in exquisite detail, the way his tongue swirled around my clit. The way his fingers felt, curling into me, like they'd been so close to doing sitting on that window seat. The way he bent me over the sofa in front of the fire and fucked me until I almost passed out with the pleasure.

I knew, without a doubt, that one night with Jamie would shake me out of the funk I'd been in ever since Tony left.

But apparently, I was going to have to wait.

As we finished up the dessert, all surely wondering why we had to sit through speeches at the rehearsal dinner *and* the wedding, Maria appeared over my left shoulder and said, 'I'm so sorry.'

'What on earth for?'

Maria winced. 'John wants to take Jamie out with the other lads for a last minute stag do in the town tonight.'

I glared at her. 'Tell him my need is greater.'

'I would, but …' Maria bit her lip. 'Turns out my cousin Stacey's planned a surprise girlie night in for me here, too. I need you there.'

Maria hates her cousin Stacey. Chances were, the evening would be an orgy of pink drinks and painting each others' nails. Maria and I would both rather be in the town drinking with the lads, I was sure. But apparently that wasn't an option.

'You owe me,' I said, grudgingly.

Maria flashed me a smile. 'I'll make it up to you. I promise.'

I looked up across the table, and saw my own frustration mirrored in Jamie's face.

Tomorrow, he mouthed at me, before he followed John out the door.

Apparently, the resurrection of Lucky Lucy was going to have to wait another day.

The morning of the wedding dawned bright and warm, the Tuscan sun beating down on the flagstones of the courtyard where the guests congregated, sipping bucks fizz and eating canapé sized breakfast pastries.

It was the biggest day of my best friend's life, and all I could think about was my own problems.

It had seemed so simple last night. One more night as Lucky Lucy. But in the morning light… Could I really do it? Could I really be that person again?

'Where's Jamie?' Maybe if I saw him, I'd know the right thing to do.

'I think he's helping John get ready this morning,' Maria said, emerging from her bathroom. 'They seem to have become fast friends over too much grappa in the tavernas last night.'

Rifling through one of the deep drawers of her antique dresser, Maria pulled out a shiny silver gift bag. 'I've got a present for you.'

'Isn't it traditional for the groom to give presents to the bridesmaids in the toasts?' I sat down on the bed, curious.

'You'll get one of those, too. This is just from me to you.' She gave me a mischievous smile as she sat beside me and handed over the bag. 'Besides, you'll need it before then.'

Eyebrows raised, I pulled out an exquisite, obviously expensive, lace corset, with suspender straps and silk stockings. I blinked. It was beautiful. And far, far sexier than anything I'd worn in the last three years. I loved it.

Then I realised … 'No knickers?'

25

Maria shrugged. 'I didn't think you'd need them. Besides ...' She wrapped her arms around my shoulders. 'I think it's time to find the old Lucy again, don't you? The one who was always far too good for an idiot like Tony, anyway.'

And suddenly, I felt like that Lucy again. The one who knew how to cut loose, how to have fun, how to be herself, not the Lucy someone else wanted. And I knew there was no way in hell I was waiting until the party was over to get Jamie inside me.

Lucky Lucy was back.

'I think you're absolutely right,' I said, hugging Maria. 'Thank you.'

Maria chuckled. 'Well, now I'm going to be old and married, I figure I'll have to live vicariously through you.'

'That's not going to be a problem,' I promised.

The wedding ceremony itself was held in the villa's extensive gardens, the sultry scent of wild flowers floating in on the breeze from the meadows beyond. Maria looked stunning, of course, and I'm sure the ceremony was beautiful. But to be honest, from the moment I followed her down the grassy aisle, all I could see was Jamie, dark hair curling over the collar of his suit jacket, his hands in his pockets as he stood, pulling the fabric of his trousers tight over that fantastic arse. Then, when he spotted me, the wicked, wanting smile he gave me as his eyes took in my strapless lavender dress.

I smiled back, as serenely as I could manage. Just wait until he got a look at what was underneath.

The vows and such are a complete blur in my memory. Instead, I remember the way my stockings brushed together as I shifted, and the feel of my bare bottom under the satin of my dress. How naughty I felt, standing knickerless up at the altar. The way my pussy moistened as Jamie's eyes lingered on the very low neckline of my dress. The way the sun made my skin so warm, and my mood so languorous. The daydream I indulged in of dragging Jamie off to that meadow of wildflowers, lying him down and climbing onto his beautiful hard cock and riding him for hours in the sunshine.

But mostly, I remember the moment I spotted the summer house.

It sat a decent distance away from the main house, far enough, I was sure, that you couldn't see it from any of the reception rooms. It was on the edge of the meadow, slightly hidden by a row of Cypress trees. And yes, OK, it had huge windows on all four sides, making up most of the walls, but probably no one would come looking for us, right?

It was perfect for a Tuscan afternoon rendezvous. And, I told myself as Maria slipped a ring onto John's hand, it was exactly what the old Lucy, Maria's Lucy, Jamie's Lucy – Lucky Lucy – would do.

Of course, Maria was still my best friend and I wasn't about to ruin her special day by absconding half way through the proceedings. So I posed and smiled for the photos, made polite chit chat in the receiving line, and pushed my food around my plate, all with Jamie's gaze heating my blood from across the room.

But by the time I'd swallowed a couple of mouthfuls of chocolate torte and considerably more wine, I was done. There were only the speeches left to go and, honestly, I'd heard enough of those at the rehearsal dinner.

Maria was off circulating with her guests, so I couldn't ask for her blessing. But since she'd given me the damn corset, I was pretty sure I had it. I politely and demurely excused myself from the top table – Tony would have been so proud – then caught Jamie's eye and smiled.

That was all it took. As I let myself out of the side door, I already knew he was following me. And as the door clunked shut behind us, taking the noise and the chatter of the wedding party with it, his hand wrapped around my waist, warm and possessive and lovely.

'Where are we going?' he asked, tugging me against his side.

I flashed him my best flirtatious smile. 'You'll see.'

'Will I also see you naked?'

I thought about the corset. It would be criminal to waste the corset. 'Maybe not entirely.'

Jamie shrugged. 'I'll take what I can get, since I guess we don't have too long before we're missed.'

I nodded. 'I hope you still work well under pressure.'

'Just try me.'

It only occurred to me as I led Jamie up the wooden steps to the summer house that it might be locked. Luckily, it seemed that Lucky Lucy's powers still held, because not only did the door open easily under my hand, but what we found inside was just perfect for a lazy afternoon's seduction.

I looked up at Jamie and watched the smile spread across his face as he took in the daybed in the middle of the little wooden room, piled high with cushions and throws. The stand full of umbrellas and stack of board games on top of the cupboard that sat either side of the door suggested that the summer house was more usually used as a wet weather shelter.

The sun still blazed down outside. No one would be coming here to escape from the rain today. And I had a much better use for the room.

Jamie gave a little shove to the small of my back and said, 'Get on the bed. I've been dreaming of stripping this dress off you all day.'

I obeyed, a frisson of heat thrumming through my blood as I imagined his reaction to Maria's gift. I leant back on my hands, and Jamie prowled forward, his hands on the zip at the side of my dress almost before he was standing between my legs.

The lavender fabric fell away from my body, and Jamie groaned as the lacy cups of the corset came into view, holding my breasts high and full. In one swift moment, he had me pressed back against the pile of cushions. I sank into the softness, letting my head fall back as Jamie's clever mouth kissed its way down my throat to the curve of my breasts, then tugged down the cups to let my nipples free.

A moan escaped my mouth as he sucked the first one in, swirling his tongue around the sensitive nub, pulling too much blood into it until it throbbed. Then he let it go with a pop, grinned at me, and repeated the move on the other side.

My breasts ached from the attention, even as he flicked his tongue over the too sensitive flesh, sending shudders of pleasure through my body, directly down to my clit. If we'd had the time, I'd have let him carry on all day. As it was …

'You know, this outfit gets even better further down.' My words were breathy, desperate, and Jamie raised an eyebrow at them.

'Does it now?' His hands swept down over the lace covering my sides, making me shiver, and pushed the dress over my hips. 'Oh, yes,' he breathed, as the lavender fabric puddled at my feet, revealing the full glory of my corset, stockings, no knickers combination. 'It really, really does.'

Dropping to his knees between my legs, Jamie wrapped his arms around my thighs, kissing the exposed skin just above my stockings. He ran his tongue up to my hip, tracing the line where my leg meets my body, then swapped sides, tasting the skin of my other leg. And in the middle, my pussy throbbed, ached, soaked through and desperate for attention.

'Please,' I begged, and he laughed against the curls covering my mound.

'Patience,' he said, but he started to kiss lower, his mouth mostly closed against my pussy, just enough pressure to make me need more, urgently.

Then, finally, his tongue darted out, parting my lips,

tasting me for the first time in years. 'You're still so sweet,' he murmured, and the vibration of his voice made all the muscles in my stomach tense.

There were no more words, after that. Jamie's arms clamped around my legs, holding me tight up against his mouth. His clever, loving tongue swirled around my clit the same way it had my nipples, sucking it into his mouth until I had to pull a cushion to my mouth to keep from screaming. And when he stopped, it was only to dive deeper, his tongue plunging inside me, fucking me with all the dedication he would use with his cock. My body pulsed with the need to come, spiralling higher and higher until I thought I would break. Then, without warning, Jamie released my legs, sweeping his tongue up along the length of me, back to my clit. I gasped at the sensation, and he curled his fingers inside me, pressing up and in until I screamed into my cushion, my whole body arching up off the bed as I clenched and pulsed around his hand.

'Oh God,' I mumbled against the fabric as I sank back down.

I heard Jamie laugh as he pulled away, and when I managed to open my eyes to peek, I realised he was still fully dressed. He glanced away, out of the window, and said, 'Maria's coming. Think we might have been a little longer than planned.'

He held up my dress, and I looked at it in confusion. How could he possibly expect me to stand up, let alone dress myself, after that? 'What about you?' I asked.

Jamie's smile was wicked. 'Trust me, I expect you to make it up to me later.'

I grinned. 'I will.'

Lucky Lucy was back. And she loved weddings.

New Orleans When It Rains
by Maxim Jakubowski

Some cities smell of diesel fumes, others of cats, and then there is the smell of the sea, or mown grass, or the sharp odour of curry cooking endlessly in basement flats, or again the acrid combination of industrial waste and low-hanging fog.

New Orleans smells of spices, the humid twang of nearby Mississippi bayous and swamps and, in early morning, the unpleasant waft of stale beer on the Bourbon Street sidewalk following yet another night of drunkenness and minor-league bacchanalia before the high speed hoses complete their work and sweep away the detritus of the previous evening's boisterous excesses. Mardi Gras adds yet another dimension of smells and spills and noise, or the Jazz Festival or New Year's Eve when it can take almost a quarter of an hour to walk through the massed crowds from Jackson Square to the corner of Toulouse and Bourbon. A cocktail like no other.

Even the music rising from bar to bar on each side of the street, battling for your attention, blues against jazz, show-tunes fighting hard rock, Broadway schmaltz wrestling with tentative folk melodies, it all seems to hold yet more fragrant promise of sensuality unbound.

There is no place like New Orleans.

And, year after year, I kept on coming back.

It was a city that talked to me, whispered to me from faraway through to my European shores of melancholy and I

31

would treat myself again to the long plane journey, with the customary stop-over in Chicago or Atlanta (and once Raleigh-Durham) to catch the right connection, arriving at Louis Armstrong Airport as night was falling, bone tired but my mind on fire, my senses waking with a sense of delight to the smells and sounds of the French Quarter.

Some cities are male. Others are distinctly feminine. New Orleans was assuredly the latter.

The way it tempted you, caressed you, kissed your emotions, licked your soul, fed you with sumptuous plates of jambalaya, warmed your stomach with okra-sticky but succulent bowls of gumbo, and its raw oysters once split open made you think of a woman's cunt as you sucked on them with undisguised greed and swallowed their juice and spongy flesh in one swift and easy movement.

It was a city I had brought women to.

Often.

In a spacious 12th floor room at the Monteleone I had undressed a preacher's wife from the Baton Rouge suburbs I had met on the Internet. She had driven down in her SUV to join me and timidly tapped on my shoulder while I examined the shelves at Beckham's on Decatur, where you could once often find some interesting first editions amongst the morass of worthless book club editions. That was where we had arranged to meet. I turned round.

'Martin?'

'Hi ...'

She was voluptuous, a lovely face, somewhat bigger than I had expected from the photos she had sent me but I knew those curves and the demure clothes she was wearing concealed terribly guilty urges and a determination to be bad.

Once in the hotel bedroom I stripped her and buried my face between her high but generous breasts, licked and bit her nipples to gauge her reaction while I cupped her cunt with my hands. She was terribly wet. Her kisses tasted of

32

cotton candy.

When I undressed, she looked down at my half tumescent cock and exclaimed that it was so big. Which warmed my heart of course, although I knew it wasn't particularly so, just that her husband's (she had known no other man, she had once confessed) was smaller.

I drowned in the folds of her flesh, my thrusts inside the cauldron of her innards setting off concentric waves of shimmering movement across the surface of her skin.

We fucked ceaselessly, between walks through the Vieux Carré in search of beignets and praline-led sustenance. She only had two free days before family duties required her to be home.

'Where have you told him you are?' My finger inserting itself into her anus, feeling her squirm with added pleasure.

'It's not important. I don't want to talk about him.' Her regal thighs clinching me in a mighty vice, her hand roaming hungrily across my balls, nail extensions dangerously grazing me.

Even though she lived barely a couple of hours away, it was only her third time ever in New Orleans. A city of sin that represented everything that was evil in the eyes of her social set. Which made her brief affair with me even more of a thing of the night, and a temptation her frustrations had been unable to resist. Meeting a foreigner with a quaint accent, for purposes of the flesh, in such a den of iniquity somehow felt right. We would never meet again after those frantic two days but before we lost contact I heard that she had left her husband and shacked up with a pharmaceutical salesman who was happy to fuck her once a day at least unlike the monthly diet her religious fanatic of a man had restricted himself to, and always in the dark at that. I had, inadvertently lit the fire and set her on the right (or wrong) path.

Then there was Natalia, a Lithuanian waif and single parent who lived in Delft in Holland, who had been a regular

33

fuck buddy back in Europe. My evocative stories of New Orleans and its sweet craziness had convinced her to accompany me across the Atlantic. She made it a regular habit to meet men she came across in chat rooms and I knew all too well I was not her only sexual companion (I was aware of the Korean business student she had been giving Russian lessons to; the English engineering export rep; the married car dealer who wanted to leave his wife and live with her; and the many others she had no doubt omitted to inform me about).

She fell in love with New Orleans. The hotel I had booked us into upgraded us to a suite and she wandered naked and free across the lush carpet, the angle below her pert white buttocks always just that touch apart, a sheer invitation to grab her and do my worst. She was playful, capricious, deliciously wanton. No post-coital sadness for Natalia: the moment I'd withdraw from her following each frantic fuck, she was up and about, eager to go out and sample more French Quarter atmosphere, tip-toeing away from the bed on her heels towards the open window and looking out from the balcony in the buff, attracting whistles and cries from the street beneath on most occasions, and then rushing back with a cheeky smile on her face at having exposed herself and straddling me, or standing above my still exhausted form on the bed, her legs obscenely spread, affording me a voyeuristic close-up of her still wet cunt and her luxuriant and curly dark pubic thatch.

One morning, she had arranged for a local pen pal to pick her up from the hotel in his car. We shook hands, both introduced to each other as just friends. He was supposed to take her for a drive along the nearby bayous, but I suspect they spent most of that morning in his bed. No matter, it gave me a handful of hours to rest from the fucking.

In my memory, Natalia and New Orleans went hand in hand in perfect harmony. The fragrance of southern flowers, magnolias et al and the intoxicating smell of her cunt. The delicate curlicues of wrought steel of the Crescent City balconies and architecture and the cheerful curve of her snubbed nose and the gap between her front teeth. The Queen of the blow jobs who always insisted on going pantie-less when we went out for walks or to eat. I'm still in touch with her. She finally gave in and married the car dealer and had a son with him although it hasn't worked out and they are now separated.

Another bittersweet New Orleans memory is the Finnish interpreter from Seattle. High cheekbones, square jaw and a monstrous tease it took me ages to finally get into bed proper (days of foreplay and petting until she finally agreed that having spent an eternity in bed naked together, we should finally fuck …). She knew of my attraction to New Orleans and suggested I join her there; she was in town for a conference and had a large room in one of the massive impersonal hotels on Canal Street, with a view of the Mississippi from her window.

By then, she was beginning to lose her looks and I was no longer as much attracted to her, I must shamefully confess, but the lure of New Orleans was too much to turn the opportunity down. I entered her from behind, her pale body squashed against the bay window, suspended above the void, like in a bad erotic movie (which is probably why I enjoyed fucking her thus …). Her plaintive voice endlessly calling out my name, invoking it in fear, in lust, as I dug roughly into her, slapping myself into her, against her. She liked it rough, made you know wordlessly that she wished to be manhandled, to end up with bruises across her arms, her rump after the deed was done, although in private conversation before or after, during meals, or normal social interaction, she would always refrain quite religiously from raising any matters sexual. She still sends me birthday and Xmas wishes every single year.

And then there was Pamela, who was married to a famous experimental jazz trumpet player. We'd met in New

York at a party. She was a friend of a friend. We would get together on every trip of mine to Manhattan where she shared a flat with a girlfriend near the Columbia campus. Her husband was always away on tour somewhere. God, Pamela, so many years ago now! Dark, lustrous, long hair, sublime arse, heavy breasts, how we fitted together so well! She joined me for a Bourbon Street Mardi-Gras folly, walking up and down the alcohol-soaked road at snail's pace, screams from the balconies for women to lift their tops and show their tits and be rewarded with cheap, colourful beads. Which she did, roaring with laughter, on a couple of occasions. Her breasts so shapely. Dead drunk, we finished up in someone else's hotel room with a group of local acquaintances of hers, which ended in a fumbled orgy in which all present ended up in bed together; I even think her husband might have been there too and watched us fuck before dutifully taking his turn with her, while I was being indifferently blown by his blonde companion, my cock likely still coated with Pamela's sweet juices. New Orleans madness!

All this to explain the guilty attraction for New Orleans that simmers uncontrollably beneath my skin.

The spicy food, the oysters and crawfish diet I could live on, the voodoo fumes, the rumbling and heavy flow of the river, the fireworks off Jackson Square on New Year's Eve as all the riverboats on the Mississippi toot their horns on the stroke of midnight as the traditional glitterball concludes its descent on the sidewall of the old Jackson Brewery, the drunks and druggies in Louis Armstrong Park, the endless causeway across Pontchartrain Lake, the antique shop windows on Royal Street, the antebellum mansions of the Garden District, the halting tramways, the diners dotted across Magazine, the sounds of every conceivable sort of music filtering like smoke from the bars and clubs, the noise, the warmth, the humidity, these have all become the foundation stones of who I am and entrenched New Orleans in my blood.

Why I always go back.

Even when I have no reason to do so.

No touristic urges.

No woman.

When it rains in New Orleans, it pours. The skies open wide. It's the climate, you see, a sheer avalanche of water. Within a minute or so, the streets are like rivers. It never lasts very long, and in late spring or summer, within minutes, it has all evaporated as if by magic.

But if you happen to get caught, you're drenched from head to toe in the blink of an eye. Best take shelter fast.

I was wandering aimlessly through the French Quarter, smelling the smells, drinking the sights, my mind both at rest and empty, although my soul, as ever, yearned for things unsaid. I'd already strayed beyond the main Vieux Carré area which is always so full of bars and stuff, and walking by mostly boarded-up buildings and all-night groceries. I recalled that there was a small park a few blocks further to the north. Maybe I'd sit for a while, collect my thoughts, read a bit from the old pulp paperback I'd picked up earlier at the Rue Dauphine Librairie Bookshop.

My short-sleeve shirt stuck to my skin and sweat painted a sheen on my bare skin. I took a sip of water from the Coke bottle I carried along in my tote bag and looked up at the sky. A mass of dark clouds was passing across the sun, and there was a touch of electricity in the air. A big storm was nearing. I knew from experience how quickly it could break and looked around for possible shelter. The park I remembered was too far, even if my memory of its location was correct.

A drop of water cascaded over the tip of my nose. None of the buildings nearby extended canopies across the pavement, unlike in other areas of the French Quarter. I darted down a side street, hoping for a bar or a store where I could take refuge. The sky darkened.

There.

A small neon light advertising something just fifty yards away on the other side of the street. I hastened my pace. Reached the door of the joint just as the heavens opened, water splashing against my loafers.

Inside, the smell of stale beer and centuries of cigarettes impregnating wood and bodies.

I'd thought it was just a bar but noticed the small badly-lit stage at the back of the room. A titty bar! A strip joint away from the normal beat. The sort of place I'd never really cared for much, whether in New Orleans or elsewhere. Muted sounds of a Rolling Stones song shuffling in the background. 'Sympathy for the Devil', I recognized. My eyes were becoming accustomed to the ambient darkness.

Men along the bar, or at small tables, nursing drinks, hushed conversations. I found a gap at the bar. Ordered a Coke and was told they only had Pepsi. Fine with me. 'No ice, please.'

As the barman, a swarthy red-haired bull of a man, delivered my glass, the lights illuminating the stage area at the back were switched on proper. The music on the juke-box fell to an abrupt halt and with an asthmatic click the club's sound system came to life. Conversations ceased, punters shifted in their seats, glasses clinked.

Just as the new music took flight, I briefly heard the monotonous sounds of the rain outside beating against the pavement and the club's unsheltered windows. It was a big one.

As the sound of the echoing rain quickly faded into the distance I realised that the music now spreading like a wave through the room was not the sleazy sort I'd somehow expected. No sweaty rock 'n roll, or brassy big band tune or jazzy effluvia. It was actually classical. I closed my eyes for an instant in an attempt to dredge some form of recognition from my memory. Lazy strings, shimmering beaches of melody lapping against each other, Ravel or maybe Debussy.

A spotlight appeared out of nowhere.

Highlighting a dancer who had also materialized from the undefinable contours of the surrounding darkness.

Again she was not some identikit stripper, all crude make-up, vulgar attitudes and gaudy minimalistic apparel.

She was clothed in billowing white gossamer material, a flowing dress or sheet suspended in an imaginary breeze. Reminded me of Isadora Duncan in photos I'd seen in books or magazines, or maybe from a movie. Her own face was even paler than her thin dress. Just a savage slash of red lipstick, like a still bleeding wound, highlighting a set of perfect features. Cheekbones to kill for. Eyes deep with ebony darkness. A luxuriant jungle of blonde curls like a royal crown, falling all the way down to her shoulders, framing her face in total harmony.

She was almost motionless at first.

I looked up.

Met her eyes.

An endless well of sadness.

Her face expressionless.

The billowing white dress concealed any hint of the shape of her body, just thin legs and delicately-shaped ankles above her bare feet.

Again skin of abominable pallor.

One shoulder moved imperceptibly to the rising beat of the strings carrying the melody.

I held my breath.

Hypnotized.

The next five minutes saw me transported to another time and place altogether as I watched the young woman's set. Similarly, every other spectator in the room had fallen silent as we all watched transfixed by the spectacle of her dance and gradual disrobing, as her movements invisibly accelerated and she began to dance, sashay, sway, shiver, perform, display herself, lullaby of desire, conjugating the geometry of her sexuality to a factor of infinity, stripping, moving, flying even, suspended in the winds of desire, spreading herself with both grace and total obscenity and making the whole spectacle a thing of innocence and unashamed pornography.

Her slender neck.

Firm small breasts. Nipples adorned with the same fierce shade of lipstick. Fiery. Hard.

Her washboard stomach. The miniature crevice of her navel where the steep descent towards her delta began.

Her shaven mons.

The highlighted straight vertical scar of her cunt opening, again defined by the scarlet hue of lipstick. The coral depths peering with every other movement inside her as she floated between the billowing flow of the thin white material of the dress she had now shed and swam through a world of emptiness and gauzy material to the quiet, peaceful beat of the music.

Darker, brown inner labia, teasing our eyes.

An imperceptible tattoo just an inch or so along to the left of the opening of her cunt. Looked like a gun, or maybe more traditionally a flower.

The harmony of her thighs. The golden down in the small of her back caught by the spotlight. The symmetrical orbs of her arse. The darker pucker of her anal opening as she bent forward and spread herself wide for our edification.

It could have been offensive, vulgar, dirty, but it was anything but.

She was confident with her body. Knew how beautiful she was, Remained in control of every square inch of her immaculately white skin and she was gifting us with its vision.

At no moment did she stray more than a few metres from the fixed spotlight. No need for wasteful movements or poles for acrobatics or seeking tips from the audience. Not that there was anywhere they could be tucked as she had been quite naked underneath the white Grecian-like dress. No exotic lingerie or suspenders or garter belts. No superfluous items of clothing. Once she was naked, it was something so natural, the way a woman should always be.

And her face, ever expressionless. Distant. At peace.

The melody began to fade, the strings shimmering as the journey ended. I felt as if my heart had stopped.

The young pale blond woman's motion slowed.

Her legs opened at a revealing angle.

Her arms spread wide in both directions.

Christ-like. Crucified.

I held my breath.

The spotlight sharply disappeared and the darkness that took over the room was blacker than ever.

By the time our eyes adjusted, the dancer was no longer there and the small stage was empty.

Every spectator present was silent.

I finished my drink and walked outside.

The storm had passed and the street was almost dry already, thin clouds of steam rising from the gutters as the rain evaporated in overdrive.

It was late afternoon.

In the distance the calliope of a steamboat on the Mississippi chimed.

Damn, who was she?

I walked all the way back to Toulouse and then, impulsively, trackbacked to the small strip club. The stage was occupied by a black girl with silicone tits and an over-prominent Jennifer Lopez arse and the customers now few, as if all the previous punters knew no one could properly follow the blonde and there was no point lingering.

The barman glanced at me. His eyes twinkled with malice. 'She only dances once a day,' he said, predicting my question.

'Oh …'

41

'She's dressing right now. Should be coming out any moment,' he added.

'I'll wait, then.'

Away from the stage, she appeared even taller, straight backed, imperious if fragile, now that she had wiped the savage lipstick away, her whole face a symphony of whiteness. I was unable to recognize the fragrance she wore.

She seemed to be still wearing the white gauzy dress she had begun her dance in, under a floor-length transparent plastic mac. And she was still barefoot. A large canvas bag hung from her shoulders. It appeared to be full of books and silk scarves in every colour of the rainbow.

'Loved your set. Can I offer you a drink?'

'I just had some water in the dressing room,' she said. 'No thanks.' Looked at me blankly.

'Going home?'

'Maybe ...'

'Hungry?'

'A bit. Dancing does eat up all your energy,' she said.

'My treat. Anywhere you want to go.'

She agreed to share an oyster po' boy at the Napoleon House.

Even now, I remember very little of our conversation although we must have spent more than an hour together eating and conversing. She never would tell me what her name was or anything about her life. I recall discussing books, she loved F Scott Fitzgerald and let slip she had once lived in Manhattan. Every attempt on my part to find out how come she was now a stripper failed. She wasn't rude or offended by my questions, just indifferent. The time passed quickly and I assume that yet again I must have done too much of the talking, and bored her stiff with my usual stories and feeble anecdotes and jokes.

We walked from the Napoleon House to the small Faulkner House bookstore in the alley by Jackson Square where I failed to find a copy of a book I had been singing the praises of and had hoped to buy for her.

'Sorry.'

'It's fine,' she said, with a faint smile. 'So?'

'So?'

'Do you wish to come back to mine?'

My heart skipped a beat.

'That would be lovely,' I replied.

It was a walk-up in a decaying building that might once have been a mansion's slave quarters just off Dumaine.

She closed the door and took my hand in hers.

'Kiss me,' she asked.

How could I say no?

It wasn't fucking. It was making love in the most absolute sense of the term. It could only have happened in New Orleans.

Her bed became our battlefield.

I knew how pale her skin was but never guessed how soft and pliant her body would prove, a feathered cushion firm and languorous, a perfect treasure offered up for plunder and worse. Oh, the satin of her skin, the marrow-like texture of her lips, the way her fingers caressed my cock with shameless impunity and coaxed it to full length and thickness before she took me into the oven of her mouth, nibbling, teasing, biting with kindness, her tongue delving into my pee-hole with exquisite, measured probing, riding my lust, controlling it.

Her cunt, a map of untold treasure. Yes, it was a tattoo of a gun there, no larger than a nail, a Chinese miniature in the heavenly pornographic landscape of her intimacy, inner and outer folds delineated with mathematical precision, a medical sketch where every feature was drawn with close attention to detail and colour. Beckoning me. Opening for me like a flower of the tropics, swallowing me whole, feeding on me, feeding me.

New Orleans night.

The sound of her moans, the tightness in our throats as

we pushed boundaries and held each other in the darkness like orphans in a storm. Every single woman I had touched, loved, brought to New Orleans led to this moment, this epiphany.

Fuck! Why wasn't it always like this?

Morning. Lazing spread-eagled in a crazy geography amongst the tangled sheets of the bed. Our smells mingling, our sweat a potent cocktail of spent lust.

'Hello. Shouldn't I at least know your name?' I asked, a fingertip lingering indecently across the ridge of her cunt lips.

'Good morning, lover.'

She rose from the bed, brushing away my greedy hands. Regal. Pale. Naked. My cock hardened again in an instant, despite its rawness.

She smiled and tut-tutted.

'Later,' she said. 'Offer me breakfast.'

We dressed and walked out into the hesitant early morning sun to Jackson Square for traditional beignets and coffee at the Café Du Monde.

She still wore the white, billowing dress, a tall, pale ivory figure making her way across Decatur.

Wiping away the powdered sugar that had spilt across my dark shirt, I looked up to see the sun fading.

She followed my eyes.

'Seems like another storm is on the way,' I said.

She nodded.

We began to make our way back to her apartment, hastening our pace as the dark clouds gathered menacingly above.

But only made it halfway there before the heavens opened.

I laughed as the first drops fell on my tousled hair, turned towards her expecting a similar smile. But the look on her face was one of terror.

'It's only rain, water,' I said.

44

And, one final time, I witnessed the despair that lingered deep down in the dark pit of her eyes.

The rain fell, implacable, surrounding us, submerging us.

Quickly soaking the thin material of her thin dress, instantly revealing the sweet contours of her body, the now transparent gauze sticking to her skin, betraying the dark hardness of her nipples and when she attempted to move, the cleft of her cunt. At any other time, I would have found this highly erotic and arousing. But not at present.

As soon as her total nudity beneath the dress was betrayed, she began to fade.

It only took a few seconds.

Fading.

Like melting in the rain.

Her contours losing their firmness, their definition. Her pale skin disappearing with every new drop of rain.

I stood there with my mouth open.

Her lips parted as if she wanted to tell me something but not a sound emerged and then she was gone.

The rain beat against the pavement with monotonous regularity, cutting through the air where once she had stood. And soon, as ever, the storm passed, and the water just evaporated and disappeared in little swishes of thin steam. Just like she had. And I was left alone, on the corner of Conti and Royal, standing like a fool in front of the Federal Building.

I didn't know what to think at first.

Was this a joke? Was this illusion, magic?

My mind in a tizzy, I ran back towards her apartment but was unable to find it again. But then, in New Orleans, so many houses look alike and my mind had been on other things when we had first made our way there.

I tried to compose myself.

Went to my hotel to change clothes. Take a shower, reluctantly washing away her scent from my body, from my cock.

Then rushed out to look for the strip joint where I had first come across her. Half believing it also would have disappeared from the map.

But it was there. In the same place as the previous day.

Closed. It was still only mid-morning.

I found a secondhand copy of "The Beautiful and the Damned" at the bookshop on Dauphine. Hadn't read it in decades. It helped me pass the time until the bar opened.

Standing on the opposite pavement, late afternoon, I saw the blinds rising and the click click of the door's lock.

A short, greying man was wiping the tables clean with a wet cloth, and no sign of the customary barman.

My questions hit a blank wall.

No, it had been ages since they'd featured dancers.

No, they no longer had a licence.

Elderly regulars slowly streamed in.

None of them had any memory of when, if ever, the place had been a strip joint. Just a good place for a quiet place for a drink these days.

Somehow, it was what I expected.

Made a strange sort of sense.

I finally sat myself at the bar and asked the middle-aged woman now serving for a drink.

As she bent down to get the bottle from the lowest shelf of her glass-fronted fridge, I caught sight of a fading framed photograph crookedly stuck to the large mirror which formed the back wall of the bar.

Squinted.

Recognized the pale features of my heavenly blonde stranger behind the sepia tones.

'Who is that?'

'Oh, that … Just an old photo taken some sixty years ago when the bar was a thriving private club for gentlemen,' I was told, 'must have been one of the dancers.'

I gulped down my drink and walked out.

*   *   *

Tomorrow, I will check out of my hotel, stroll down Royal Street and head towards Canal, leaving the mighty flow of the Mississippi behind me, and I will wait for the rain to come and maybe I will melt away and meet her again on the other side of the humid New Orleans curtain of rain.

For sure.

Gulliver on Lillipussia
by John McKeown

The doc wants me to write this, thinks it'll help. She's very nice but she thinks I'm crazy, permanently delerious after those weeks adrift at sea. But I'm not. I'm NOT! It all really happened. I can understand why she might believe my story's just sexual hallucinations, given my history, which I told her about, which she lapped up; and I'll admit, before the ship wrecked I was hornier than a rhino's tusk. But I never had much of an imagination, so I don't see how I could've produced anything as crazy as what happened to me. OK, to follow doctor's orders then:

After the liner went down (I don't want to go into that because it's been in all the papers and on TV) I drifted for days; no sea charts, no flares, no radio, nothing but enough food and water for about a month. I'm not one to panic though – not enough imagination! Heh heh – I just hunkered down and waited to hit the shipping traffic, thinking what Mabel the poledancer at The Marie Celeste was going to do to me when I was rescued.

One minute it's pitch black, with the stars shimmying up in the sky, the next I'm eating sand and warm salt water, face down on a hot beach, the sun beating on my bare back.

'Must've overslept,' I muttered, hoisting myself up and looking around: palm trees, beach, incoming surf. Then it all spun round and I blacked out again.

When things came back into focus I thought I must've died and gone to heaven. There's a group of bare-legged, long-haired lovelies, in short, low-cut sarong-type outfits, whispering and cooing and stuff, right in front of me. One approaches and bends down to me and I see right down into the warm compressed curvatures of the most beautiful pair of knockers I've seen for months. I'm instantly alert. And I suddenly notice something odd. All of these lovelies, though fully-formed, mature young women, are no bigger than three feet high. The one bending over me's about 3' 4" or 5".

Then she speaks.

'Welcome to Lillipussia, Mr …?'

As though it was the most normal situation in the world I answer, 'Gulliver, Lawrence S Gulliver. Warrant Officer First Class.'

(I think I can be excused under the circumstances, for giving myself a little promotion. I'm actually just a humble ship's grease-monkey).

My hostess was very polite, genteel even, as they all were, at first. But that all evaporated pretty quickly, I have to say, what with the fact that I was the only man they'd had on the island for ten years. To put it bluntly, those lovely little women were starving for some cock. And when I say little, I stress, they weren't midgets, or deformed in any way, they were all perfectly, mouth-wateringly, formed; Playboy centrefolds in miniature.

You can imagine my state then. There I was, barely able to contain the massive boner that had been dogging me for weeks, surrounded by these gangs and crowds of *very attentive* females whose heads barely reached my balls.

I know what you're thinking, I know … I'm getting to that.

It began on the second night. Three of the little ladies had been assigned to attend to my wounds – just a few bruises and cuts from the wreck. They slept on mats around the edge of the palm shack they'd brought me into with much ceremony. It was getting harder and harder to sleep, listening to them whispering and shifting, and seeing their tight little arses cavorting across my sleepless mind. Suddenly I heard tittering and felt little hands patting my feet and legs. The fine reed mat that covered me was drawn off and the hands began smoothing and stroking my legs. I raised myself on an elbow but could see nothing.

'We check you all OK all over? OK?'

'OK with me, nurse. Check away.'

'Lie down please.'

I lay back and felt the hands slipping light as pattering streams of water up my thighs. Automatically, I opened my legs. And the little cool hands, getting warmer by the minute, stopped and then folded around my balls.

'We need light. Nurse!'

A light was struck. And what a scene!

My three nurses were stark naked. The blonde one had her hands on my exposed balls, smiling, while the other two knelt on either side of me, their eyes, shining in the light, hungrily taking me all in. I have very big balls. In the blonde's hands they looked as big as overripe coconuts in a five-year-old's.

She started squeezing them while the other two bent lower and lower, their big (for their size) breasts hanging, as they stooped in fascination.

Then my boner started stiffening with a vengeance. The three of them looked at each other then up at me with pleasurable alarm.

'You OK, Larry?'

'Me OK.'

'Can you show us? We medical doctors. No worry.'

'I'd be glad to oblige.'

I pulled it out of my shorts and they fell back with a real gasp of terror. The thing was even bigger than usual, in fact, it seemed to have grown a couple of inches.

'It looks very sore, Larry. Me lick it, make it better. Yes?'

'Oh … Yes, OK.'

The blonde one took it in both hands and began pecking it at the tip. It was a bit like being pecked by a soft-beaked bird, quite pleasurable, but quite frustrating too. There was no way her mouth was big enough to take it in. They could sense my disappointment.

The other two began stroking it, and purring.

'Poor Larry!'

That was a lot better. I lay back. While the blonde kept pecking and licking the tip, the dark haired one squeezed my balls and the redhead ran her hands up and down the shaft with increasing speed and intensity. She started moaning, and chanting some primitive song, and then, playing her wet little mouth along its bulging cords, she wrapped her long, long little shapely legs around it. I was seriously excited now. I don't like to moan like a teenager, but what the hell, this was a once-in-a-lifetime experience, Larry, let rip. So I set to moaning, and that really got my nurses senseless. Dark-hair pulled red-hair off and got her legs around it. Then blondie pulled her off and started rubbing it into her breasts. It went back and forth between the three of them until my head was spinning. Six titties rubbing against it, tanned thighs jacking it, three tongues licking and tickling. I was about ready to explode. But I wanted to explode *in* something.

They could read my mind.

The three of them lay down and spread their legs wide. *Wide.* Three beautiful soft red jewels glinted at me like tearful eyes. Beautiful but too small! I pressed my cock against each of them for form's sake though. When I got to the blonde I almost felt it was going to go in. But she was wincing, and not with pleasure, and hey, I may be a grease-monkey from Port of New Orleans, but I'm a gentleman.

I looked down at them. They were stroking their own little pussies, little fingers slipping in, and trickles of juice slipping out. I had to start whacking myself off. We did it in time, a Lillipussian chamber quartet.

51

Then, we all had a eureka moment.

They stood up, three opened mouths, six fingers probing deep into three tightly weeping pussies; the three mouths formed the action of one on my cock. I closed my eyes. It was BEAUtiful! Three warm wet greedy suction cups slipping and sliding and suckering all over it. Their finger action got quicker. Their mouths wove my head in a net, touching and sweetly stinging like it was dipped in a hive of honey-mad bees. I felt my feet coming off the ground, tremors shooting up and down my legs. I swept them up in one armful and threw them on my rush-bed, bent and kissed them all over, toes, legs, sucked at those pussies till they screamed, licked those breasts like a kid with fresh-pulled dollops of ice-cream. Then I leaned back and as they watched, panting, jacked all over them. Gouts of spunk flew out like gouts of Jackson Pollock paint between jerks. They grabbed at it, smearing it over their faces and hair and into those greedy little cock-starved pussies.

A real tsunami of sexual frenzy took over the island of the little women then. It would take more time than I have to describe the things we all got up to together, en masse, as the Frenchies say. I'll just tell about the biggest gang-bang before I managed to escape.

They took me up to the extinct volcano in the centre of the island – a big hollow shallow crater – and filled the damn thing with all kinds of flowers that gave off a savage aphrodisiac aroma. They were all naked, and all drinking this home-brew that was enough to blow your head off just getting a whiff of it.

They had this lotion that had a numbing effect, a sort of anaesthetic, that they smeared all over my cock, this would delay my ejaculation, allowing as many of them to get a piece of me as possible.

I have to say here though, that cock of mine really had grown another six or seven inches, and about four inches wider. It was massive. I put it down to the radiation. From what the Chief told me there were atomic tests in that part of the Pacific years before. It certainly accounted for their small size and my inflation. The weird thing was, though, as I got bigger, they seemed to get smaller and smaller. It made them even crazier with frustration, as there was no remote possibility of my cock getting inside any of them. I think the smallest of them was the size of a Barbie doll.

Anyways, they laid me down in the centre of that crater, stark naked, with my cock smeared with the anaesthetic and my head full of the home-brew. Then they all retreated to the slopes, arranging themselves in a huge circle. Three of the most luscious ladies stayed to work me up into a towering hard-on. The smallest of them used it as a pole to do a wild pole dance, while the one with the biggest arse, bumped her big little soft arse against it, until her juices broke and dripped over the big red head like a pierced orange. Despite that anaesthetic I was about ready to shoot it up to the moon and the stars that were already appearing. The teaser-tasters disappeared then, and all was silent. Then I heard a long WHOOOOOOOOOOOOOOOOOOOOOOO-OOOOOP! And the earth started to tremble with several hundred little feet running and jumping toward me.

They swarmed over me! I was like a wounded wasp fallen into a red ants' nest! One of them burrowed up my arse, and stayed there, doing I don't know what, with I don't know what, but it made my cock as hard as a concrete bridge support. They twined around it, they slid up it, they slid down it, they jacked themselves off, they jacked each other off, they tongued each other, they tongued me, thirty at a time, they massaged my balls with their feet, they stuck their arses in my mouth, I made a line of them come by sticking my nose up their cunts! (Why hadn't I thought of that one before?).

It was high time for me to blow off.

Suddenly they all drew back. And you wont believe this.

They started to climb up on each other, like five hundred naked little acrobats, they climbed up, they twined together, all sinewy, and musculaturely ... What were they doing? They were forming themselves into one giant woman! When they finished, with quite a few dropping off in sheer exhaustion, she was about twenty-five feet high, with huge PULSATING breasts, hair made of flowing naked legs, thighs rippling with little glistening breasts like hundreds of pink and brown moons, and, as I watched, breathless, a BIG gaping cunt, its lips rippling with a hundred pink red mouths, and surrounded by waving tresses of multi-coloured hair!

She aproached, surprisingly nimbly, toward me. A hand made of hands reached out and lowered my cock, she bent, both hands made of soft soft hands, angled it into that rippling, opening and closing cunt. It was in!

She straddled me. The whole mad machine started to pump and gyrate, pump, swivel, gyrate, suck, withdraw, blow, pump, swivel, twist, gyrate, and the *moaning!* It was like fucking ten whole girls' choirs at once!

The choirs moved faster, I moved faster, what a sight we must've made!

The really amazing thing was that they all seemed to feel as ONE WOMAN. They were like iron filings all aligned in the same direction by the magnetic waves of my big surging cock.

I closed my eyes. It was like a river of warm raspberry jello surging. It was like hot firm custard. It was like Mom's apple pie, and how Mom's sister used to spoon in the innards of Mom's pie with a big silver spoon in front of me, when Mom wasn't looking. And how she licked it! That long red glistening tongue brought to a point, lifting off the last tiny fleck of soft, perfectly cooked apple ...

AHHHHHHHHHHHHHHHHHHHHHHHHHHHHHHHHHHH HHHHHHHHHHHHHHHHHHHHHHHHHHHHHHHHHHHHHH HHHHHHHHHHHHHHHHHHHHHHHHHHHHHHHHHHHH!!!!!!

!!!
!!!!!!!!!!!!!!!!!!!!!!!!!

I came. It blew through the giant woman like a geyser erupting, ripping and scattering her constituents apart. None of the little women were hurt seriously when they landed, I don't think!

That was the peak of my sexual adventures on Lillipussia. There was plenty of horsing around afterward, but, I was getting bored. Fantastic though Lillipussia was, and I'll take my memories of the place to my grave, I was still hankering after Mabel my friendly neighbourhood pole-dancer. But how was I ever going to get away from Lillipussia and its legions of hungry little pussies?

As my mom was always saying: Necessity is the mother of invention. And boy, when I heard what the Lillipussies had planned for me next, I came up with an escape plan quicker than the snap of a pimp's purse.

The little women were getting bored with me too. I was lavished with love just the same, but there ain't nothing better for a pussy than a cock that more or less fits. I don't blame them for wanting something closer to their own size. I do blame them for the solution they came up with.

The Head Witch Doctoress brewed up a big vat of the special shrinking potion their ancestors used to shrink heads with. She reckoned that if my dick was pickled in this for a few hours it'd get me down to a manageable size. One of the ladies who'd been assigned to me the first night broke ranks to warn me about the plot.

What to do? I had to get off the island, but on what? No boat. It would take too long to make a raft. What then? Fly, burrow, float? … Float!

One moonless night my little friend got me all worked up with whispers and dirty little stories, and I kept remembering Aunt Flo, spooning in the hot entrails of apple pie, and Mabel, her lovely big butt twitching on that pole under the flood of red light. My clever little friend smuggled in a super large dose of that anaesthetic I mentioned earlier and covered my erection in it so it wouldn't deflate. Man, it was as big as a dinghy.

I grabbed a bag full of supplies, stuck my little friend inside – if I left her behind she assured me that she'd be torn apart and fed to the miniature wart-hogs – and ran, or, actually, tottered down to the beach. The tide was peaking, and would soon be going out. I put both hands round my cock and jumped into the breakers. It worked! We floated further and further out. I lashed the thing to me with some cord and used my hands to paddle us out into the deep ocean. This time we had a compass, so we knew where we were going. But I kept thinking of Auntie Flo and Mabel, and the big rippling pussy of the giant woman that had eaten me a few days before, and my little friend kept me stiff and buoyant with her expert little tongue and fingers and toes, and a huge feather duster she'd brought to tickle me round the base of the foreskin, Christ that always drives me crazy …

Sadly my little friend didn't make it. One morning I woke to find her gone, but luckily the feather duster was still there, and dry, so I tickled and fantasised and steadily paddled my way on to dry land three days later.

There's a lot more to tell, particularly about the BazzookaBazooms, the giant women who inhabited the island I was washed up on next.

But reading over this I don't think there's much point, I know no one will ever believe me!

The Warmth of His Touch
by Viva Jones

It started as a dare. When Belinda confided in her best friend, Mia, about Alistair, the new man in her book club, and his quiet good looks, his reserved nature and his intellectual demeanour, she'd jokingly admitted that he was about as far from her type – which was rugged and sporty – as he could possibly hope to be. Mia had got very excited, quoting from the last self-help book she'd just read, and said that it was precisely *because* he was against type that she should date him.

'We keep repeating mistakes,' she'd insisted paraphrasing the book's contents, 'and looking for the same guy, only to find he has exactly the same faults as the last one. Until we break this pattern we'll never move forward and find happiness. Think of your last three boyfriends – they all screwed up in the end, didn't they? So try Alistair. Go on, I dare you. You never know, he might surprise you.'

Less than convinced, Belinda ensured that she sat next to him at the following book club meeting, and as he analysed and assessed the latest Booker winner (of which she'd only managed the first two chapters), she gazed into his soft grey eyes and studied the lines of his rather too thin lips. When she cracked a joke he didn't laugh at her heart sank. There was no way she could last a whole date with this man, she thought. If they couldn't laugh together, which certainly seemed the case, then they didn't stand a chance. But she remembered Mia's words, and persisted. A dare was a dare, after all, and Mia herself had just chosen against type and was already on her second date with Mike, an aircraft engineer. ('Think of all the free flights,' she'd exclaimed.)

The book discussed and reviewed, the group broke up into convivial chat, and Belinda turned to Alistair and asked about his life. He was a financial analyst, he told her, and had recently returned to the UK after a spell in Frankfurt. He lived alone, having broken up from his German girlfriend, and had a love for the arts, regularly attending concerts on the South Bank. His family originated from Norfolk and his parents owned a ski chalet in Austria. After the arts, skiing was his passion. All the time he was speaking Belinda ensured she watched him with a rapt expression on her face, and avoided revealing how low-brow her own tastes were, and that her favourite programme was *Strictly Come Dancing* and the last concert she'd attended was Kylie Minogue's. He was a nice guy, she decided, if a bit stuffy. The sort of guy her parents would approve of. She could imagine them being very impressed. She and Alistair had nothing in common (although she'd love to learn to ski), but if she could just get one date out of him the dare would be won.

A week later, the date was suggested: a low-budget French film followed by a late supper at some Japanese place he knew close by. Subtitles were not really her thing, but Belinda managed to follow the movie (at least she enjoyed the glorious Parisian backdrop and the stylish clothes) and pretended to be interested as he gave it his assessment over bowls of steaming noodles and a cup of Japanese tea. She ached for a glass of wine but thought it inappropriate to ask for one.

Leaving the date with a quick peck on the cheek, Belinda told herself she'd never see Alistair again outside the book club. He was boring, somewhat on the self-engrossed side and they really did have nothing in common. But a few days later she found herself attending a recital with him, and

58

pretending to enjoy it, followed by a stroll around the National Portrait Gallery. Was he trying to educate her? She tried making him laugh – a speciality of hers – and he'd allow her an indulgent smile, like a father being kind to an overexcited child, and on her way home Belinda told herself that was it. She'd refuse his next invitation, if indeed it was forthcoming. She'd had enough. She'd fulfilled her dare, he hadn't changed her life (just slowed it down a little) and now it was time to move on.

On his next phone call, however, Alistair invited her to his family's ski chalet in Austria. 'It's very modest,' he insisted, 'but comfortable and cosy, and there are some gentle slopes nearby making it perfect for beginners. Normally it's rented out, but we got a last minute cancellation, and I thought it too good an opportunity to miss.'

As did Belinda. Telling herself she'd enjoy learning to ski, and that just maybe there'd be a bit of brandy about to ease the conversation, she decided to let him have one bad shag and then call it a day. Alistair would be wooden and awkward in bed and she was convinced she'd get nothing out of it, but it would mean she could walk away knowing she'd contributed to the weekend in her own special way. If Belinda was confident about one thing, it was her own sexual ability.

Meeting him at the airport, she was pleasantly surprised to see how good he looked in civvies – she'd only ever seen him in his work suit before. Now he was in jeans with a quilted jacket, his hair looked less groomed and he hadn't shaved, and she began to see another layer of Alistair revealing itself in front of her. She liked the way he insisted on carrying her bag for her, and at security she even got a smile out of him with her striptease quip as she removed her belt, boots and jacket. On the plane they drank coffees and shared a pack of shortbread fingers, and, despite her misgivings, Belinda began to think that maybe the weekend wouldn't be quite as dull as she'd imagined.

On their arrival, he hired a small car and they drove for half an hour up into the hills, through snow-clad forests and chocolate-box hamlets, to where the family ski chalet was based. Belinda had never seen such pretty scenery before, and was sorry that this would probably be the only time she experienced it. As they drew nearer, the chalet was everything she'd been expecting, with its broad snow-covered roof, shuttered windows and dark wooden balcony, and she persuaded herself that Alistair was someone she could maybe fall in love with after all.

'It'll be cold at first,' he warned her as they entered. 'But I'll have the heating on in a jiffy and by the time we're back it'll be toasty, I assure you.'

Just the words "jiffy" and "toasty" were enough to make her doubt the weekend all over again.

The chalet was indeed cosy, however, with quilted throws over the sofas, lots of wood furniture and big old lamps, rugs that slipped a little on the polished wooden floors and a pretty kitchen that almost made her want to bake apple strudel.

Alistair deposited their luggage into the main bedroom, she noticed, saying they could sort their things out later. 'Let's hit the slopes first, eh?'

He had gear for her, his mother's old skis and a suit belonging to his sister, and in no time Belinda thought she looked like a pro. Once on the slopes he was surprisingly patient with her, guiding her along, giving her gentle demonstrations and correcting her position. She found she liked him more, as if he was the caring brother she never had, and the more she relaxed the better her skiing came along. Once, when she nearly took a tumble, he caught her, and as he held her in his arms, she felt the tiniest jolt of electricity between them.

But then he'd say something like, "You're doing awfully well for your age", and all her misgivings would come hurtling back, faster than an out-of-control snow-boarder.

One minute she fancied him, the next she couldn't wait to get away.

Towards the end of the day, however, she felt guilty about holding him back, and urged him to head for a tougher slope while she enjoyed a hot chocolate laced with rum. Happily he obliged and when, a good hour later, he returned, skiing expertly right up to the café, she was reminded of James Bond, or some kind of action hero, and she reckoned that, with the help of two large tots of rum, he'd just got that little bit sexier.

She'd still dump him after the weekend, though. Deciding you weren't totally bored by someone wasn't a good enough excuse to keep seeing them.

When they returned to the chalet in the fading light, instead of finding it warm and toasty, as Alistair had promised, it felt even colder than before. 'What's gone wrong here then?' he asked, checking the radiators and the thermostat. 'Damn it, the boiler must have broken.'

He spent a while complaining to the management company while she huddled on a sofa, under one of its quilted throws.

'Belinda I am so sorry,' he told her once he got off the phone. 'I feel terrible about this. Let's go out for supper and warm up in a restaurant.'

They did so, and enjoyed a hearty stew and a good bottle of red wine, followed by a glass each of the house wine. They were in for a cold night, after all. He was mortified about the heating, he kept telling her, and Belinda kept repeating that it wasn't his fault, and that she'd be all right. But on arriving back at the chalet, it felt so utterly chilled that she didn't even want to change into her night clothes.

'I don't want to sound presumptuous, but if we share a bed we'll get warmer,' Alistair suggested, as she nodded bleakly, the buzz of the wine dissipating in the cold air.

While he was in the bathroom, Belinda took a deep

breath, pulled off her clothes and threw on her deliberately unsexy pyjamas, adding a pair of thick socks for good measure. Then she climbed into bed, lying flat on her back and pulling the thick duvet up around her. Alistair emerged from the bathroom in his pyjamas, and climbed primly into bed beside her.

'I'm so sorry about this,' he whispered, lightly touching her hair. 'Tomorrow we'll spend the day skiing and then we're on the evening flight home. We'll survive.'

'It's OK,' she whispered back. 'I've had a wonderful time.'

'Good.' He leant forward and kissed her gently, a peck on the lips, and Belinda braced herself for what was to come. She might as well let him have sex and get it over with, she decided. What was the harm?

He kissed her again, and this time his tongue poked through to meet hers, and she felt an instinctive darting feeling between her legs. His tongue was surprisingly adept, and she began to relax into the kiss, folding him in closer with her arms. His right hand crept under her pyjama top towards her breast, her nipples already firm due to the cold, and as he touched them she gasped – so warm were his fingers as they stroked and played with her nipples that she could feel her skin immediately reacting to them. He then climbed on top, dislodging the thick duvet as he did so, and allowing more cold air to embrace her body. He pushed her pyjama top right up and took each breast in his hands, and although this meant they were exposed to the cold air, his hands kept them warm, and the difference in temperature was exciting in itself. There was an element of pleasure and pain here, and Belinda didn't know which she preferred, so chose to lose herself in the sensation.

Then he slid down and started to kiss her breasts, and to suck and gently flick at each nipple with his tongue, and once again his warmth stirred her, and she felt it flooding inside her, permeating her skin, and if there'd been an infrared camera poised above her, it would reveal her blue skin gently turning a soft red. He began kissing her tummy now, moving gently but persistently down her body, teasing her by taking his time, and Belinda felt herself becoming wet with desire. When he reached the waistband of her pyjama bottoms, he hesitated, but by now Belinda was in no doubt and wanted him to go further. She raised herself up a little so that he could pull them down, and he took the initiative, kissing and nibbling her further along her body, on her tummy, the front part of her hips and the tops of her thighs.

He paused again, as if unsure whether he should go further, and she whispered, 'Go on,' while opening her thighs in encouragement.

Soon Alistair's head was above her pubic mound, and his tongue persuasively searching between her thighs, and Belinda gasped as she felt his heat tickling her, dipping inside her like a searchlight, gently probing and exploring her pussy lips, flicking at her clit and all the nerve-endings surrounding it. She opened her thighs wider and he readjusted, placing his hands – now positively hot – under each buttock and lifting her off the mattress, so that his tongue was free to explore her more deeply. And with every kiss she felt herself warming, with every flick of his tongue she felt her will softening, and every time he scored a direct hit on her clit she felt herself quietly exploding. Even though the air was bitterly cold, she could feel warmth spreading from his tongue to her pussy and further outwards across her body. It was as if she'd been trapped under an avalanche and Alistair was rescuing her: breaking through the ice, digging out the snow, warming her with his very breath.

He inserted his index finger inside her and it was like a bar of heat warming her to the core, and she longed for his cock.

'My turn,' she whispered, manoeuvring him off her and onto the bed beside her. As she climbed on top of him, she gasped as the cold air hit her back, and then slid down to where his cock was straining inside his pyjama bottoms. She released it within the open fly and took it in her mouth, where once again she was amazed at how hot it was, like a beacon of heat, and as she licked and sucked him and took him as deep inside her mouth as she could, she felt like an ice sculpture coming to life, as if previously she had been just a form with neither emotional nor spiritual depth, but with his heat her brittle exterior was melting away, and she was becoming a complete and sensitive and emotional living being.

He pulled her up and sat upright, and she straddled him, positioning herself on his cock, and then slid herself down on it, so that he filled her and her pussy became the centre of her warmth, a life-force in itself, and she rode him and they kissed, exchanging fluids and juices, warmth and tenderness, and he held her by her buttocks and she clung onto his back, and when one of his fingers slipped inside her butt she thought she was going to explode, and their kissing became more frantic and feverish, as if without it they would both die of cold, and he pushed her over so that she was on her back and he plunged deeper and deeper inside her, taking control, pummelling her as if without his cock her life would surely slip away, and she came in such an outburst it almost took her breath away, crying and screaming and holding him hard and pulling him inside her until it felt he might split her in two, and then he came, crying out in what seemed like anguish, his heat-force extinguishing, his power subsiding, and he slumped over her and their bodies lay as one, dripping in sweat, and they kissed each other gently, laughing at the strange urgency of their sex, and a need that was greater than them both.

The next morning, nestled against his body under two thick duvets, Belinda wished she could stay that way for ever. Who needed central heating when there was a man like Alistair around? In the rising sun they made love again, more tenderly this time, and she enjoyed seeing his body in the new light, the firmness of his muscles and the smoothness of his skin. For an office-type he kept himself pretty trim, she noted, and although most of her previous lovers had boasted the thick-set physique of rugby players, she now appreciated his slender form.

'Breakfast in the café and then shall we hit the slopes again?' he suggested and, suddenly ravenous, she agreed.

And while they ate, dipping their croissants into hot chocolate and laughing at the resultant mess, Belinda wondered about the overwhelming sense of love she suddenly felt for this man. He was, after all, everything a woman could ask for: he was steady and loyal, he had a love of the arts, he was kind, he made decent money, *and* he had a chalet in Austria – and she couldn't understand what had held her back until now. Why hadn't she seen what had been staring her in the face? Was she so shallow that great sex was all it took?

And with that thought came a new question: was the sex great because she loved him, or did she now love him because the sex was great? Because Belinda knew with a sudden and fierce conviction that she really did love him. As if black had become white, and fire had turned into snow, everything he did and everything he said attracted her. He seemed to smile more, and his conversation had grown lighter and wittier, as if he was no longer trying to impress her with his intellect. His reserve had melted, revealing a quiet confidence that was so much more alluring than the braying beer-swillers she'd found such fun until now. Suddenly Alistair stood out from the crowds, as if there was a glow around him, and his features, which she'd deemed on the bland side before, had become handsome and dashing and sexy.

In a revelation that shocked and excited her, Belinda knew with certainty, over that breakfast, that this was the man she must marry, and that this was the father of her children.

And when it clouded over, chilling the temperature by several degrees, theirs was an easy decision. With two hours to kill before they had to leave for the airport, they climbed back into bed, and once again she was struck by the warmth of his tongue and of his touch, and she knew that with Alistair in her life, she'd never feel cold again.

The Invitation
by Maria Lloyd

Thursday morning I noticed the gold-bordered envelope in my pigeonhole and wetted my already dry lips. Tried to act casual as I collected my mail and took it back to my office.

I work at a well known college, the security is high, yet this envelope had not come through the post – there was no stamp, no franking – and it had no markings from the college's internal post. It was cream, rich and heavy, edged with gold. Only my initials marked upon it in dark blue ink by a thick-nibbed fountain pen.

How does he do it? He likes to keep me on my toes. Maybe he had attended a meeting in the conference rooms, and had slipped this across. Maybe he had watched me as I arrived at work this morning, had passed me in the corridor while I turned to check my mobile for text messages. I always dress so prim for the office. My intellectual armour against any emotional entanglements and it seems to work. Always a linen blouse with a high collar, long pencil skirt, French flat shoes. And I always pin my hair up. I wear minimal makeup, lipstick a nice neutral shade. All so different to how I am with him …

I placed the envelope squarely on my desk. Took a sip from my cup of coffee. I rifled through my handbag and reapplied some lipstick carefully using my handbag mirror. Then I opened the envelope.

An air ticket to a Greek Island leaving late Friday night. Confirmed booking for a single room overnight stay at a hotel the same night. A car hire docket for the next day. And a leaflet for some botanical gardens, a tourist attraction inland on the island. Scrawled in ink on a thick white piece of card.

Saturday 7 p.m. Wear your red dress.

I felt weak at the knees and wet between the legs. My heart thudded at the very idea of another date with my secret lover and master.

I could hardly concentrate all day. I negotiated Friday afternoon off, and the Monday, just in case. I finished work as soon as I could and hurried back to my flat to make arrangements. Find that red dress and all the other things I may need. Cancel my attendance at a dinner party, at a private view. Book a taxi to the airport.

As always I had to rearrange my life at his whim but it was always such a delight, a pleasure to do. For the rewards were great.

It meant we would have precious time alone together and who knew what that would mean?

The flight was a red eye and I ended up getting to my hotel in the early hours. I was grateful for the short sleep, the hearty breakfast which included honey and Greek yoghurt, and the power shower to wake me up. I wore my red halter neck dress, my corset and stockings, my Louis Buton shoes just as he had specified. Applied my fifties style makeup, the livid red coco Chanel lipstick. Left my hair loose in frothy blond waves that reached down my back. I was ready to collect my hire car by mid morning and I decided to drive straight out, worry about provisions later. But by the time I had studied the map and negotiated the mad traffic rules, the dusty roads, and made a few wrong turnings even with my satnav, I ended up stopping for lunch, and much needed coffee. I reapplied my lipstick in the taverna toilets, aware of glances from the locals. I blushed behind my sunglasses as I took off again, some kind of scarlet woman travelling alone. But the sea breeze on the coast road cooled my cheeks and

68

freed my inhibitions. No one knew me here; I had used the supplied alias all along. I sang along to Louis Armstrong favourites as the car snaked beside a sparkling Aegean sea.

I enjoyed the searing light even through my sunglasses, the heat on my bare arms, and the sound of jazz on the CD player. All of this lifted my spirits after a damp and chilly British summer. So it did not matter so much that I did not arrive high in the mountains until late afternoon.

The final road was full of hairpin bends, and I almost gave up. But I was determined to make it, despite the inches between tarmac and sheer drop into heavily forested valleys. I loved the smell of dust and vegetation. It felt wild and free.

I saw the sign for the Botanical Gardens and it intrigued me. Visit the pleasure gardens bio project, declared the handwritten sign. An impressive array of flora and fauna open to the public for the first time, the sign announced. I wondered if this was a new and obscure project my lover was involved in. Well it looked the right place from the leaflet. Good enough for me.

I reached the Gardens half an hour before closing time, and my car was the only one in the car park. There was a taverna, built with an all round balcony to enjoy the views, and a small ticket booth which was empty.

'Hello?' I called not very hopefully when I noticed someone at the far end sweeping the floor. He was tall and dark, dressed in striped T-shirt and jeans, a deep golden tan. He paused, put his broom against the wall, and strolled over. It was too hot to hurry after all. I could smell his fresh sweat, see it beading his brow. He looked at me a little in surprise but spoke politely in perfect English.

'Hello. You wish to visit the pleasure gardens?'

'The botanical bio project gardens yes. I hear they are very impressive.'

'Yes, we grow many exotic things here in this microclimate. You are a student?'

'Yes' I lied and gestured to my handbag just about

containing my A5 sketchbook, and my mobile which doubled as an excellent digicam.

He smiled. 'I am also here to study the flora and fauna for the summer. I am Max'

'Hello Max. I am Juliana'

'So you are here for inspiration?'

'Yes. You could say that ...' I trailed off, unnerved as I noticed him watching my lips and the nape my neck with vampire-like intensity. My red dress and heels were still having an effect, something which always surprised me.

Then his mobile rang and he answered swiftly. Sounded like he was talking to his boss in Greek. Then he hung up and turned back to me.

'Good luck with that,' he said 'I am to let you in free. The path is over there,' he gestured before he returned to sweeping the floor of the taverna.

I took a dusty path that wound into what seemed like a jungle. I was relieved by the shade but overwhelmed with how profuse everything was. There were figs, lime and lemons, bougainvillea, and everything seemed bursting with fruit or bloom. Soon I was walking under a trellis, vines full of bunches of grapes suspended from its wooden slats. I reached up and picked some, as though I was in the Garden of Eden, and they tasted so bright and sweet – bursting with all the goodness of the hot sun.

The more I spiralled up the path the more I spotted – bright multi coloured lizards sunning themselves, massive crickets in all shades of khaki rasping loudly as they flitted from stem to branch, and massive honey bees drinking nectar from large blooms. I imagined how delicious that honey would be with Greek yoghurt. No wonder this had been the cradle of Western civilisation. Anything seemed possible here in this kind and fertile land.

I stopped to sit on a large flat rock to sketch the view of the valley. Up so high, it was so hot and still. I wanted to capture the late afternoon light on the greenery before the sun's path behind mountains brought shadow to the valley.

There was a faint breeze where I sat, perhaps from the silver glimmer of sea in the distance. I took out my mobile to snap the view and almost dropped it when it rang.

It was him.

'Hello, darling.' At last his beautiful voice, so warm and yet commanding.

'Hello,' I said throatily, my mouth dry with nervous anticipation.

'Turn around, lean back a little. I want to see you.'

I turned around and obeyed. I could see lush vegetation above me, a nearby summit, but no sign of human life. Was he there, or was there simply a hidden webcam to watch me with? He always kept me guessing.

'Pull up your skirts, darling.'

'But someone might—'

'Discover you? Unlikely this close to closing time but always a possibility. Never mind. Do it.'

He loved to shock me out of my comfort zone. Trembling a little, I obeyed. Just as instructed, I wore stockings with my heels, but no panties. My shaven cunt was on full display, my arse bare to the warmth of the sun baked rock and the soft breeze.

'Play with yourself,' he said.

He knew it was just exactly what I wanted to do. I let my fingers stray across the swollen lips of my sex and dip into my wetness, and I groaned in pleasure.

'Very good. Now stop.'

I whimpered a little in protest but I obeyed.

'That's good,' he breathed, 'now carry on up the path a little. There's a sculpture, can you see it?'

'Yes.'

Two tall twisting shapes of smooth wood which suggested the horns of a bull. I stroked their contours, appreciated the grain of the wood. I could see a lizard dart to one side, and butterflies visiting the lavender blooms along

71

the path, its scent heavy in the air like incense. The whirr of crickets' chorus rose and fell while bees droned by.

'Lean against the sculpture, darling,' he murmured thickly, 'Lower your top. Let me admire the view.'

I undid the halter neck to expose my naked breasts. I was in the shade of an olive tree and its branches dappled my pale skin. My nipples were erect in the breeze at the thought of him somewhere, watching me. Was he on his laptop in a hotel room on the other side of the world or here on this mountain top with me?

'Beautiful', he said, 'That red really shows off the creaminess of your skin. You're a work of art yourself. A Helmut Newton maybe.'

'Thank you,' I shifted a little, eager for his next move. 'What else should I do?'

He laughed, evidently pleased at my impatience.

'Put on your blindfold then do nothing. Just wait.'

I rested my handbag at the foot of the sculpture, took from my handbag the blindfold I had brought and carefully applied it. I could hear the crickets' loud chorus rise and fall once more and strained to hear a twig snap, a footfall, in case anyone approached me now that I was this prone and vulnerable. Yet just waiting for him, like this, turned me on so much. I knew he was listening to my short shallow breathing over the mobile, enjoying the effect he had on me.

Then I did hear a twig snap behind me, and I jumped as a soft feather stroked my neck, my breasts. I gasped at the sensation. Then a leather paddle was smoothed across my skin, with its silent threat of worse, and I arched my back against it, with a soft moan.

My mobile blipped, making me jump.

'Hello?' I said anxiously, fearing we were disconnected. Then I checked my voicemail.

'Turn around and bend over,' he said.

Trembling, I obeyed. I felt my skirt tucked higher to expose my arse. Now I was all but naked in the dappled

72

shade, the warm golden air thick like honey around me. I felt soft leather and feather against my skin. It was delicious torture, to have each texture stroked randomly across my nipples, my sex, and my arse. Who was this? Was it my lover or a proxy? He had threatened to send someone else in the past, and although I only wanted him to do these delicious things to me he knew that I would obey him.

When the leather paddle paused across my buttocks I tensed.

'You can hang up now,' my real solid lover whispered softly in my ear and I smiled with delight and relief. I could smell his woodsy cologne, his soft fresh sweat as he took the mobile phone from me.

I waited, bent over, buttocks swaying slightly. Now that I knew he was the one here, how I longed to be punished.

'Have you been very wicked since we last met?' he whispered.

'Yes,' I said, feeling wet with longing.

'What do you say?'

'Please. Punish me.'

I gave an involuntary cry at the first strike across my buttocks that jerked me forward, almost over the edge but he caught me, his strong forearm a barrier, and I trembled against him as the fire licked my buttocks. He gently inserted a gag.

'We don't want to call too much attention to ourselves, darling,' he murmured as he applied the paddle once more, swiftly across my buttocks, until my heart thumped and I moaned at the shock and pleasure. It made my cunt throb with longing, the way he punished me, and I leant against him as he stroked the stinging flesh with the smooth leather. The hurt, the humiliation, the danger of being discovered all turned me on like crazy and he knew it. His fingers explored my sex slowly, with satisfaction as I writhed against him in longing.

'There,' he whispered, 'that will make for a tender

73

reminder of me for a day or two. Just a moment, I'll take a picture of your predicament for my album.' I heard him use my mobile's camera. Then I moaned as I felt his cool tongue lap soothingly across my buttock's stinging flesh.

'Delicious.'

He continued to lap at my skin, and my cunt, until I whimpered with the need to come. Then he withdrew his hands, his tongue so that I whimpered in disappointment

'Give me your wrists, darling.' I held out my wrists and he bound them together. The restraint of the smooth, wide tape made me shiver. He gently tugged me upright and pulled until my wrists were above my head, hitched me somehow to the sculpture so that I was almost suspended, on tiptoe with breasts jutting forward. He brought my ankles together and bound these too. I was helpless and I loved it, to be so completely offered for his enjoyment. I felt the breeze against my skin, against my erect nipples and sore buttocks. I longed to feel his touch again, but waited in silence for his next move.

Then he began to tease me slowly all over. The nape of my neck, my breasts, my flat tummy, the base of my spine, my instep. With little nips and a teasing circling tongue, all caressed in turn and stroked to some kind of frenzy. Finally he stroked my cunt, and circled into me with that jutting teasing tongue which made me rock and moan. Bound, I could not separate my legs to let him have deeper access and I quivered with the sweet frustration of it. I rocked and moaned, seeking release.

Finally he removed my gag.

'What do you say?' he asked sternly.

'Please. Please. *Please* ...'

I felt my bonds slacken as he took me down, pushed me gently to my knees on the dusty path. Then I felt his prick nudge against my lips and I licked gratefully along its shaft, admiring how taut it was, gently encasing the swollen glans and circling with my tongue to softly suck.

74

He moaned. Clearly I was not the only one half mad with longing.

'Stop,' he ordered at length and I stopped with a little whimper. I had wanted to make him come but he had other plans.

He pulled me down to all fours, balanced precariously. I could hear him circling, admiring me from all angles.

'Please, please, please,' I whispered, beside myself with lust, a red haze of longing before my blindfolded eyes. I wanted him to take me any way he wanted.

Finally I felt him crouch behind me and release my ankles, splay my knees apart to expose my tender sex. When he entered smoothly, firmly, my whole body quivered with pleasure at being held and possessed by him again. With my wrists still bound I could not balance well and relied on him to cradle my waist, position me just so. Slowly, carefully he circled and thrust, and I shivered every time he pressed against my tortured buttocks, every time he nipped and suckled my neck or rolled and pinched my nipples. He was teasing me into a tempo of submission I could not control, until I begged to be fucked to oblivion, begged to come. He ignored my entreaties, taking me to another plateau of abandon then another, until we finally came together, bucking and writhing like one animal, our naked bodies glistening with sweat.

Eventually he released my wrists, took off my blindfold, and we kissed tenderly like the long separated lovers we were. I gazed upon him hungrily, his blond hair and smiling blue eyes, the honey tan, his long solid body wrapped around me so fluidly, those wonderful hands and lips that had taunted my body for so long.

He took a bottle of water from his knapsack and I drank thirstily, more parched than I had realised.

'So you own this place? Is this your way of giving me a tour?' I asked.

He smiled

'I also own the villa a little way up the mountain. I thought it could be our home away from home. Will you stay a couple of nights to think it over? I have cheese and olives, yoghurt and honey, fresh figs, fine wines, a swimming pool and well ... a few other things. And lots of time I want to spend with you.'

I smiled a slow, happy smile. 'Thank you. That,' I said, 'would be a great pleasure.'

And it is.

The Oregon Trail
by Landon Dixon

He said he wanted me to find his daughter. He showed me a picture. He showed me a lot of pictures. And the family resemblance escaped me. He was short and squat and swarthy; she was tall and thin and slightly Asian-looking.

But his money made everything nice and familiar. Two thousand up-front, and five hundred a day on the trail. My bank account was at a low ebb, my scruples along with it.

He'd traced her from the east coast to the west – Portland, Oregon. My town. I assured him I could find her.

Her name was Amy Lin, twenty-five years of age. She had long, sleek black hair and hazel-coloured, slightly almond-shaped eyes, tan skin. She had a dancer's body and an erotic dancer's bustline. My client said she had money, liked a good time. She had disappeared on him and he needed to talk to her. I was the bloodhound.

I carefully folded his dough into my pocket and then took the light-rail from my office across the Willamette River into downtown. I hung around until dark, people-watching, then went on the prowl. It was a Friday summer night, and the nightclubs were doing a booming business. I did more club-hopping than I'd done in years.

And just when I thought I'd come away with little more than a headache from the music and a hangover from the liquor, there she was – at The Vibe, out on the strobe-flashed, writhing dance floor.

She was wearing a silky black dress and very little

underwear, a wild expression, gyrating to the overpowering techno beat, flinging her arms and body around, dancing with everyone and no one. I fought my way through the mob and yelled, 'Amy Lin! Your father's looking for you!'

Her long, lithe arms came down and her long, lithe legs stopped prancing around. Her eyes narrowed and darkened, and she yelled back, 'I don't want to see him!'

I knew that already. So I hooked onto her elbow, nice and gentle and firm, started steering her off the dance floor, through the crowd. Her skin was tawny and smooth, warm to the touch.

She started screaming, as loud as she could, staring me in the eyes. Her shriek pierced the thundering air like a siren.

Bouncers barged onto the scene from all corners, and gallant gents stepped up into my face on behalf of a damsel in distress. Strong, rough hands grabbed onto my arms and held me tight. As Amy Lin melted away into the crowd.

Explanations failed me. So I head-butted the guys on either side, kicked the bouncer in front in the groin. My arms came free and I grabbed onto the bent-over bouncer and drove him forward like a tackling dummy, using his big body to clear a path through the sea of unfriendly humanity.

I burst through the aluminium doors of the joint just in time to spot a rental car roar out of the lot and bounce onto the street. I had a hunch who was driving.

I tailed her out onto Route 30, heading west. Not too close and not too far behind, just in range of the resourceful lady. If it hadn't been nighttime, our trip would've been a scenic one, through the deep, green forest that crowded either side of the highway, along the mighty Columbia River. All the way out to the Pacific Ocean – the picturesque, historic town of Astoria.

Amy checked into a motel on the hilly, wooded outskirts of town, bedded down. I waited until daybreak, then slipped out of my car and into her room.

She had a spectacular view of the Columbia emptying

into the ocean. The wide river gleamed bright blue down below, the forest all around emerald-green. Two long bridges crossed the river at different points, one high, one low. In the distance: the vast, placid, grey-blue waters of the Pacific Ocean.

The town had been founded by John Jacob Astor, 19th century fur baron. Lewis and Clark had camped in the area circa 1805; 85 straight days of cold winter rain.

But it was warm and sunny now, the air fresh and clean, pine and salt-scented. The scenery was a sight to behold, outdoors and in.

I left the curtains slightly open and pocketed my lock-picking tools, walked over to the bed and looked down at the long, luscious, caramel-coated and mound-titted body of Amy Lin stretched out asleep on the bed. Her little black party dress lay puddled on the carpet. I touched her bare shoulder.

Her eyes instantly fluttered open, narrowed, cat-like. She sighed and stretched her arms and legs, shuddered, kitten-like. She didn't seem the least bit surprised to see me standing there, violating her privacy.

'You're a hard man to shake,' she murmured, emphasising the soft rise and fall of her breasts.

'I'm habit-forming, all right. Getting paid to be.'

She smiled, bathed her plush lips with a shiny pink tongue. 'There are other ways to be paid.'

She reached out a long arm and latched slender fingers onto my belt buckle, pulled me closer. I could've slapped her hand away and reached for my cellphone, called the number where my client could be reached, was waiting impatiently to hear from me. But the sight of that stunning body, the scent of her sweet body spray in the air, the feel of Amy's scarlet-tipped fingers drawing my fly down and my cock out, was too much for a man of dubious ethics to ever resist.

She laced her fingers around my shaft, her palm

79

squeezing warm and wonderful. 'Jesus!' I exhaled, watching the silky woman swing her body around on the bed so that she was sitting up on the edge, the sensual swirl of her hand drawing me closer to her lush, parted lips.

She cradled my balls out of my pants with her other hand, gently cupping, fondling; caressing my cock out long and hard and throbbing right in front of her.

Now, I'm not a bad-looking guy – medium-height and build, blond hair and blue eyes, a cleft chin and youthful expression – but Amy was a lady normally out of my league. She was exotic and erotic. The things she did with her hands on my genitals made my head spin and my body burn.

And when she fully flowered her crimson lips and flowed them over my mushroomed hood, poured them down two-thirds of the length of my swollen shaft, staring up at me with her sparkling eyes, I just about blew my top then and there.

But, somehow, I held on, and off. I shot my fingers into her shimmering black curtain of hair and grabbed hold. Her head moved in my hands, her wet, hot mouth gliding back and forth on my cock, sucking me tight and tender with ease and expertise. I groaned, glaring down at her. Her lips smiled around my shaft, her beautiful head bobbing on and on.

'Jesus! I can't–'

I couldn't even finish the sentence, complete the dirty thought. My balls boiled out of control in Amy's grasping hand and my cock surged wildly in her sucking mouth. I clutched her hair and thrust out my hips, jerked, jolted by joy.

She sucked firmly and calmly and sensually, taking every white-hot, body-shaking blast I let loose. I emptied everything I had into the woman. Then almost swooned over the top of her.

She took me down onto the bed and in between her legs. 'Your turn,' she teased, looking over her humped tits at my

80

reddened face. She licked her glossy lips, swallowing the last of my semen.

I had to give back, reciprocate best I could. She deserved that much. There'd always be time to call my client.

I gripped her taut, golden thighs and stared into the soft, darker folds of her pussy. She was shaved clean expect for a downy black tuft of fur at the top of her slit. Her pussy lips glistened with moisture, the scent and heat making my dizzy head spin all over again. I stuck out my tongue and licked her.

She bucked, grabbing onto my head. Her breasts thrust up huge between her arms, nipples jutting high and hard. I flattened my tongue and lapped at her pussy, stroking from deep down over her puffy lips all the way up to her swollen clit. She shivered with each drag of my licker, her lovely body sexually tensing.

I dug my tongue in, squirming the thick, wet, red appendage right into her pussy, writhing it around inside the woman's satin pink tunnel. She vibrated on the end of my tongue, wrapping her thighs around my neck, her eyes wide and staring, nostrils flared.

I pulled my tongue out of her slit and popped her clit up with my fingers, slapped the hard little pink button around with my mouth-organ.

'Oh, God! Yes!' Amy cried.

She arched up off the bed. I just had time to seal my lips around her clit and suck on it, before she screamed and squirted hot juices against my chin. She bounced my head up and down, clawing at my scalp, drenching my face, her clit pulsating in my mouth to the frenzied beat of her orgasm.

Then she really choked me with her thighs, twisting my neck with a sharp snap.

When I came to, she was gone.

Cannon Beach is a gorgeous, mile-long expanse of sand

dotted with treed outcroppings not far from shore, about thirty miles down the coast from Astoria. The town itself is slightly tacky, with a touristy, carnival feel. But the beach at low tide is something to behold – stretching out, shimmering, seemingly forever to the far-off, hazy blue horizon of the ocean.

I located Amy's rental car in one of the parking lots just off the main drag, thanks to the tracking device I'd attached to her undercarriage before I'd busted into her motel room. I found Amy down on the beach faraway from the madding crowd of kids and their parents, sunning herself in a hot-orange bikini, stretched out on a tiger-striped beach towel. She was just as stunning in the bright light of day, buff and busty and gleaming bronze.

She lifted her designer sunglasses and looked up at me when I cast a shadow and called out her name.

'I was his mistress. That's why he wants me back. He's the violently jealous type, brutally possessive.' She gracefully lifted herself up on her elbows. Her breasts surged outward, straining the thin material of her bikini top, nipples just about poking right through. 'I won't go back to him. I can't. I …'

She left it hanging, like she had me.

'I'm not going to force you, Amy. I'm just going to tell him where you are. That's my job.'

She bit her lip and narrowed her eyes, gazing out at the sparkling water way off in the distance. 'Maybe.'

She rose to her feet and took my hand.

I let her lead me out onto the beach. It was a long, hot walk to the water with the tide out, the sand getting wetter and stickier, the air steamier. The screams and shouts of the other beachgoers faded away. As we strolled hand-in-hand all the way out to where the ocean lapped shallow and gentle and warm at the sand.

The heat was intense, heavy, the air hazy and humid.

Amy turned and faced me. She unbuttoned my shirt and

pushed it off my shoulders, unbuckled and unzipped my pants, pushed them and my shorts down. I stood there in a trance, dripping with sweat, burning inside and out, my cock swelling up and jutting out like before, like never before. The hot, salty air caressed my nude body with languid moisture, as I watched Amy slip the thin straps of her bikini top off her shoulders and let the overfull cups drop. As she unsashed her bikini bottom and let the thin strip of orange fall.

We stood naked on the damp sand at the ocean's edge, glowing with heat, beating with passion. I grabbed the beautiful woman in my arms and flung her and I down onto the sand. She coiled her arms around me, and we kissed, frenched, our tongues exploding out of our mouths and entwining.

Amy dove her hands down my back and onto my buttocks. She clenched the flexing pair, as I pumped my hard cock into her soft belly. 'Make love to me!' she moaned, breaking away from my devouring mouth.

I clutched up her breasts and kneaded the hot, heaping mounds. Amy rolled her head side-to-side in the sand. As I sucked up one rigid, rubbery nipple and tugged on it, bobbed my head over and urgently sucked on her other nipple. Until she pulled my head back up and mashed her lush mouth against mine again, and we wound our tongues together in a frenzy.

I lifted up. Amy grabbed onto my cock, washed my hood back and forth through her pussy lips. She was breathing as hard as I was, her face and body dewed with perspiration. She bit into my tongue and sucked on it, slotting my cock into her cunt.

'Yes!' we groaned, both together.

Amy grabbed onto my ass again and sunk her claws in, urging me to fuck her, glaring into my eyes. I met her lust head-on, pumping my hips, my cock back and forth in her wet-velvet tunnel. We swirled our tongues together, she grasping my ass, me her tits. I pounded into her faster and faster. She sank into the sand, the water lapping against us.

Amy arched up and shuddered wickedly, her fingernails tearing at my buttocks. Hotter, stickier juices coated my plunging cock, and I cried out my own ecstasy, spraying searing come into the screaming woman.

We reluctantly pulled ourselves out of the sand and dressed, walked back up the beach.

Amy ran away from me as soon as I had my back turned to gather up her towel and bag.

It took ten minutes of dogged jogging up and down the wood-plank sidewalks of the small beach town before I finally caught up with her again. She was standing in front of a cotton candy concession, holding a young boy by the hand.

'This is the real reason I have to get away from your client,' she explained calmly, lifting the boy's hand in hers. 'This is Andrew, my son. His father recently died, and I have to look after him now.'

The kid stared up at me with his big brown eyes. He had short black hair and a cute round face and a plump little body. He looked unmistakably Asian. He smiled at me.

Amy pleaded with her eyes. And I nodded, watched them walk away. Then I phoned my client and told him the trail had gone cold.

'Look, asshole!' he bellowed. 'I didn't tell you before ... but that bitch has $200,000 of my money. She stole it from me when she took off, and I want it, and her, back. So you fucking find her! I'll give you 10% of the dough that's recovered – as a finder's fee.'

Just then I turned a corner, and spotted Amy handing over her "son" to a couple of Japanese tourists down the block. The man and woman were sitting in an open-air tent eating corndogs with a larger group of their countrymen. The kid ran over to them, cotton candy in one hand, Amy's fifty-dollar bill in the other.

'I'm on it,' I growled into the phone.

Amy showed actual surprise when she found me leaning against the side of her rental car. She still looked luscious in the bikini, with the beach towel wrapped around her hips. But I wasn't having any of that any more, when she wound her arms around my neck and kissed me wetly on the lips. The prospect of twenty grand changes a man's priorities.

'You stole some of his money. He wants it, and you, back. And I don't care what he does when he gets you back.'

Her arms slid off my neck. 'What about what he does to *you*, when he gets me back?'

'Let's go. It's a hundred mile drive back to Portland.'

She pushed her sunglasses up into her lustrous hair and adjusted the straps of her bikini. Her breasts jostled deliciously, full rounded curves shining bronze in the hot sun.

'I wasn't lying about him being the violently jealous, possessive type – when it comes to money and women.' Amy bit her lip and batted her long, black eyelashes. 'If I told him you seduced me in my motel room, and on the beach – ate me out and fucked me – there's no telling what he might do to you.' She smiled, like she had it all planned out from the start.

I stared into her dark, duplicitous eyes; then shrugged. 'We can have a pretty good time for a couple of weeks – on his money. While I stall him along.'

Her smile turned wet and warm. 'You know, this is actually my first time in Oregon.'

I took her hand, grinning. 'Well then, let me show you around.'

Escape
by Clarice Clique

It's hot. Searing. Burning. Sticky. Heavy.

A raw heat that reaches into my body, boiling me, stripping me to the bone, leaving nothing but my essence exposed for all to see.

I am no longer the clothes I so avidly choose from fashion magazines, not my beloved Stella McCartney handbag or treasured Jimmy Choos. I am not carefully applied layers of natural looking make-up, nor the scent of some Hollywood star's mass produced perfume.

I am long red tangled hair. I am dried out skin. I am broken unpainted nails.

I am Tits. I am Arse. I am Cunt.

Silver5 tells me that this is the Sahara at her gentlest after the rainfall. I see the air thick with mosquitoes, carelessly carrying malaria; death and disease a wing-beat away. I see nothing gentle.

Silver5 digs his rough hands into my arms and pulls me back into our tent.

I have to constantly remind myself that he's not really Silver5, that I should call him his true name.

'This is real life now,' he growls in my ear, 'get my name right.'

This hazy world of camels and sand dunes *is* real life.

So why does it feel like a dream?

Not as true as sitting in my dark, cool, basement room on

the edge of London, typing one-handed messages to strangers; telling one I'm spreading my butt cheeks, and another I'm thrusting my favourite vibe into my pussy, all while I sip a mug of low calorie carrot soup and casually watch two men suck each other off in a porn video playing in the background.

I have to constantly remind myself that this heat is reality, the other thing is a life of the imagination; a virtual life.

But still in my mind the man who thrusts his hand down the front of my shorts is Silver5. Even as I cry out the right things, night after night, day after day.

'Dave, oh, Dave.'

'You're so big, Dave, almost too big.'

'Harder, Dave.'

'Please. Dave. Please.'

'I'm coming, Dave.'

'Thank you, Dave.'

Dave was a disappointment when we first met.

No, not a disappointment, that word is too harsh. He was just different from what I was expecting.

He said on his profile that he was forty-two. In person he could be ten or fifteen years more than that. Maybe it's just all the time he spends outside; the sun and rain and wind marking him as one of their own. Even if his age is a lie, it's not one that matters. I like, I yearn for and seek out, experienced men. His body is firm and hard, compact and strong. As soon as I saw him I knew he could fulfil all the fantasies we'd shared online.

As stupid as it sounds, it was his name that made a little piece of my heart sink. I fantasised about being fucked by an exotic world-renowned photographer, not a man called Dave, who despite his travels, carried with a definite pride the remnants of the London accent I heard every day in my normal life.

All the countries he'd been to, all the things he'd seen which the majority of people could only ever experience through his photographs, and he summarised it in the women he's slept with: thirty nine different nationalities.

But these things excite me as well.

I like the stubborn roughness of his voice as he orders me onto my knees.

And when I watch his cock slide into me, I think of all the people who have preceded me: a petite geisha; a Hungarian shot putter; a dusky Brazilian prostitute; a French high society lady; and so many more from countries I couldn't find on a map. I wrap my legs around Dave's waist and all those women exist for me, I feel a part of them and through them somehow connected to the billions of people in this world. For beautiful eternal moment I'm more than just another lonely insignificant collection of atoms.

He rips through the loose cotton of my shirt and twists me onto my back. His hands grip my wrists, his weight pins me down and his teeth bite into the delicate flesh of my breasts. In the furnace of the tent, sweat drips down both our bodies. I am coated in his scent, he is coated in mine. Is this what it means, two becoming one?

He grinds into me and my skin bruises inside and out. All who have gone before, all his other women, all my other men, fade away. My mind is white light. There is no Dave, no Silver5. I have no thoughts, no fears, no past or future.

Nothing exists but our entwined limbs and the infernal desert heat.

This is freedom.

This is my escape.

This is proof that I am more than the secretary typing out endless divorce proceedings, making infinite cups of coffee for men who have stopped loving their wives, passing countless tissues to women who have started hating their husbands.

*   *   *

'What's Niger?' my best friend asked. 'Are you sure you don't mean Nigeria? And why do you want to go there anyway? Everyone is starving in Africa, aren't they? It's all thieves, murderers. And worse.'

'Aren't you a little late for a gap year? This is what you're planning, isn't it, however you want to dress it up,' my boss said. 'You are doing very well here, Chloe. You have the opportunity for a good career. I'm afraid I'll not be able to hold the position open for you.'

'Darling,' my beautiful caring mother said squeezing my hand, 'you know I'll always support you whatever you want to do, but think of the danger. Going to an unknown country with an unknown man, and whatever you say chatting to a stranger through a computer does not mean that you know them, you'll never convince me otherwise. Will you please think about it some more. For me, if nothing else. You probably don't feel it, but you're still very young. Be patient and I'm sure you'll meet a lovely solicitor, or maybe a lawyer. Seeing that you don't seem to mind older men, perhaps there might be a single judge waiting out there for you. Of course if he's single you'd have to think there might be a reason that he hadn't got married, a widower will be better. That comes with problems of its own, but nothing like trusting someone you don't know from Adam.'

With Silver5 it was easier, despite his early protests.

Me (as **Scarletgirl**): I am coming with you on your next trip.

Silver5: How many times do I have to tell you? It's not happening. I don't do commitment. You know that's why I've never got married. I've always been honest with you, Scarlet. I just want sex between jobs. Read my profile again. If you've forgotten. NSA=No Strings Attached.

Scarletgirl: I don't have any strings attached. You can examine every part of my naked body yourself to check.

Silver5: I will do that and a lot more. In England. Not Africa.

Scarletgirl: I'll be your whore, your bitch, your hooker, your courtesan, your slave. You're hard for me without even meeting me. Think what it'd be like in real life. You can do all the things you want, spank my pussy, bind my tits, fuck my arse. And I'm certain there is more, you haven't told me everything. And you don't have to. You can do it all. In Africa. Not England.

Across the years, across the world, women and men have traded their bodies, their love, for a lot less.

And everything he said he wanted, everything he's done since we met, has fulfilled my own desires.

Each time my thighs part and I accept him into my body, the greatest aphrodisiac, *power*, surges through me. He wants me, he *needs* me. He twists my limbs around, he slaps my tits, spanks my pussy, forces his fingers between my buttocks, and all the time I'm alive with an incredible sense of control.

In those moments it seems like that is the only reason I am here, the only reason I keep taking every heavy step, every panting breath. In this heat, life seems slower but in the desert, surrounded by millions upon millions of grains of sand; it is like being thrown into a middle of a metaphor.

Silver5, Dave, is here in Niger, where the world seems too close to the sun, like any second we are going to spin into its fire and the whole human race will return to ash, to photograph the Gerewol festival.

'It is what it is,' he says with a shrug. 'It's been too overexposed now, everyone knows about it, going to have to get something really special to make it stand out.'

I nod as if I sympathise, as if he cares about my opinion.

All I know about the Gerewol festival I saw in a couple of YouTube clips and I read in the Wikipedia page on the Wodaabe tribe.

I just wanted to be away from London, I didn't mind where. But still …

But still something stood out about women being allowed to be sexually promiscuous and take other married men to their bed.

Would my boss lose all his business, would marriages in England be happier, if we had the same tolerance?

I ask Silver5, Dave, that question. His reply is a disinterested shrug.

I watch his hands finger his different lenses as if they are living, feeling things, and am both aroused and jealous.

I brush my hand against the fine hairs of his arms.

He pauses, staring at me, before he finally shakes his head. 'I'm working.'

The passion and wonder I experienced typing to him before we met surges through me; a sense of love and admiration for his world where work is playing with pieces of a camera. No office. No eternal paperwork. No lunch break with your colleagues, where veiled bitchiness masquerades as friendship.

I look around at the vastness of the sand, seeming to shimmer in the heat. It all belongs to him and his camera. This dream that I can't grasp is his life.

'You haven't taken any photos of me yet.' I undo the buttons on my cotton top revealing my naked breasts.

He glances at me and frowns.

I swallow hard. There is no one about, but under his gaze I suddenly feel like a naughty little schoolgirl about to be banished to the tent for the rest of the trip.

He bites down on his lip. 'All of them. Take all of your clothes off.'

His hands continues to fondle his camera as I remove my shorts and knickers and shoes, letting them all fall into the sand, then look around me, unable to meet his eyes. Dave has told me that Niger contains some of the most beautiful sand dunes in the Sahara, in the world. I have nothing to compare them with, but I am awed by them.

Silver5, Dave, is able to navigate them. He says it's a gift he learnt over many journeys with an old tribeswoman. They all look the same to me, but that somehow increases the smallness I feel standing naked, an interloper in their midst.

Is it possible to feel so empowered and so insignificant at the same time for the same reason?

Dave appears unaffected by the natural beauty that surrounds us. He points for me to stand in a different spot.

'You know nothing about light, Scarlet.'

'How comes I have to call you Dave but you can call me Scarlet? You know my name is Chloe.'

He doesn't bother to answer and I obediently walk to the spot he indicated.

The sand burns my feet; I try not to show it.

I pose like a supermodel, one foot in front of the other, hip thrust forward, pouting as if my beauty is a burden, staring into the distance as if my beauty disconnects me from the ordinary world.

I pose like a glamour model, my hands on my tits, tossing my hair, parting my lips, a glint in my eye, teasing the whole world into wanting to fuck me.

I pose like a porn star, my fingers pulling on my nipples, flicking my clit, delving into my velvet passage, as if I care about nothing but my own pleasure.

Silver5, Dave, stares at me, there is an obvious bulge at his crotch, yet he does not take any photos.

'What do you want me to do?' I ask exasperated, my hands falling to my side.

'On your back, legs spread.'

I feel a momentary twinge of hurt that I haven't done enough, or haven't found the right thing, to make him want to capture me for all eternity with his lens. But it is overpowered and destroyed by the sexual energy that flows through me in response to his simple command.

I drop onto the burning sand and part my thighs. He walks over to me and now I hear the click of his camera.

I stay still and pretend I am not conscious of him. Pretend

that I am not aware of every grain of the desert sticking to my back and legs, a thousand embers searing my skin.

He stands above me, his monster of a camera is hanging around his neck on a thick strap, he supports it in one hand, the other hand is unzipping his fly and pulling his hard cock out.

'Squeeze your tits together,' he says and I obey.

I stare at the drops of precome glistening on the head of his cock, in the desert all water, all liquid, takes on a magical quality beneath the continual glare of the sun. Drops of sweat from his brow drop onto my stomach.

He wanks in long motions from the tip of his cock to the base, his strokes get faster and I move a hand down to my own sex, rubbing my whole hand over my pussy.

I think of being at home huddling under the duvet on cold, dark winter nights, caressing myself between my thighs and being amazed at the heat as the rest of my body shivered. Here the warm moistness of my cunt is nothing under the dominating rays of the sun.

In London it would be the beginning of autumn, the slight hope of a summer that never appeared fading into a constant fine drizzle. Legs and chests that had been bared a couple of weeks earlier would now be safely protected under coats and trousers, the city would sink back into the greyness that it wears so naturally.

I think of the oranges and yellows and reds of the dying leaves. Here in this arid landscape where plants and animals have to struggle for every moment of life, where the sky and sand stretch out into eternity, everything is so much brighter, somehow more alive.

So why do I yearn for home as Dave's spunk shoots out over my stomach and breasts.

I rub his come into my skin, it easily merging with the hot stickiness of my sweat. Licking my fingers clean. He gives me a nod and walks off as I slowly put my clothes back on. I do not attempt to brush the sand off. I want it to scratch at my skin, to scratch me inside and out. I want to be part of this world, to feel that somehow I belong.

I'm relieved when we get close to Ingal. The barrenness of the desert becomes busy with people moving towards the festival. I think of the bustle of London, but instead of cars there are barefoot children leading donkeys and the sound of traffic is replaced by the lowing of cattle.

I am genuinely shocked when I see a white face, freckled and tanned to a light hazelnut, amongst the elegant African features.

'Who's that?' I ask nudging Dave.

Dave swears under his breath. 'I'm working. Don't make me regret letting you come.'

'Don't you pretend for a moment that you could ever regret letting me come.' I wink at him but he's focused on a world that doesn't include me.

I hope I am not breaking any ancient tribal etiquette as I weave through the figures, who pay me little attention, and fall in beside the white woman.

She smiles at me. 'You're a tourist? Come for the Cure Salée?' She speaks with a French accent but her English is perfect.

'I'm here for the Gerewol festival. My friend is a photographer.'

'Yes,' she says as if I'd just agreed with her, or confirmed what she already knew.

'What about you? You're a tourist too?' Looking at her, my question seems ridiculous. Her skin is lighter, her hair a fine white-blonde and she's shorter than the tribe around her, but the way she walks and holds herself makes her part of them in a way that I could never be.

'This is my friend, Doulla; he is one of the leaders.' With a small hand movement she introduces the man standing next to her.

The tall slim man gives me a wide smile, revealing

94

perfect white teeth, but there is something inconsolably sad about his face.

'Hi, Doulla I'm Chloe.' I give him a little wave as if we're saying goodbye rather than meeting for the first time. I savour the feel of his name on my tongue, exotic and fresh. Then I blush with the realisation that I know nothing about his culture, no words of his language, no idea of the polite way to behave.

'It's a pleasure to meet you, Chloe.' His accent is thick and he speaks slowly.

'You can speak English? Well, of course you can, you just did. I'm sorry. I don't mean to appear so ignorant.'

Doulla speaks to me in his steady English as I journey on in the midst of his tribe. I don't understand it all, but it doesn't matter. In the heat of the day his voice washes over me like a trickle of soothing water.

The French woman only speaks occasionally to help him remember words and to expand excitedly on how they met in Paris.

I want to ask him how he got to Paris, why he returned here to the hard life of a nomadic tribe surviving on the little the desert offers. But the questions do not matter so much as listening to the continual flow of his voice.

It's only when the tribe begin to settle for the night, making up an elaborate array of beds, which I yearn to be invited to lie down on, that I worry about finding Silver5, Dave. And then I am not as concerned as I should be. If I don't find him I'll lie down on the sand and let the insects feast on my blood and the sand mould around my body.

But he is there on the edge of everything. He gives a small nod to indicate I go into the tent.

I tell him about Doulla and the French woman, Christine, I think she said her name was.

'She lives with him, walks with him everywhere. He was in France, for some reason, somehow, but he came back here to be with his people. Isn't that amazing?'

'It is.' He puts a finger under my chin. 'And all you could think about was what it would be like sucking on his big black cock.'

'No, no. It wasn't like that. It was peaceful and beautiful and wonderful, having a conversation with someone from such a different way of life.'

'Lie to me if you want, but don't lie to yourself. The attraction between us, the reason I was willing to break all my rules and bring you with me, is based on the fact that we're two people who are entirely centred on sexual pleasure. People talk all sort of artistic guff about my work, but the real reason they like it is because it lets them glimpse how I see the world, which is the same way that you see it; sex. And it's opposite, death.' As he speaks his hands grope my breasts as if they have a will of their own.

I stare into his old eyes that have seen so much. My own hands pull at his fly.

It's true. Whether I am typing four letter profanities to strangers in the safety of my home, or sweating under a foreign sun, it is all about sex to me.

I find his thick cock and wank it, all the time staring into his eyes. With my other hand I pull my own shorts down. I take his hand and place it on my sex. He rubs his thumb over my clit and pushes a finger inside me. I gasp and step closer to him.

'Do you wish I was your new African friend?' He gives me a half smile.

'No.' I lick my lips. 'While you're fingering me, I'm imagining that he is out there fucking the French girl.'

'Me too.' He kisses my neck and then pulls me into him.

His cock grinds into my pussy. I think of the lovers I've had who've fumbled around not knowing what to do, not caring what I want. I grind back into Dave, closing my eyes and seeing Doulla on top of the French woman, whispering to her all the secrets of the desert.

Neither Dave nor I come. Or we come multiple times.

Through the night we cling to each other, our limbs entwined. And for the first time I think I understand what I'm doing here so far from home.

I watch the Gerewol standing by Dave's side. The men have spent hours getting ready. Covering their faces in red make-up, their teeth are so white and their eyes are wide as they dance, rocking on their feet, and sing in voices that reach into my soul, before the women that will judge them. Dave says they take lots of stimulants so they can dance like this all day, he tells me that some tribes have to travel hundreds of miles to get the pigment for their make-up.

There are a small handful of tourists, leaning against a jeep, snapping photos. There are more people just wandering around, sometimes looking over at the dance, but mostly talking and busy with the concerns of their own life.

I wish the whole world would stop and look at how beautiful these men are. How paradoxically masculine they appear when by western standards they have feminised themselves.

I press into Dave's and feel the sweat of his body through his clothes. I breathe in the desert air and I breathe in the scent of the man who has taken me to this old world where everything began, this land of sex and death.

It is December. I shove the scribble list of things I need to buy for Christmas into my pocket. I wrap a scarf around my neck and cover half my face ready to hit Oxford Street. Before I leave, on a whim, I check my e-mail for a final time.

I smile when I see something from Silver5. I open it and a photo of my naked body lying in the desert sand flashes up. I stare at my parted legs, my hands resting across my chest and stomach, and my face. I am looking away from the camera, staring into the distance as if I can see something no one else can.

He has written three words.

Peru in February?

I shut the computer down, wrap the scarf round my face a little bit tighter and venture outside. A north wind hits me with all its cold wet power, but I don't stop smiling.

Burning Woman
by L A Fields

Owen will remember his time at Burning Man as a week of merrily twirling color. Taking 'shrooms and watching people ribbon dance and spin umbrellas in his face, put on light shows, finger-paint their naked bodies like children, unsexually, unselfconsciously. Owen appreciates their pure souls for the first few days, but in the three years since he graduated from college, he's missed more about school than the casual bald intimacy of people on drugs. He misses sex. He misses sex with creative people, girls who make clothes out of rags, girls who make art of their hair, girls who look really happy in their bodies, and who like him enough to share that joy with Owen.

This trip was something he and his friends had always talked about doing. Everybody knew about Burning Man, and half the parties on campus seemed to imitate all they knew about it – trippy decorations, people running around in horns and fake fur, music made out of the noise from didgeridoos and Theremins and rain-makers. It was all amusing then, but after graduation it became much more important to keep that youthful whimsy in their lives. Phone calls back and forth between his buddies were sad laundry lists: my job sucks; my apartment sucks; no I don't have any friends like you guys; and no I haven't met any girls.

They all met at the airport and rented a car out to the festival. They all agreed:

'This is going to be awesome.'

'Yeah it's been rough, but this trip is going to put it all in perspective.'

'Man, it is so great to see you guys again, we haven't betrayed who we wanted to be at all.'

But it isn't three days before Owen discovers just how much his friends have changed, and in their mirror he realises sadly: he must have changed too.

Ron is engaged, and though Owen doesn't really want to hold that against him, it's just that twenty-five still seems so young, and Ron talks about it exactly the same way that his other buddy, Harrison, talks about grad school. Like it's an investment, a business decision. If you want to get married, live in a house and have some kids, you've got to get started before you're thirty, and right now it's a buyer's market because most people their age are only just pairing off.

'We're not that young any more,' Ron tells him. 'This is pretty much my last hurrah.'

'Cool,' Owen replies non-committally. He feels like he hardly started having hurrahs in school before it was supposedly time to leave them behind. But not everyone takes life seriously, Owen knows. That's what he's here to learn about.

These people ... what could they possibly do for a living? The guy with tattoos on his face and ironic breast implants? The woman who is sixty years old if she's a day with crazy neon troll hair, a bejeweled bellybutton to match, and an X over each sagging breast's nipple made out of black electrical tape? When did *they* grow up? What's *their* retirement portfolio going to be worth in forty years? Who lied to Owen and told him there was a "right" way to live when *clearly* these people do nothing more illegal than the occasional hallucinogen, and are still out roaming in the world on their own free terms?

Owen admires every flamingo and scarlet ibis and peacock he spots while wandering through the festival. He participates whenever someone needs a partner for

100

volleyball (or chicken volley ball, or a game of Questions played over a net like in Rosencrantz and Guildenstern Are Dead). And yet ... well, it turns out beggars really can be choosers.

He looks at every girl twice, once as a stranger in a strange land, trying to categorize them, see who they really are, who they want to be perceived as, etc. Next he measures them like a discerning grocery buyer: too green, too ripe, too bruised, too pricey, too good to be true, and even a few he deems rotten. For days the only girls he even speaks to are the ones he meets through their boyfriends, and although several of them seem open and eager to welcome Owen to a threesome, it just isn't the sort of thing he's shopping for.

But after a while he spots someone. You'd think in the riot of colour you might not notice one girl's hair, but in a sea of artificial dyes, this girl has naturally remarkable hair. It's ginger-bronze. It's a copper-berry. It's amber waves of champagne.

This girl, she isn't perfect either. She's at least thirty pounds overweight, but Owen likes a girl with some heft in her breasts anyway. She's as pale as fear and burnt red or peeling everywhere the sun touches her skin. When she dances she drips like someone who's trying to sweat out a fever, but no matter what Owen sees, he finds a way to like it. She's drinking vodka straight from a plastic jug? She knows how to party. She's making out with two guys at once? She's friendly. She decides to sing along loud to someone's radio? Well, she's got a great voice, and that's not even wishful thinking on Owen's part, not some lustful illusion, she really is good. In fact when Owen finally works up the nerve to speak to her, the first thing he learns is that she's a singer in band.

'We were staying with some guy in Reno who was planning to come out here, so of course we tagged along. Haven't you always wanted to go to Burning Man?'

'Yeah,' says Owen. 'So you're another virgin then? I

keep meeting all these old-timers.'

'Virgin, yeah!' She laughs in a voice much deeper than the one she sings with. 'It's nice to be a virgin again at something. Lord knows it's been a while otherwise.'

'How old are you?'

'Twenty-three,' she tells him. She's resting on something that might be a mangled desert rock or might be somebody's art, there's no way to tell for sure. She was leaning there for a while before Owen came up, her head moving as if to music, though there were no headphones in her ears.

'Did you just graduate?' Owen asks, thinking he's finally found someone he can relate to.

'Naw, I never even finished high school.'

She smiles blearily at him, looks him up and down slowly, sizes him up. Owen hopes his tan is even, that his clothes seem cleaner than they are, that he comes across as earnest, but aloof.

'You wanna hang out?' she asks him, and with that Owen knows: he's made muster. He's in.

She shares a tent with a beautiful guy, tall and Nordic this guy, teeth like he's sucking on a string of pearls. Owen is relieved to discover that this guy is gay, and that he's got somewhere else to be.

Missy invites Owen into the cocooned heat of the tent, and in response to that heat, she pulls out the simple bow that's been holding on her entire light halter dress. It falls to her waist, pooling around her like shallow water.

Her breasts are heavy, and her skin has the cold sear of a way-too-hot bath, the kind of hot your brain almost interprets as freezing. Or maybe her skin is clammy-cool compared to the covered air in the tent. Owen doesn't spare more than a moment trying to figure it out.

She lifts a knee, her dress still covering the crux of her body, the hottest place on any girl. She combs out her hair with her fingers, settling that around her too, just like the puddles of her dress. She watches Owen patiently, and why

102

she tolerates him is unknown to Owen, because he can feel his jaw slacking open, his eyes glazing stupidly, his fingers fumbling as he reaches towards one of her nipples, as if to pluck a strawberry.

Owen has forgotten his feet outside the tent. He's leaning on one hand and cupping an ample, hangdog breast in the other. He doesn't envelop totally into this bud of a space until his date hikes her skirt back, and Owen desperately needs his other hand to explore her molten core. Yesterday Owen met a glassblower at the festival who told him every detail of the process, and yes, reaching into her is like dipping a piece of himself into a furnace. If she is a crucible, Owen is a blowpipe. Even her patch of hair is a dark orange flame. Even the condom she hands him has the viscous transparency of liquid glass.

There are patches of sand in the bottom of the tent, in and out of the snake pit of sleeping bags twisted around each other. It starts to sparkle and dot her hair as she writhes beneath him, using her head and neck as leverage to arch further towards Owen. He clutches at her in thick handfuls, he smothers himself in one of her breasts as if into a pillow. In the moment of his climax, Owen knows with certainty that he would happily suffocate himself if she'd allow it.

In the moments after however, he discovers that she wouldn't.

'Wow,' Owen says as he lies back on the ground. 'And I don't even know your name.'

'What good would it do you?' she asks him with a tired sort of amusement. 'I bet you never see me again after this week.'

'Well, yeah,' Owen says, realising of course how improbable it would be to carry on any sort of relationship with someone who might live anywhere in the country, but almost assuredly nowhere near him. He accepts that disappointing reality with an adult's practised ease. 'Still, there's no reason for us not to be friendly, right?'

103

'We've been friendly enough already,' she says with a more genuine smile. She pats him on the shoulder as she gets up and starts to retie her dress. 'You can count yourself as one of my friends.'

Owen comes to find out by the end of festival that this girl has a lot of friends. She's got a name too; she's actually not that stingy with it, since all the other guys call her by it. Missy. He keeps spotting her by that magnificent hair, and whenever he sees it he approaches it, a moth to the flame.

But soon enough (too soon enough) it's time to return home again. His friends want to leave early to beat the traffic and get back to the comforts of a hotel room, and truth be told, Owen gets tired of Missy's statuesque friend looking at him pityingly, like he's just another one of many. Owen decides to bow out gracefully, packs up his good time, and gets into the car for the trip back to the real world.

The windows are lowered as they're pulling away, so they can see the last of the sights. Owen spots Missy one final time by the turn of her head, and he smiles quietly, keeping it with him as they start home, feeling a little bit better even if he doesn't feel quite like his old college self, the kid he used to be … the one he came out here to find.

Owen is looking at Ron and Harrison, thinking that this vague disappointment isn't the *worst* thing in the world; nobody stays young forever, right?

But before they're totally quit of the festival, there's one last big cluster of people. They look like they're in their late twenties, maybe early thirties some of them, but Owen can't see their faces too clearly while moving past them, and their clothes are wild and ageless. They're standing in a circle, all hands in, and a huge bearded man in a tie-dyed halter dress and combat boots is yelling at the top of his voice like a coach about to send his team onto the court. He's saying something Owen thinks he's heard in an English class or two. The people around this bearded leader stamp their feet and shout with his every line, getting more and more frenzied:

'You have NOT slumbered here! These visions DID appear! TAKE this weak and idle theme! NO MORE YIELDING, *LIFE'S A DREAM!*'

And what Owen was about to let go of? The magic he was about to put down to vacation syndrome? The warm hope that comes from idolizing a girl he'll never really get to know? Well, Owen decides to keep all that with him, to hold onto it as hard as he can ... because why can't real life be like this too?

French Kissing
by Josie Jordan

There I was on my back, with my legs in the air, sliding down an icy slope.

'Help!' I cried, but all I got was a mouthful of ice-chips.

The legs of skiers and fellow snowboarders flashed past as I accelerated downwards. Just as I was about to slam into a fir tree, a strong pair of arms gripped hold of me, bringing me to a stop.

'*Ca va?*'

Through the snow-covered lenses of my goggles I saw the lift attendant peering down at me. '*Ca va,*' I said weakly.

When I removed my goggles, I saw him properly for the first time. What was it about some people that made them irresistible? Their smell? Their body language? Or just that mysterious element known as chemistry? Whatever it was, he had it.

He helped me to my feet.

'*Merci,*' I said, blushing furiously.

He must have sensed how unstable I was, for he kept hold of my gloved hand. 'Engleesh?'

'Yes,' I said, annoyed my accent had given me away already.

I'd come to this small French ski resort with my boyfriend, Jake. It was our first day snowboarding, so perhaps it wasn't surprising that we'd fallen off the tow lift barely fifty metres up. But I thought snow was supposed to be soft! My bottom throbbed from where I'd landed on it. In fact I felt like I'd had a good spanking.

Jake limped towards us. 'You OK, Rach?' he shouted.

'Yeah, I'm fine,' I called. 'You?'

'Yeah.'

The lift attendant shifted his Oakleys to his forehead. Was it my imagination, or was there more interest than there ought to be in his huge dark eyes? Flustered, I busied myself brushing the snow off my jacket.

'My name is Mathieu,' he said.

'I'm Rachel,' I replied.

I had a split second to prepare myself before his warm lips pressed against my frozen flesh. They were soft with a hint of stubble. Four kisses: two on either cheek. And by now Jake was right in front of us. Being French though, Mathieu got away with it, especially since he then turned to Jake as if to kiss him too.

I saw my boyfriend tense, clearly fearing the same. But Mathieu just slapped his back in a friendly manner and Jake let out his breath in relief.

Anyway, that turned out to be the limit of Mathieu's *Engleesh*. Luckily I spoke reasonable French. Ignoring the muttering of people waiting on the lift, Mathieu showed us how to hold the T-bar.

'Open your legs,' he told me, and I felt myself flushing again. I clung to his shoulders for support while he eased the T-bar between my thighs. He was a big guy, broad as well as tall, yet he had a surprisingly gentle manner.

He helped Jake into place beside me. 'Now hold on tight,' he called and started the lift running again.

This time Jake and I managed to stay upright.

'I wonder if all the lift attendants here are that friendly,' Jake said, as we slid on up the mountain.

The following day when we were queuing for the lift, Mathieu came bounding from his hut to greet us. 'Jake! *Rachel!*'

I loved how he said my name. There were four more kisses that made my stomach burn up despite the sub-zero air temperature, and an invitation to his New Year's party.

'Nice bloke,' Jake said.

'Yeah,' I agreed, glad he hadn't noticed the effect Mathieu had on me.

Up to now, I'd always considered myself the faithful type. I was about to be put to the test.

That night, Mathieu wore loose-fitting dark jeans and a black silk shirt instead of his red and yellow resort uniform. We were the first to arrive. There was wine for me and beer for Jake and a tour of the small wooden chalet.

'I built it,' Mathieu told us proudly.

'No way!' Jake exclaimed.

'It's beautiful,' I said.

Mathieu smiled. 'I lived all my life in this valley and I'll never leave it.'

I sucked in a little breath when he led us down the pine-panelled corridor to his bedroom. What exactly did he intend here? *Menage a Trois* was a French term, after all.

The covers of his double bed were drawn back invitingly. I wanted to jump right in.

The two men stood by the window. As Mathieu pointed out at the snow-dusted fir trees that glowed in the light of the moon, his shirt rode up to reveal a glimpse of bare midriff. His other hand rested on Jake's shoulder, a move I could tell Jake wasn't altogether comfortable with.

Physically the two men couldn't have looked more different. Jake was lean and blond – a metro man, if you know what I mean. I could see how other men (if they were that way inclined) might get the wrong idea about him. He got his bum pinched in nightclubs on a regular basis.

Did Mathieu want to fuck my boyfriend? I imagined him groaning away on top of Jake and my knees went weak. But sadly there was little chance of this happening. Jake was staunchly hetero; there was no way he would even kiss another guy.

Perhaps Mathieu hoped he and Jake could share me? I'd never had two guys at the same time, although I'd fantasised about it. Jake fucked me in the arse occasionally, when he was in the mood for it. Yet after five years, his dirty side came out less and less often. Which of them would I take up the arse this time? Presuming of course that Jake was OK with the idea … which I very much doubted. I felt a mixture of disappointment and relief when Mathieu led us back to the living room.

'More wine?' he asked.

In front of a roaring log fire, he told us stories of winter storms and avalanches. I sat between him and Jake, translating. Every time our eyes met, I felt butterflies. And our eyes seemed to meet a lot. But I was with Jake and Mathieu clearly respected that.

One by one his friends arrived. Mathieu introduced Jake and me as though we were guests of honour.''Appy New Year, Rachel,' he said at midnight, bending his head to kiss me. I got a blast of his spicy aftershave and couldn't help myself; I turned my cheek and met his lips with mine.

He jolted but didn't pull away. Perhaps I thought it would get him out my system, yet when I pressed my tongue into his mouth and tasted him, I realised immediately that it wouldn't. It only made me long for more.

Afterwards, we just stood there looking at each other. Wrong place; wrong time. I felt guilty and torn. Luckily nobody had noticed – Jake was dancing in the corner.

'Really nice bloke,' Jake said as we staggered back through the snow to our hotel.

I shoved him to the bed the moment we got to our room.

'What's brought this on?' Jake asked as I ripped off his clothes.

'Shut up and fuck me,' I demanded.

I lay on my stomach, my face buried in the pillow. When

he entered me, I moaned in delight. Poor Jake. As he pumped his cock into me, he had no way of knowing what I was imagining.

For the rest of the week, I steered clear of Mathieu's ski lift. I didn't trust myself. Yet we couldn't leave without saying goodbye. So on our last day we returned to his little chalet and Mathieu scribbled down his contact details in ornate French handwriting.

He gave Jake a warm embrace. 'Take care of Rachel for me.' Then he kissed me and said, '*Au revoir.*'

Until we meet again. I so wondered if we would.

There was a lump in my throat as we loaded our bags onto the coach. Every fir tree, every metre of descent took me further away from him. Too soon I was home and back at work. Life returned to normal and the mountains seemed a whole world away.

Yet I couldn't get him out my head. Jake and I began to argue, worse than we'd ever done previously. When we broke up a few months later, I suspected that Mathieu had a lot to do with it.

I spent the summer moping and my mood only picked up in autumn. A friend of mine was working in France as a chalet girl that winter, so I arranged a trip out to visit her, knowing in the back of my mind that Mathieu's resort wasn't far away.

I hesitated over whether to call him. It had been nearly a year after all. Then I remembered his kisses. And as soon as I heard his voice, I knew I'd made the right decision. He sounded delighted to hear from me.

'I'm visiting a friend in Tignes,' I told him.

'Oh, but you're very near. You must come and see me.'

As my train chugged and screeched its way across the Alps, I pictured his liquid brown eyes and wondered if they would still hold the same magic. I reminded myself not to get my hopes up – I barely knew the guy.

It was mid January. Four o'clock, and the sun had long

since sunk behind the mountains. A lone figure waited on the poorly lit platform. He was there!

He took me in his arms for his customary four-kiss greeting. '*Salut,* Rachel! So good to see you.'

'And you,' I said breathlessly.

A chunky white flake floated from the sky.

I cupped my hand to the heavens. 'It's snowing!'

'There'll be a storm tonight. We must hurry or the road will be blocked. Come.'

Slipping his gloved hand into mine, he led me to his car. He jammed my snowboard between the seats, cleared the windscreen with his sleeve and climbed in.

The snowflakes flew at the glass as we drove up the valley. The road surface was covered already. I squeaked and gripped the dashboard when the wheels skidded around the first of the hairpins.

Mathieu covered my fingers with his larger ones. 'Don't worry, Rachel.'

'Keep your hands on the wheel!'

He chuckled. 'Is normal for me, this snow.'

Further up it was several inches deep, and on the track to his chalet deeper still. I clung to his fingers as we bumped along, expecting at any moment to have to get out and push.

When he turned off the engine there was a strange silence. We looked at each other shyly.

'Ready?' he asked. 'Run!'

Dragging my suitcase and snowboard bag between us, we rushed inside. I breathed in the familiar smell of wood smoke and felt like I'd come home. It seemed only yesterday that I'd been there. The place hadn't changed at all. But had he?

He tugged off his boots and crouched in front of the fire. Soon he had a flickering flame which grew stronger when he fed it with kindling. I felt its warmth on my forehead.

Looking satisfied, he stood up. 'You are hungry?'

I noticed the table was set for dinner. 'Wow, have you

111

cooked for me?'

'Of course. Would you like some wine? No – sit down, relax.'

Expertly, he uncorked a bottle of red. The wine added to the heat in my stomach. From the sofa, with the fire crackling in the background, I watched him at the stove.

His rich tomato and ham pasta was accompanied by a fresh green salad.

'You've gone to so much effort,' I said, touched.

'It's nothing.'

Our eyes met.

He reached across to top up my wine. 'How's Jake?'

'He's fine, as far as I know. Actually, he's engaged to a girl he works with. We broke up.' I couldn't read his expression. 'How about you?'

'I dated a Parisienne for a while.' He shrugged and smiled. 'They're *complique, les Parisiennes*. And she wanted me to move to Paris.'

'You didn't want to?'

'I belong here in the mountains.'

'Right.' I certainly couldn't imagine him in a city. He'd be a fish out of water; too big, too alive to be confined by concrete.

Outside the window, the snow gave off a ghostly orange glow. The glass had steamed over, so I wiped it clear. 'It's still snowing.'

'Yes,' he said. 'We might be snowed in all day tomorrow.'

'Really?'

Again our eyes met.

He put his wine glass down. 'Shall we go outside to watch the snow?'

'Sure.'

The icy blast when he opened the balcony door made me shiver.

He unfolded a blanket and held it out to me. 'Come here.'

I stepped towards him and then we were kissing. We stood at the railing with the blanket wrapped around us, exploring the insides of each other's mouths with our tongues. French kissing. And he was the most amazing kisser.

'Rachel,' he breathed when he finally came up for air.

I blinked, dazed.

'I wanted to do that for so long,' he said.

'Me too. It was just bad timing before.'

'It doesn't matter. You are here now.'

I nodded. I had the strongest feeling that this was meant to be. Events had lined up to bring us together, halfway up a mountainside in the middle of a snowstorm. I touched his lips with my finger and his mouth descended on mine.

The tip of his tongue swirled and probed. I imagined how it would feel elsewhere and our kiss became frenzied.

He pulled away. 'You want?' he asked in English.

My stomach flipped. I knew exactly what he was asking. 'I want.'

Wordlessly he picked me up and carried me down the corridor. Inside his bedroom, he kicked back the bedclothes, deposited me on the mattress and stripped me to my knickers.

I loved his urgency. The wait was over. I was his for the night and he was mine. Once he'd pulled off his sweater and stepped out of his jeans, he climbed into bed with me, pulling the duvet over our heads. His tongue found its way back into my mouth. Against my belly I felt the cool silk of his boxer-shorts. Inside them he was hard already.

His hand slid into my knickers. Whenever Jake had touched me, it always felt like he was fumbling for the light switch. But Mathieu knew exactly where my switch was and how to work it as well. He looked down with his big dark eyes as he slicked his finger back and forth.

When he pressed the finger into me, I arched my back and closed my eyes, aware of nothing except his finger. He

113

added a second finger, making me twist and writhe. Then his thumb got in on the act, rubbing in tiny circles. He kissed my open mouth and I came in a short sharp blast.

Still quaking with aftershocks, I ripped down his boxers and burrowed under the covers to take his swollen cock into my mouth. He tasted soapy sweet and I couldn't get enough. His hands stroked my hair while I sucked him deep into my throat.

Now he was the one gasping for breath. He caught me by the shoulders. 'I want you, Rachel.'

In the darkness, I saw him holding a condom. When I nodded, he ripped it open. His expression was serious as he lowered himself over me. He pushed my hands to the bed, level with my head, his fingers entwined with mine. His eyes searched my face as his cock nosed into place. It was as though he feared, even at this late stage, that I might change my mind.

I shifted my hips to accept him. Inch by inch he slid in. I was so wet that I squelched. He bit his lip and held himself still inside me for a moment. I bucked my hips, desperate for more, but he shook his head in warning and drew back.

Only when I relaxed, did he begin slowly fucking me. His lips parted, his eyes closed. I wriggled my hands free so I could hold his hips as he moved. His movements became more urgent. He buried his face in the pillow and panted into it as he thrust away. I dug my fingernails into his buttocks to urge him on.

He muttered something under his breath and came to a stop. Eleven months ago we'd had to hold back. We didn't have to hold back any longer. I wrestled him over so that I was on top of him, pressed his shoulders to the bed and rode his cock, hard as I could. He lost it and thrust upwards to meet me, biting into the side of my neck as he did so. With a groan, he made one last deep movement and his body spasmed.

He pulled me to his chest and we lay there, his cock still

114

jerking away inside me.

A while later, I raised my head to look at him. 'Remember when we came to your New Year's party?'

'Yes?' He cupped my breasts in his hands.

'You brought us into this room and I thought …'

He squeezed my breasts gently. 'What?'

'Well, for a start I wanted you to throw me down in bed and take me.'

He smiled. 'You don't know how badly I wanted to do just that.'

'But I was trying to work out where Jake would come into it. Like, you and Jake doing me at the same time?' The thought was still enough to make me hot.

'I admit I thought about that. But I didn't get the feeling Jake would be into it.'

'You're probably right.'

'How about you, Rachel? Did you like the idea?'

He could tell from my face that I did. He laughed and pinched my nipples. 'Naughty girl.'

I squeaked and rolled off him.

He gripped hold of my waist and pressed himself up against my back. 'Now you've made me hard again.'

I felt his cock pressing against my buttocks.

'The other thing was,' he said gruffly, 'I didn't want to share you.'

I pushed my bottom into his groin.

He groaned. 'I want you, Rachel.'

'Then take me.'

'Soon.'

'Now,' I begged.

He shook his head. 'You make me too crazy. I won't be able to hold, so first …'

He slid under the covers and showed me another form of French kissing. The tongue that had been so expert in my mouth proved equally adept on my clit. As he dragged my folds this way and that, I decided then and there that I could

115

quite happily marry the man.

After he'd made me scream, he hauled me out of bed and plonked me on top of his chest of drawers, before turning away to put on another condom. I saw the wild look in his eyes when he turned back round. Roughly he spread my thighs; I braced myself. He shoved his cock in and pumped away in a frenzy. I wrapped my legs around his waist and clung to him until he came.

In the morning, I sat at his kitchen table dressed in one of his thick woollen jumpers while he prepared breakfast. Coffee mixed with the smell of wood smoke. I watched him squeeze oranges and spoon jam into a bowl. My mountain man was actually quite domesticated.

He placed a plate of croissants in front of me. 'Happy, Rachel?'

'Very.'

Over breakfast we talked of our lives, carefully picking our way around the idea of a possible future. I hadn't told him as much yet, but the prospect of me moving to France wasn't out of the question. One weekend clearly wasn't going to be enough. I had a feeling I'd be coming over here on a fairly regular basis for some more French kissing.

The snow on his balcony was several feet deep and it was still coming down hard.

He saw me looking at it. 'I think we're stuck here,' he said.

'So what will we do all day?'

His eyes sparkled. 'I don't know. Do you have any suggestions?'

I had a lot of suggestions. In fact the prospects seemed endless. I leant across and kissed him urgently.

He gave a soft laugh. *'Encore?'* Then he turned off the coffee maker and led me back to bed.

An Argentinean Tango
by Troy Seate

Jacob Smiley sat at a small table in the heart of Buenos Aires. Before him, men and women twirled and whirled to the heartfelt rhythms of the Tango. He found the exotic Argentinean dance only a step away from fucking. As far as earthly pleasures, there was almost nothing like the sight of bare, shapely legs in high heels to shovel more coal into his boiler. *Those little Latin bastards can do a seduction number that Gringos could take a lesson from*, he mused, doing everything he could to take his mind off his problem, trying to succumb to the seductive music and the bare thighs whipping around the legs of male partners.

Only a few days earlier he had celebrated the moon landing touch-down in the manner that he liked to celebrate all aerospace accomplishments: He had fucked a secretary on his boss's desk.

'Your lift-off was fab,' the secretary had told him. 'And your rocket propulsion packed plenty of thrust per square inch.'

'That's what they pay us for – to get our ships off the launching pad and into the unknown.'

Janice had climbed off the desk and straightened her skirt. 'You can shoot your rocket off in my direction any time, Smiley.'

Smiley watched her wiggle toward the door. 'Don't forget these, sugar.' He held up her bikini panties and twirled them around his finger.

'Keep them to remind you of me,' Janice said. 'They're the first I've given away since I threw a pair at Elvis. See you around, JS.' She left the room wearing a coquettish smile instead of underwear.

'Same bat-time, same bat-channel,' Jake called to her.

God, but these were great times. It had taken two years, but the summer of love – in attitude if not in dress – had finally infiltrated even a tight-ass outfit like NASA. It was as close to a James Bond lifestyle as Smiley would ever get and he savoured the rewards. Space launches, security clearances, cool cars, and hot chicks. You didn't have to be an astronaut to get plenty of action. In his high-profile position, he sometimes even fancied himself as James Bond's Yankee cousin, particularly when there were women who practically pulled up their skirts and said, 'Here it is,' like Janice. Once, he'd been the recipient of a masterful blowjob at his open workspace without detection from a hot little number who worked in Security. But an office provided less risk, and what better office than the one belonging to the big cheese. Hugh Hefner might have his mansion full of bunnies, but those in the space program had nothing to complain about. The celebrity of being a part of Mission Control in Houston brought the local girls bunny-hopping.

The astronauts were safely off the surface of the moon. Smiley's job was done for the time being. After lift-off and touch-down with Janice had been successful, he had turned his attention to the sojourn to Argentina. NASA had sent him to Buenos Aires for a conference about space flight. The moon landings had turned even the technicians into high-profile, sought-after personages. Still, it could have been a boring week if not for Tango watching and the parties.

Everyone in the space program had secrets. Even those they kept from themselves. Jake was no exception, and secrets were how he had gotten himself into a fix. He'd met

Rosalina at a party thrown by no less than the Russian Ambassador to Argentina at a plush residence on the outskirts of the city. Jake knew the party would be the kind that ambassadors liked to throw – lots of waiters, plenty of beautiful ladies, and a night that held possibilities for a mid-level celebrity. Mental breaks from Mission Control were like pages in an unfinished novel – the next page waiting to be written – a world in which he could have a tryst that would be no more romantic than a five-minuet carwash, or as awe inspiring as falling in love.

Any number of sweet young things of every nationality grazed around the mansion chattering and fizzing like opened, inexhaustible bottles of champagne. But the woman who caught Smiley's eye stood alone on a huge deck that overlooked the lights of the majestic South American city. His eyes fixed on her face, slid down her body and then climbed up again completing the inventory. She looked like a forties movie star with her raven hair, her heavily mascara-laden eyes and two-toned eye shadow. Her hands were dramatically posed on the railing as she seemed to study the flickering of city lights that offset the glow of the quarter moon.

He made a beeline toward the vacant space beside her. She glanced at him suspiciously as smoke from a Virginia Slims leaked from her nostrils and one corner of her mouth. As their eyes met, he could feel his nerve endings sizzle.

'Just room for one more,' Smiley said.

She looked at Smiley more closely, searching for something she couldn't seem to find, appraising him. Finally, she said, 'So, can you see this doodad in the sky at night?'

Smiley turned his gaze to the pinpoints of twinkling light. Due to his line of work, he appraised the heavens often. On this night the stars were as bright as ice chips flung across the sky. 'Afraid not,' he answered. 'That doodad is orbiting the moon. It won't be headed home for a while yet.'

She cocked an eyebrow. 'Are you someone of importance?' Her accent was heavy. She sounded like Natasha on *The Rocky and Bullwinkle Show*, but her looks and figure were stunning.

'I'd like to think so,' Smiley said. 'And how about you? A Russian spy here to steal all our space secrets?'

She smiled at that. 'How did you guess?'

'Maybe by the cut of your jib – the skirt slit up one side and the sleeveless, oriental-style top. Very Tokyo Rose. Or Mata Hari, perhaps.'

'So you've found me out. Aren't you the clever one? Perhaps if you get me a drink, I'll let you tell me about yourself and your secrets.'

'The name's Smiley. *Jacob* Smiley,' he said with just a hint of a smile, trying to be as mysterious as she.

The events were exceeding Smiley's expectations. Back home in Houston, he'd make the rounds with the cute cowgirls and look for one that could be cut out of the herd for a ride in his phallic-shaped XK-E convertible. And later, he'd offer to provide a tour of his bachelor digs with its impressive spacecraft models and pictures complete with a photo of him shaking hands with the President. But this exotic bird's company suited him just fine because he liked the enigmatic. If she were Cat Woman, he'd be happy to play Batman. It would be a refreshing change from country-western.

Rosalina Lapierre, at least that's what she called herself, said little but beguiled Smiley just the same. He wandered into her universe like a passing asteroid captured by gravitational pull into her orbit, for one night at least. She had no interest in a moonlit stroll, but after two dozen martinis between them, she did agree to accompany him back to his hotel.

The mansion was in full swing when Smiley escorted Rosalina from the party. They trundled down the steps to the first in a line of waiting automobiles provided for guests.

Before climbing into the backseat with his new companion, he looked into his bread-and-butter sky. He gazed at the quarter moon, curved like a shepherd's crook, and thought about the man circling it and the men on its surface. Their adventure was world news, but his adventure with Mata Hari forecasted earthbound delights. And upon this blue bauble where humans resided, Smiley was anxious to fill in unwritten script.

For most of the drive, Rosalina had smoked in voluptuous silence which added to her mystique. The couple was dropped off in front of Smiley's hotel. Inside his suite was a bottle of expensive champagne. He popped the cork and made a toast to space travel and beautiful women.

'Jacob Smiley.' Rosalina said his name slowly as if she were seeing how the words tasted inside her mouth.

Smiley knew exactly what would look best in her mouth. Something far tastier than those long feminine cigarettes she had a thing for, or good champagne. 'All my friends settle for Smiley.'

'Whatever you want, Mr Important Man.' As she stood before him, one thigh peeking out of the slit in her dress, he could almost picture her gorgeous, naked body displaying two perforations across her midsection from staples in a *Playboy Magazine* gatefold.

'Nice suite they gave you, Smiley,' she said.

'You want music and the nickel tour?' he asked.

'No, I want you,' she answered huskily. The cobweb of a kiss clung to his lips – a promise of things to come. She wrapped her arms around his neck. 'Drink up then show me the bedroom.' She kissed him again. Her tongue plunged into his mouth and slithered about.

'Are you Commies all so impetuous?' he asked, coming up for air, feeling a bit like James Bond himself.

'Let's say I like the way you fill out your trousers, much the way you like the slit in my dress. No more talk now, *patushkin.*'

Rosalina was like an itch Smiley had to scratch. He drained his glass and led her by the hand into the adjoining room. He unzipped the back of her high-necked blouse and unhooked the black brassiere. She turned toward him so he could watch the garments slip over her head to reveal her admirable breasts, young and firm. He led her to the edge of the bed where he undid the skirt and pulled it down over her high heels. Then he locked her against him, his face between her breasts. He nibbled lightly then slid his face down her supple flesh.

Rosalina wore a black garter belt that hitched to her nylons. But beneath the lingerie resided a pert pussy covered in curly blond hair. That seemed strange. Smiley rose and took a closer look at the countenance of his female party-favour. He gripped her hairline and tugged. Beneath the wig of raven hair were curly blond locks, not dissimilar to her pubic hair.

'Methinks something is amiss, my pretty.'

Rosalina's come-hither look faded a bit. She shrugged her shoulders.

'So what's the real story here, Rosie?'

The woman suddenly lost her foreign accent. It was replaced with a hint of the familiar Texas twang. 'Several girls were dressed up. I guess you glommed onto me so fast you didn't notice the others.'

'Guess not. So you were hired for the party?'

'Three of us from home. Your boss figured that'd be enough for NASA guys looking for some company. Help keep you away from anything that might embarrass one country or another.'

'Hookers?'

'I beg your pardon,' she said with faux arrogance. 'A very upscale escort service, thank you.'

For once, Smiley was stumped for a quick quip.

'I'm taking acting lessons. How did I do, Daaaaling?'

'Oh, you did fine. What's your real name? Connie Sue something from Houston?'

'Close. Tammy Lee from Beaumont.'

'I kind of liked the idea of an Iron Curtain bitch trying to suck and fuck national secrets out of me.'

'We can still play. We were hired for the duration and I know you like my looks whether I'm a brunette or a blonde.'

Rosalina/Tammy Lee slipped out of her belt and stockings. Smiley didn't like getting fooled, but guessed it to be innocent fun and a big "haw-haw" on the part of his big-spending boss who had sent him to South America in the first place. Tammy Lee was still a lot of woman in her own right, even if she wasn't Natasha or Rosalina, or whoever.

'OK, let's play,' he said.

'You want I should stay in character or just be myself?'

'Whichever way you're the hottest.'

Tammy Lee left the wig off and smiled. She pushed Smiley down on the bed and pulled off his trousers and shorts. 'I think I can satisfy you better if I'm my little ole self. My, that's some booster rocket you had in your pocket.'

Smiley smiled at the golden triangle between Tammy Lee's thighs and gave it a kiss. With the Natasha bit behind her, she giggled like a good ole Texas gal rather than a Russian spy. 'You know, a hard cock sort of looks like a rocket with its passenger cone sitting on top,' she said teasingly. 'Maybe you should paint USA on your shaft.' She bent over so her tongue could do to his cock what it had done in his mouth – darted and probed. First, it teased the cone's slit then the helmet's rim. His cock became her lollipop and her vagina his honey pot. *James Bond would be proud*, he had thought.

'I have a condom. You can take off into the wild blue yonder, but you need to keep your little men in their capsule.' Tammy Lee opened the package and efficiently rolled the rubber down Jake's cock. Then she mounted him

123

like so many cowgirls had done before. Like she'd dropped a quarter into the slot of the little wooden horse outside of a Woolworth's, she started her gallop.

'You gettin' over the fact that I'm no more than some hot Texas stuff?'

'No problem,' Smiley groaned. 'We all wear masks of some kind.'

'Besides, everything from Texas is bigger and better.' She lifted her bouncing tits to prove her point.

Smiley had no objections. Tammy Lee's wild pink yonder of a pussy felt more than county-fried chicken fine. She was one of the best, if not *the* best, pieces of tail he'd ever had – a semi-pro all-American, schooled in the fine art of giving men pleasure.

After his first orgasm, Tammy Lee climbed off so that the swimming little men in the rubber capsule could be captured and tossed aside to fend for themselves. She held out a hand and pulled him off the bed.

'Dance with me. You said you liked the local stuff. Let's try it.' Tammy Lee wrapped her bare legs around Smiley's waist. He bent her back toward the floor as if they were a couple of naked dance-partners doing the Tango, sort of. She took time out for another cigarette and to refill their champagne glasses, but soon returned to the task of nurturing Jake's phallus. Smiley went at her doggie-style for their next coupling.

'Girls want to be ridden, Spaceman, whether they admit it or not,' she said over her shoulder.

Smiley rode Tammy Lee long enough for the cows to come home, but the drinks were finally taking their toll. After he pulled out of his partner's wiggly cunt, he dropped onto his bed feeling a bit out of it.

'Didn't mean to wear you out, but I think we're both getting your boss's money's worth.'

'I'll have to remember to thank him,' Smiley said groggily.

Tammy Lee led Smiley toward oblivion by dropping back on her knees and giving his cock and balls the old Spic 'n' Span cleanup. Her rosy reds attached themselves to the head of his captain like a vacuum cleaner extension. He almost expected her to start humming *Deep in the Heart of Texas* as she snuggled up against his scrotum, the last thing he would have expected in the land of the Gaucho and the Tango. She gobbled his prick, tongue swirling within gentile sucks. Her head moved up and down on his shaft slowly as its veins thickened and again achieved the hardness of the barrel of a six-shooter. She pulled her rubies back to the tip of his glistening lead pipe and held it like a peeled banana. In no time Smiley filled her mouth with his ejaculate, thick and hot as shaving cream. Some of it bubbled out around her lips like fast-acting Burma Shave.

'There, buckaroo. You go to sleep now,' she whispered.

With this delightful spectacle complete, Smiley slipped into Never-Never Land with thoughts of dancing, drinking, and fucking the night away in this love-nest, warm and safe, set to the music of Argentinean guitars.

Smiley had fallen into a deep, trance-like sleep, but not too deep for his subconscious to be titillated by current events. In his dream, he was the astronaut to follow Armstrong out of the Eagle space capsule onto the lunar surface. The landing module was shaped like his XK-E, long and phallic. Like most dreams, there were many bizarre twists. He'd found something miraculous – a moon woman, just like in some tacky fifties sci-fi flick.

She told him he wouldn't believe how good fucking could be in an atmosphere with only one-third the gravitational pull of earth. No matter that she possessed two heads and four tits. There was only one pussy between her legs and it was covered with blond curlies just like Tammy Lee's. But before he could take another giant leap for mankind and become the first earthling to fuck a moon woman, his sleep tumbled further into the black void beyond even the moon and its neighbouring blue bauble in the sea of night.

Vertical strips of sunlight painted Smiley's face as he awoke. He reached out across the bed for his most recent companion, but she wasn't there. He sat up and tried to remember when he'd zonked out. His head was swimming, but it wasn't from the booze although he had drunk plenty. It felt more like he'd been drugged with something more potent than alcohol.

'Rosie,' he called out.

No answer.

'Tammy Lee from Beaumont!'

Nothing.

Something was wrong. Without searching for clothes, he stumbled to the suite's work area. He couldn't find his satchel that contained any number of technical schematics and propulsion estimates.

'Shit,' he said. He searched for his plastic-coated ring of access cards and high priority identification badges.

'Fuck!' He grabbed the telephone from its cradle and dialled the hotel's front desk. The spiral cord stretched to its full length as he searched for other missing items.

The phone rang four times before the concierge answered. 'I'm placing a call to Houston, Texas,' he shouted and gave the man the number. Smiley tried to calm himself and waited for the big cheese to pick up. His boss finally answered.

'Those girls from the escort service you sent down here to keep up company, boss. I think there may be a problem.'

'What are you talking about?'

'One of them came to the hotel with me.'

Smiley heard his boss slurp down a sip of coffee then softly chuckle. 'Someone said you left with a real looker. You just never get enough, do you, Smiley?'

126

'But she was with the escort service.'

'I don't know if getting our baby off the moon has crossed your wires or if you had too many martinis and too much poon-tang, but there was no one from any escort service that I know of. I don't have time for a true confession at the present. I'll see you at the shop in two days so we can get our boys home.' His boss hung up.

Double-crossed and counter-spied by Rosalina or Tammy Lee or whoever the babe was with the curlicue pubes and the sweet pussy, the best ever. She'd certainly taken his ass for a ride. It was a low-tech intercept. He supposed that his bed-partner was looking for microfilm and gathering up charts while he was off trying to score with the two-headed, four-titted moonchild. Whatever she'd slipped into his drink hadn't been without some reward.

He tried to figure the logistics. If she scored at the party, there had probably been an accomplice she could call to pick her up while her target was in Never-Never Land. She'd even taken her Virginia Slims cigarette butts with her. She'd blown smoke both from her mouth and up Smiley's ass. He felt a lot more like Maxwell Smart than James Bond at this juncture. His name might be Mud. Jacob Mud. *The wild blue yonder, indeed.*

The southern-simple act had been the one that was the put-on. He would have to become more proficient with tools other than his dick and more perceptive with women who seemed a little too willing. 'Damn, but those spies can hold their liquor as well as they can suck dicks,' Smiley mumbled. Didn't Bond get burned on occasion when playing with fire? But Bond was wiser than he was, perhaps not with propulsion estimates or space coordinates, but with the sense to kill sexy spies when he'd finished fucking them.

He showered and dressed while pondering his course of action. It certainly had turned out to be an eventful evening, quite a new page in the unfinished novel of his life – a crisis that he hoped would have a not-too-unpleasant resolution.

He tried to think what to do about stolen NASA information and about explaining how he had been duped by a blond bush. He was Jacob Smiley after all, James Bond's Yankee cousin. He was down but not out. He decided he could do his best thinking by going back to the dance hall and watching the Tango dancers applying their passion for upright fucking. Life was often a Tango dance, and he would have to learn some new steps to dance around what had happened the night before.

Fly me to the moon, Smiley hummed on his way out of the hotel.

Romanesque
by O'Neil De Noux

Just as I finished snapping a picture of the Romanesque statue of the three nymphs inside the rear archway of *The Arena*, a woman walked through into Verona's ancient Roman coliseum. Suddenly, the naked bodies of the buxomly nymphs looked like pudgy boys to me.

The woman moved smoothly, catlike, her long black hair swirling behind in the northern Italian breeze. Her low cut mini-dress did little to hide a beautifully sculptured body – tall and thin with oversized breasts that took my breath away.

As she walked past me and up the concrete steps that led up to *The Arena's* time-worn seating section her short red dress rose and I saw she wasn't wearing panties. I almost fell off the steps where I stood, my trusty Nikon in hand. A voice called out behind me. I turned as a man came through the archway where the woman had entered. Two cameras dangling around his neck, the man called out, much to my surprise, in English. 'Slow down,' he said as he hurried to keep up.

The woman slowed, looked back over her shoulder and smiled wickedly. She looked to be about five-ten. The man trailing her was about three inches shorter, a lot heavier and wore glasses. He looked around, noticed me and nodded. Looking back at the woman, he pointed up the steps to the seating area. He hurried past her and led the way up.

As the woman ascended, she looked at me for the first

time and flashed a warm smile. I took the smile as an invitation to follow those sleek legs and that nice round ass up the steps to where her photographer had set up.

She stopped and turned and the breeze lifted her skirt again. I saw her neatly trimmed bush and felt a tug in my crotch.

'Stand right there,' her photographer said as he bent at the knees and took a picture.

The woman raised her hands and put them behind her head and I could see up her dress clearly as I snapped a quick picture. The man turned to me, and I asked, 'Is it OK, if I take a picture?'

He looked back at the woman and she said, 'Sure. It's nice to meet another American here.' Then, incredibly, she pulled the straps off her shoulders and bared those luscious breasts, her dress dropping to her waist.

I focused on her breasts, on those small nipples and pink aureoles and took several pictures. I was mesmerized, staring at the perfectly matched pair. Heavy and wide, they seemed huge against her thin frame. I was breathing heavily.

She giggled and sat on the stone arena seat and pulled her feet up next to her, her knees high. She posed for both of us. I scrambled to get her arse and bush and those incredible breasts in the picture. I made sure to also capture that gorgeous face – deep red lipstick on full, pouty lips, dark brown eyes. She threw her head back and, as if on cue, the breeze took her long hair.

She brought her knees even higher and opened her feet slightly. I could see her pink slit. My crotch throbbed as I carefully focused and snapped another shot.

The man turned suddenly and introduced himself as Lee and told me the woman was Carrie, his wife. Nodding at her, he said, 'Not bad, huh?'

'She's gorgeous!'

Carrie dropped her left knee, giving us a clear view of her pussy. We both took several shots. She laughed a deep, sexy laugh, then moved again, sitting cross-legged. A mischievous smile on her face, she reached down and lifted her dress to her waist to expose her pussy completely. She leaned back and turned her face to the bright sun.

'Take your time,' Lee said as he noticed me hurrying my shots. 'She's not going anywhere.'

'Yes,' she agreed, 'I'm not going anywhere.' Her voice dropped an octave. 'I may come, but I won't go.'

Lee told me they were from St Louis. I told them I was from New Orleans and Carrie said they went to Mardi Gras last year. She flashed her breasts all day on Bourbon Street.

Her husband looked around and said, 'OK. Let's go for it.'

Carrie stood and reached back and unzipped her dress. She climbed out of it and tossed it to her husband. Looking right into my camera lens, she posed for me – naked, except for her red high heels. I saw Lee move around to get us both in his camera. So that's what he was up to, getting pictures of a strange man taking nude pictures of his wife. OK. Who was I to complain?

I controlled my heavy breathing as best I could as Carrie moved slowly, raising her hands, then reaching down to cup her magnificent breasts, then reaching down to brush her bush, then turning and reaching around to cradle her fine ass as she bent over.

I kept refocusing and shooting, the flash of my fill-in light bathing the beautiful naked woman as she posed in the ancient Roman amphitheater. Built in the first century AD, *The Arena* is the largest Roman arena, after The Coliseum in Rome. At least that's what the tour guide told me before disappearing because it was siesta time.

He told me how Christians-and-lions spectacles were held in the infield below, how the wide pit was filled with crocodiles so Christians could be thrown to them. Now *The Arena* was the site of spectacular nighttime operas and concerts.

It smelled of old brick and dust. Towering above the tilted tile roofs of old Verona, it was an architectural spectacle – witnessing another spectacle, Carrie. I wondered, as Carrie sat again, if the Romans ever held orgies here.

Carrie sat cross-legged, leaning back, her elbows up on the seat above. I snapped another photo. And slowly, she uncrossed her legs and opened them for me and her husband. Then she raised her knees to give us a better view of her pink slit. I could see it was wet.

I love a hairy pussy and Carrie's was particularly hairy. I especially like those soft, silky hairs around the base of the pussy, just above her ass-hole. Carrie's looked so delicate. I had an erection that could slice steel. I moved in and took another picture, an even closer view of her breasts. I noticed small beads of perspiration on them and saw them rise with her breath.

I don't know why I was nervous. I guess I just didn't want it to end. I must say, looking back at her husband, as he photographed his wife, I felt admiration for a man who would share such a beauty.

Lee nodded to his wife and said, 'OK. OK.'

Carrie rolled to her side and lay down on her back on the seat, opening her legs and arms, spread-eagle. I stepped above her and shot more pictures. Carrie, really getting into it, began to move her shoulders and hips around. She rubbed her breasts, squeezed her nipples, then moved her hands down to her pussy.

None of us spotted the cop until he spoke.

Standing below us, a uniformed Carabinieri, he pointed a white-gloved hand and said, 'No. No.' Then he rattled off several hurried sentences in Italian.

Carrie stood up and brushed off her ass, then moved slowly down to the cop, who was still chattering. She stepped up to him, leaned forward and kissed him on the mouth. He stopped talking. She grabbed his crotch and started pulling him back to the first seating row. I had to shoot a picture. He was slack-jawed, staring at the naked woman pulling him by the crotch.

He must have been six-three. He pulled off his hat, a Napoleon-looking hat, and wiped his brow with a white glove. He had slicked-back black hair. Carrie unbuttoned his belt and pants, unzipped his pants and reached in. The cop looked around as Lee and I took pictures.

Carrie pulled out his swollen cock. Pointed skyward, it was ready. She kissed its tip as I took a photo, then licked it, then sank her mouth on it and started bobbing her head up and down.

The cop moaned and closed his eyes. He fanned himself with his hat and started pumping his ass to Carrie's sucking. I took more pictures and suddenly Lee said, 'Stop. I gotta reload.'

Carrie stopped moving. The cop looked around incredulously as Carrie's husband started reloading his cameras. I snapped another picture and hurried to reload my camera too. Carrie pulled her mouth off the cop's wet cock and started slowly stroking it with her hand.

The cop moaned again, and, just as I finished reloading, reached down and pulled Carrie up. He grabbed her breasts and pressed his open mouth against hers. They French kissed each other, their tongues probing as he continued squeezing her breasts. Then he pushed her back slowly, on the seat and moved between her legs. Carrie lifted her ass slightly, reached down to her bag, and retrieved a condom.

The cop still had a hold of her breasts as his cock slipped into her. And as we took more pictures, they fucked right there in *The Arena*, groaning and moaning, gyrating their pelvises, crying out in pleasure.

'Oh, God!' Carrie cried as the cop worked his cock in her.

The cop called out in Italian, something about his mama. I photographed Carrie's breasts moving back and forth with the humping.

'Good, huh baby?' Lee asked her as he took another picture.

'Yes,' she gasped. 'Come on. Fuck me. Fuck me good!' She reached around and grabbed the cop's ass.

They pumped away, grinding against one another. Carrie cried out again as the cop pounded her like a pile driver. Then the cop grunted as he came, his ass jerking in spasms. I moved in for a closer view. Finally, they both eased up and caught their breaths.

Carrie's husband started to reload his cameras again. I looked down and saw I had only one shot left. I took it of the two lovers, still pressed together, then hurriedly reloaded.

When I finished reloading, I move back to Carrie, as the cop backed away and started pulling up his pants. Carrie lay there as I took a close up of her wet pussy, her legs still wide open.

When I looked up at those big brown eyes, she smiled and said, 'You just going to take pictures, or what?'

Lee bumped into me and reached for my camera. I passed it to him and unzipped my jeans. Carrie was still breathing heavily, her gorgeous breasts moving up and down as she looked at me in expectation. I dropped my pants and climbed out of my jockeys. My cock was up like a flagpole and she smiled at it. She reached for another condom as I leaned forward.

I went directly for her breasts and squeezed them, then kissed each nipple, rolling my tongue around each aureole. They tasted sweet and wet from perspiration. I sucked her nipples, then opened my mouth as wide as I could, filling it with tit. Carrie guided my cock to her wet pussy and I slipped inside.

Her pussy was slick and hot and tight and grabbed my cock as we began to rock and fuck. I heard Lee clicking away; saw my fill-light flash as he took pictures with my camera too. Moving from breasts to breast I continued sucking as we fucked. Finally, I came up for air.

Carrie's face was flushed and her hair damp with sweat. I smelled semen and her sweet pussy juice. My God, she was knock-out stunning as she rocked back and forth to my fucking.

Carrie was one great loving, sexy fuck. She seemed to tune everything else out but me as we screwed. Craning her neck up, she kissed my lips and tongued me. We frenched long and hard as I rode her until she cried and shuddered and I cried out and popped inside her.

When I climbed off, Lee was already out of his pants. I eased off and picked up the cameras and shot more fuck shots. The Carabinieri was dressed and looking around as Lee fucked his wife and I took pictures.

When Lee climbed off, I moved in for more close-ups of Carrie lying with her legs open. I focused on the juice oozing from her sopping pussy. She smiled weakly at me.

The cop started chattering again, stepped forward and helped Carrie up. She kissed him on the cheek. Her legs were rubbery. The big cop deftly scooped her in his arms and carried her back to the arched entrance, to a well hidden bathroom. They went inside while Lee headed back for Carrie's dress.

Later, Carrie peeked out and asked Lee for her dress. Stepping out in a few minutes, she looked radiant. Lee took her hand and the cop led the way out. I followed, wondering if I should ask where they were staying.

As they turned a corner ahead of me, I heard the Carabinieri start arguing with someone. Rounding the corner, I saw two more Carabinieri, each nearly as tall and good looking.

Carrie pulled away from Lee, pushed her way in between the cops and kissed each of the newcomers on the mouth. The first Carabinieri took a step back. Lee focused his camera and I followed suit. Carrie wrapped her arms around the waists of the two new cops and they all turned toward the cameras. After the picture, Carrie pulled her hands away and pointed her back to one of the Carabinieri.

It took a few seconds for him to realise she wanted him to unzip her dress. The man's eyes lit up as he did. Carrie stepped out of her dress and tossed it again to her husband. And she posed naked with the cops.

The cops chattered a lot until Carrie started grabbing their crotches. The men responded and sandwiched Carrie between them. There I took some of the best pictures of those luscious breasts as each cop sucked a nipple, their hands feeling up Carrie, rubbing her ass and fingering her pussy.

It was there I took the best picture of the lot, a shot of Carrie's rapturous face with a Carabinieri on each breast, both men looking up at her face as they sucked her nipples.

It took a while for the new Carabinieri to climb out of their pants. They turned Carrie around and one slipped his cock into her pussy, doggie style, while she took the other in her mouth. Lee and I snapped away.

The three rocked back and forth in unison. The two men came together. As soon as they finished, the first cop stepped up, moved Carrie to the stone wall and fucked her standing against the wall. It was a long, grinding fuck that went on and on and Carrie was wonderful in the noises she made, little cries and gasps, along with the sound of her ass slapping against the wall.

When they were done, the Carabinieri kissed Carrie gently and dressed her.

They waved and left Carrie still trying to catch her breath.

Lee and I helped Carrie walk out to a taxi parked against the curb of the Piazza Bra.

I had to ask, 'Where are y'all staying?'

Carrie leaned forward and gently kissed my lips. She smiled and said, 'Good-bye.'

She waved as the taxi pulled away to disappear in the

heavy traffic of the Piazza.

Turning back to *The Arena*, I passed through the gate and the statue of the three nymphs. I looked at each face, which seemed caught in rapture, and wondered if they indeed had an orgy as they posed.

If so, they couldn't have had the time we had under the warm Italian sun. Romeo and Juliet's Verona will never be the same for me. It's Carrie's Verona now and those magnificent breasts and silky pussy.

And I've got the pictures to prove it.

From Bradford to Bollywood
by Victoria Blisse

Aisha had never been abroad, never been further than
London. Her father owned a successful Indian restaurant in
Bradford and she worked there. There was no other option
open to her, she was a good girl and she did what her father
commanded. Her life was boring and she often dreamed of
marriage and escape although she realised the promises of
her favourite Bollywood movies were empty ones.

One especially busy Friday night Aisha saw a man who
made her insides burn with desire. His jet black hair
billowed around his brow. His brown eyes were large and
promising. His lips were soft, juicy and begged to be kissed.
She tried hard not to imagine what was underneath his smart
suit but his broad shoulders and slim waist made her mouth
water.

'Good evening, sirs,' she said as she handed menus to the
object of her lust and his guest. 'Welcome to The Palace, I
am Aisha and I will be your waitress this evening. Would
you like a drink?'

The wiry, rat-like man replied with the name of the most
expensive wine they sold. She bowed her head slightly in
respect and went to get their order from the bar. The hot
man barely seemed to acknowledge her presence. When she
got back to their table his head was buried in the menu.

'I really must try the Chicken Tikka Masala. It is
supposed to be the most delicious British travesty. A curry
but not as we know it.'

The rat man laughed and ordered the same. Aisha smiled it was obvious who was in charge at this table. When the hot guy finally looked up his stare was heavy and intense.

'A good choice. Would you like any accompaniments?'

'Bring me your boss,' he demanded, sternly.

'My father, I mean … my boss? Why, sir, do I not please you?'

'Please just have him come to the table immediately.'

Aisha was scared witless but she scurried off and brought her father to the table. He cursed her in Urdu the whole length of the restaurant and she knew she would be the one closing up that night.

'Sir, does this girl belong to you?' Hot guy asked when they returned. Aisha dipped her head and looked at the floor so he would not be able to see her hot cheeks. Her mixed origins meant that her cheeks flushed at the merest thing, her lighter tanned skin did nothing to hide her shame and embarrassment.

'She is my daughter, yes. If you are not happy with her service I shall find someone else to serve your table, sir.'

'Oh, quite the contrary, I want to take your daughter to Mumbai.'

'Mumbai, sir?' My father sounded confused. I looked up, wondering what the man could possibly mean.

'Your daughter is perfect for the lead role in my new movie, I am Kareem Patel if you did not know and I want your daughter to be my newest star.'

'But I don't know how to act,' Aisha exclaimed, forgetting her manners in her shocked state. Her father scowled and then looked back to the director.

'She is not incorrect. She has only ever waited tables. She has never been away from home, sir.'

'I promise to look after her well and she will get a very good wage indeed, some of which I will ensure she sends back here to support her family. She has the perfect look for my heroine, her European curves and light skin tone are simply perfect.'

Much to Aisha's surprise her father gave his permission for her to go to India and her preparations passed in such a haze it was as if it was simply a cut from one scene to another.

Mumbai was a strange place. It bustled. People on the streets shouted, on every corner a *wallah* tried to sell you something. The heat was heavy and oppressive, not even in the hottest British summer had she felt any heat so constant and stifling. She was not sure she was going to enjoy the Bollywood experience at all.

It turned out that the hotel and studio had very good air conditioning so things weren't as bad as she first feared. At least she understood most of the native language, her father had brought her up bilingually with her Bradford born and bred mother. She did miss home and her mum. She was particularly despairing the first morning she had to put on an elaborate and traditional sari. Aisha wore trousers and T-shirts usually; even her work uniform was a simple two-piece affair. A sari, she feared, was a twirl too far.

'My British Bollywood Blossom, are you ready to face the cameras?' Kareem shouted through her changing room door.

'No,' she replied holding billows of material in her arms, 'I can't work out how to get this thing on.'

'What thing?' Kareem poked his head around the door. Aisha yelped and tried to cover herself with the billowing material dangling from her arms.

'Oh, that thing. OK, I'll send one of the wardrobe ladies over to help you.'

'Thanks,' she croaked, her voice hoarse with nerves.

'I'd stay and help myself but I'm not sure I'd be very good at the task in hand.'

Aisha nodded and cursed her heated cheeks. She was sure they'd be shining like stop lights. She'd never been nearly naked in front of a man before and as much as she dreamed

140

about getting naked with Kareem her practical cotton undies were not what she planned to wear. Her curves needed a little more artful decoration she thought but now Kareem had seen her in all her worn out everyday undied glory.

She was wrapped in her sari by a huffing wardrobe lady, who seemed to think it was unseemly for a Bollywood star to be unable to even dress herself. Aisha was getting used to being tutted at. Not everyone was as enamoured with her Bradford roots as Kareem seemed to be. She was an unwanted foreigner taking a job that some local beauty would do so much more justice. She wondered how they'd feel if they knew she kind of agreed with them.

Things got no better on set. Her opposite number, the very famous but highly strung Akshay Mistry, did nothing to settle Aisha's rattled nerves. He flounced off after ten minutes of her stopping and starting, cursing in Hindi about damn wooden amateurs.

'Aisha, my dove, can I have a word?' Kareem smiled, but Aisha could see the worry in the back of his eyes. He rested his hand on her upper arm as he led her to a quiet corner.

'You're not feeling it, are you?'

'No, Kareem, I'm not. I told you I'm not an actor. I don't think I can do this.' Aisha's voice was a little high pitched and warbly as she fought back tears.

'Now, now, now, don't panic.' He stroked her arm. She assumed he was trying to calm her, but the action enflamed her passion and made her more on edge than ever.

'I know you're going to be brilliant at this; you just need to let go and use your imagination.'

Aisha was using her imagination. Her fantasy revolved around them both naked: his hands holding her down as he ploughed his cock into her.

'You don't like Akshay much, do you?'

'Well I don't really know him, I'm sure he's a very nice man really but he's a bit, well he's a bit …'

'Gay,' Kareem answered and Aisha's jaw dropped to her

141

chest.

'Not that that's a bad thing, not at all, he's got a whole generation of young Indian men watching my films who were never interested before but he does not appeal to you, does he? You don't – what's the British word for it – fancy him, right?'

'No,' she replied with a shake of her head, her lip curled up with repulsion, 'definitely not.'

'Just think of someone you do fancy when you look at him, someone who makes your heart race, your lips smile and your nipples harden.'

Aisha couldn't articulate so she just raised her brows in response.

'Just pretend he's someone else; I know you can do it.' Kareem grinned and pushed her back onto set.

She found it uncomfortable at first, but once she got used to superimposing an imagined visage of Kareem over Akshay's feminine features she found the lines she'd remembered by rote rolling off her tongue with ease and emotion. The joy of Bollywood was that longing was kept mainly to glances and long introspective songs sung about one's love. There was not much touching and that suited her down to the ground. And Akshay seemed happier with the arrangement too.

Kareem was as pleased as punch with her and she revelled in every word of his praise. She saved it up and remembered it each night as she writhed on her luxury bedsheets trying to satisfy the ache between her thighs. But no matter how much she masturbated the need just intensified with every orgasm.

She danced and spun and sung and proclaimed her love each day on set but at night she tossed and turned with unrequited lust. The make-up ladies commented upon the black marks beneath her eyes, scolding her for too many late nights.

'I'm sorry,' she apologised, 'it is the heat. I am missing

142

the cold of home.'

Which was an out and out lie. Aisha was becoming an accomplished actor. She did not miss home at all. She didn't miss the monotony of serving and waiting and cleaning at her Father's beck and call. She didn't miss the grey Bradford skies and the pervading dampness in the air. Everything in Mumbai was pretty much perfect. Except for the fact she was being driven crazy with lust. Something she'd not experienced before. Yes, she'd experienced the odd crush in her schooldays but the desire created by Kareem was something new.

It was this passion, this overwhelming urge to fuck, that drove Aisha into Kareem's office one evening. Most people had gone home. She'd taken her time unwrapping the folds of sari from her body. She enjoyed every caress of her fingers on heated skin. She imagined Kareem undressing her and a wicked little idea popped into her mind.

She pulled on her jeans and smoothed down her simple red T-shirt. All was quiet and she thought it would be safe to sneak into the director's office. She looked in through the little glass window, the room was empty and so she tried the knob. It turned. She looked furtively around, listened for movement then scurried into Kareem's office and closed the door gently behind her.

She was a good girl, she really was. Kareem just haunted her thoughts every moment of the day. His toffee coloured skin, the sparkle in his burnt sugar brown eyes, the promise of his ripe lips and his subtly muscled body. Her mind was just taken over by him; she wasn't thinking straight, she was thinking sex, pure sex.

She was content just to sit in his chair at first. Big, black, leather and well-worn around the edges it was an impressive seat for an impressive man. She sat and spun from side to side gently and contemplated her next move. She could sit here on his chair, surreptitiously slip her fingers down the front of her jeans and no one would know what she was doing. She justified her behaviour with the fact no one was around anyway and if anyone did come in she could stop wanking before they discovered her. She could say she was waiting for Kareem: people would believe that she was certain.

She unbuttoned her jeans and pressed her fingers through the gap and down inside her knickers. His sweet, spicy scent surrounded her and mixed with the leather and printer ink smells of a well-used office. She wanted to close her eyes, immerse herself in a dream but she had to keep an eye on the door, she couldn't afford to be caught.

Her heart throbbed ten to the dozen and she licked her dry lips nervously. Aisha was absolutely sure that masturbating in her boss's office was probably not the cleverest thing she'd ever decided to do but she could not deny the thrill of doing something so very, very naughty. As the pleasure built she couldn't help but close her eyes. She imagined Kareem on his knees before her, his face buried between her thighs, his tongue lapping at her juices and caressing her clit, slowly coaxing her closer to climax.

'And what do you think you're doing?'

Aisha's eyes flew open and her jaw dropped in shock. Kareem stood on the other side of the desk, his hands on his hips.

'Oh, Kareem, I was just waiting for you,' she said as she remembered her well-rehearsed excuse but she forgot to pull her hand out of her trousers.

'Oh, you were, were you? What exactly did you want me for as you're sitting in my chair with your hand in your cunt?'

'I've not–'

'Oh, Aisha, I've caught you red-handed, masturbating in my office, in my chair in fact. Please don't give me excuses.'

'I'm sorry, Kareem,' she replied, looking down at the worn desk before her as she pulled her fingers from inside

144

her jeans. 'I just – oh, I don't know. I'll just go now, shall I?'

'Stay there,' he demanded, 'and give me your hand.'

Aisha looked up and into Kareem's face. She held out her left hand, the clean and dry hand that did not smell of her juices.

'No, the other one.' Kareem was not giving anything away in his stony gaze. She didn't know what he might do next but she lifted up her right hand as she lowered her left.

He closed his eyes and inhaled.

'Yes, naughty girl. I can smell your sweet juices all over your fingers. How rude to masturbate in my office–'

'Yes, I'm sorry, Kareem, I should just go, go back to my room, go back to Bradford even.' Aisha had never felt so horrified in all her life but yet she was still wet, her pussy lips still plump and throbbing with need.

'No, you didn't let me finish. I was about to say it was very rude of you to do it without me present to watch. Now let's do this right, OK?'

Aisha nodded tentatively. She felt a subtle change in the atmosphere; she was no longer petrified of what might come next.

'Stand up, *Janeman,* that's it. Now take off those jeans.'

Aisha's trousers were already unfastened so she just shimmied the material down her legs and kicked off her shoes so the denim could be completely removed from her body.

'Wow, your legs do go on forever.' Kareem brushed past her to sit in the seat she'd recently vacated. Her nipples stung from the brief contact. She wanted to beg him to hold her, ask him to kiss her, to fuck her but the words were stuck in the back of her throat. 'Now turn around, yes, that's it. Peel down those panties.'

Aisha gasped. She could feel her face heating to boiling point as she nervously slipped the plain cotton knickers over the curve of her ample buttocks. She couldn't believe what she was doing but she was gratified to hear his growled moan as the underwear pulled away from her sticky lips and fell down to her ankles.

'Back to face me now, sweetheart. And sit up on my desk yes, yes, make sure you spread those thighs wide open.'

'Kareem, I don't think I can.'

'Of course you can, you were just sitting in my chair wanking, don't try and tell me you're shy.'

'I've never done anything like this before, Kareem, I'm scared.' Aisha felt the need to tell the truth to her fantasy lover. She didn't want to disappoint.

'Oh, my sweet, sweet girl, you have nothing to be afraid of. I have wanted you from the moment I saw you but I have waited. I did not want to pressure you, my delicate Jasmine blossom. If at any time you want to back out you can, but tell me, this excites you, doesn't it?'

She nodded.

'So sit on the desk for me, show me the delights harboured between your creamy thighs.'

His silken words made her smile.

Aisha took a deep breath and pushed herself back onto the desk. The cool wood felt like sweet relief to her hot skin. She slipped back and sat demurely, her legs closed tightly together.

'OK, well maybe we have to work up to those delights.' Kareem stood and walked forward. When he pressed against her knees he kept up the pressure until she parted them around him. He pushed in until he was tight up against his desk and her wet cunt. The soft material of his loose fitting trousers tickled her thighs and the hardness hidden beneath them nudged at her pubis.

'Let's take off this top,' he whispered and ran his fingers up under her T-shirt and pulled it up as his hands skimmed up her hips, her stomach and her chest. He pulled it clear off her body and threw it behind him. Kareem looked down on her. Aisha craned her neck back to meet his gaze. His hands

146

cupped her shoulders and his face dipped forward until his jewel-red lips pressed up against her own.

Kareem's kiss was gentle at first. His mouth just rested calmly against her own until she began to move her lips in response. She felt lightheaded. She wanted to giggle in delight and moan with pleasure at the same time. She pulled him deeper with each breath, his lips hard and demanding, his tongue soft and curious. Aisha opened herself up to him and loved it. Her body felt as if it vibrated with the energy of their kiss, it was so much more than she had imagined it would be. The intensity scorched her soul, etched his name there as the first man who had ever made her feel really, truly alive.

'Now will you do it for me, *Janeman,* will you show me what you were doing when I interrupted you?' His words were jagged, breaths pulled in deeply. It gave away his arousal. He was as turned on as she was, she could feel it in his touch, in the graze of his gaze over her face.

She nodded tentatively. She bit her lip and wiggled her hips. Her fingers dipped down to her cleavage and toyed with the pretty lace at the edge of her bra. Kareem stepped back and sat down. In a moment of brave inspiration she tugged on the material and pulled until her breasts rested on top of the cups, naked to his sight. Her nipples seemed such a shocking shade of ripe plum in contrast to her latte skin. She traced her fingertips around and over her excited nibs. The moan that fell from her lips was echoed by Kareem who leant back in the chair and watched expectantly as her hands pushed lower.

She lewdly spread her thighs. It was as if her fears had fallen to the back of her mind and so much pleasure and lust was in front of it that it became only anticipation. She slid her fingers to her slit. She leant back on one hand and let the other explore her sticky lips. Her eyes closed, her breath caught in her throat as ecstasy seared a path through every cell of her body.

Kareem moved forward, gently lifted her feet and rested them on his thighs. She looked down at him and inhaled sharply when she saw the dark, hard column of flesh sticking up from the centre of his trousers. His cock was glorious. It was so hard, so vital. It made her mouth water.

She sought out her clit and flicked it purposefully. She had never been so turned on before, never so desperate to come, but she wanted more, so much more than the ministration of her own well known touch. She wanted Kareem.

'Touch me,' she gasped, 'Kareem, please, I want you.'

'Yes, *Janeman,*' He whispered the term of endearment with such tenderness, she melted inside. 'Anything for you.'

He rolled forward quickly on the casters of the chair, his mouth descended on her pussy and his tongue slipped between her slick lips. She screamed out in shocked pleasure and threw back her head in delight. He pressed back her thighs with his strong hands and held her open so that his tongue had access to all of her. She didn't want it to stop. She was lost in lust. She'd forgotten where they were, that someone could watch them. She didn't care.

'Fuck me,' she exclaimed, shocked at her own audacity. She wanted it and she couldn't hold it in any longer.

'Yes, yes, I'll fuck you.' He pulled back from her cunt and smiled wickedly. He licked his lips and as she watched he pushed away the chair and stood. He positioned himself between her thighs and pushed his dick into her slowly and purposefully.

'Kareem,' she cried and he stilled inside her.

'Are you OK, Aisha?' he asked. 'I only want to bring you pleasure.'

'You are,' she gasped back, 'you are but it's so new, I've never felt this. I can feel you inside me and it feels like … like I've never been complete before.'

'Oh, it's going to get so much better, love.' He smiled and pushed deeper. She discovered that he was not merely

148

boasting. As his rhythm built she felt as if her skin was on fire, as if her insides were molten, as if she were made of liquid passion.

'Touch yourself again,' he crooned, 'Make yourself come. I want to feel your ecstasy as I fill you, my love.'

She snaked her fingers between them. She was so very close and knew she would come soon. The desk vibrated and creaked as they rocked and shook with passion and just when Aisha thought she couldn't take one moment more of the anticipation she came. Hard, fast and with an intensity that brought a strangled cry to her lips.

He stiffened between her thighs and as she was whipped up in a whirlpool of ecstasy he came, their orgasms mingled as freely as their juices.

'Fuck,' he panted, 'I've wanted to do that since I met you in Bradford.'

'I've wanted you to do it since then too,' she admitted coyly. 'Let's keep doing it, shall we?'

He laughed heartily. 'Your wish is my command. I have to keep my leading lady happy.'

Only in Vegas
by Elizabeth Coldwell

By night, Las Vegas lights up the sky with its shimmering neon signs, and the sidewalks ring to the clatter and hum of a million slot machines in constant motion. By day, it's just another American city, stripped of its colour and vitality. Nothing worth enduring an eleven-hour flight for.

At least, that was the impression Rosalie gained, climbing out of the cab bringing her and Paul from McCarran Airport to their hotel. When Paul first suggested this holiday as a way of celebrating their wedding anniversary, she'd thought it a brilliant idea. The Zephyr Hotel and Casino was to be the venue for Swingcon, the world's biggest annual swinging convention. They'd talked about attending in the past, intrigued by the prospect of meeting so many people who shared the same attitude to sex and relationships as they did, but never quite had the courage to fill in the online booking forms. Now, married for ten years, in the lifestyle for five, the time somehow felt right to make the trip.

'And while we're there,' Paul had said, as they discussed the idea in the soft golden glow that so often follows good sex, 'we can renew our marriage vows in one of those chapels where the minister dresses up as Elvis. How does that sound?'

'Tacky but perfect,' Rosalie replied.

Now, waiting for the girl on the front desk to check them into their room, it just sounded tacky. She was sure that was just the effect of the long, enervating flight, and once she'd had a shower and a nap she'd feel much better.

'So, you're here for the convention,' the receptionist said. When Paul admitted they were, she handed him a welcome pack, her tone as perfectly neutral as if they'd been attending an event for air conditioner manufacturers. 'That'll give you all the information you need about the weekend's events. Registration takes place today and tomorrow in the Verandah Bar. Enjoy your stay, Mr and Mrs Woolf.'

A red-liveried bell boy who couldn't have been any older than twenty took them up to their room on the ninth floor. Rosalie supposed he must know they were swingers, the hotel being entirely given over for the weekend to people attending the convention. Did that change his opinion of them? Given the reputation Las Vegas had for being Sin City, she doubted it.

The Zephyr had a reputation for luxury on a budget, and their room confirmed it. Spacious and spotlessly clean, it had a view of the famous Stratosphere tower from its window, and the bed was easily big enough for three people. That fact alone would be fuel to her husband's fantasies, though whether the extra body would be male or female was open to debate. Paul was fluid enough to take his pleasure wherever he found it: he loved to suck on a hard cock just as much as he loved to watch one sliding into Rosalie's welcoming pussy. It had added so much extra spice to their marriage over the years.

While Paul unpacked, Rosalie took a long shower, sampling the array of complimentary lotions and potions laid out on the bathroom counter. When she emerged, a towel wrapped round her compact, curvy body and her red hair hanging in damp ringlets, Paul looked up from the literature he'd been perusing with an approving grin.

'Stay like that,' he told her, 'and you'll be perfect for the party in the Towel Room.'

'There's a Towel Room? Seriously?'

She joined Paul on the bed, and together they pored through the schedule of events. By day, they could visit the big trade Expo, with hundreds of stalls selling everything from fetishwear to suggestively iced cupcakes, and regular fashion shows and displays featuring male and female exotic dance troupes, burlesque performers and what was described as an adults-only magic act. The real fun began when the sun went down, with various themed parties and playrooms open to convention-goers. Beginners could attend an event designed especially for them, offering them a chance to swing with others for the first time in a safe, relaxed environment. More experienced players had the choice of the Towel Party – which, as its name suggested, took place by the hotel's spa pool and had a towels-only dress code – the Bare As You Dare party or the Toys Are Us party, which encouraged women to take along their favourite sex toys to use on themselves and others. Everything led up to the Grand Masked Ball on Saturday night; the couple had exquisite Venetian-style masks stowed away in their luggage, ready to take part in the showpiece party of the weekend.

'Tonight we'll take it easy, what do you say?' Paul said, stroking Rosalie's bare thigh where it emerged from the towel. 'Have dinner, take a walk along the Strip and maybe pop into one of the theme rooms, just to take a look at what's going on.'

'Sounds good to me,' Rosalie replied, happy to let Paul set the agenda. Deep down, she still couldn't believe they'd travelled halfway across the world with the intention of having sex with people they'd never met before. What if they didn't meet anyone they liked? Worse, what if no one liked them enough to want to swing with them? Putting the negative thoughts firmly to the back of her mind, she determined that, whatever happened, they would make this a holiday to remember.

*　　*　　*

Rosalie's enthusiasm for the city had grown considerably by the time they returned to the hotel later that evening. They'd discovered an old-fashioned Italian restaurant that had been popular with the Rat Pack, with photos and memorabilia plastered to the wall. The food was surprisingly good for such an obvious tourist trap, and they'd dined on chicken cacciatore, washed down with mellow red wine. Then they'd taken a slow stroll along the Strip, astonished by the noise and bustling crowds, so different to the atmosphere when they'd first arrived. The sights were so familiar to them from episodes of Paul's favourite crime show, they half-expected members of the cast to go hurrying past, searching for clues to help solve some improbably gruesome murder.

Jet lag was starting to kick in, but they determined to at least stick their heads round the door of the spa pool, just to see what was happening. Rosalie felt rather self-conscious making the trip down to the lobby in nothing but a towel, but when a woman joined them in the elevator on the fourth floor, wearing a babydoll nightie so sheer it revealed every detail of her big, pink-nippled breasts, she relaxed a little.

'Fake,' Paul murmured as they crossed the lobby, the woman safely out of earshot.

'I'm sorry?' Rosalie replied.

'Her tits. Fake. Nice, mind you, but you know I prefer the all-natural look ...' He gave her bum a loving squeeze through the towel.

The party by the pool was already in full flow when they arrived, people curled together on loungers, kissing and caressing, while others had shed their towels and frolicked naked in the pool and hot tub. The room seemed to pulse with a sense of erotic anticipation, and Rosalie's pussy grew wet as she took in the sights and sounds of the various couplings taking place around her. Two blondes on a lounger to her right were locked in a slow, tongue-tangling kiss, caressing each other's breasts as they ground their bodies together. If that wasn't exciting enough, a black

153

woman sat on the lip of the pool, legs spread wide to allow a muscular, shaven-headed white man to give her pussy extensive oral attention. Rosalie shivered with lust at the sight of the man's head burying its way even more deeply into his partner's crotch.

When she ran a questing hand down over the front of Paul's towel, she felt his cock jutting out beneath the material, clear proof he was as turned on as she was.

'I'd love to play,' he told her, 'but I'm so tired.'

'Me too,' she replied, letting him wrap a brawny arm around her shoulders and hold her close.

Fortunately, it seemed their fellow swingers were more than happy for them to watch, with no pressure to join in. They were approached a couple of times, but when they explained their situation, no one saw their refusal to play as a rebuff. Instead, they found themselves being complimented on their cute English accents, with promises being made to look out for them at the Masked Ball.

'Though how they'll recognise us if we all have masks on, I don't know,' Rosalie said, as they made their way back up to their room.

'Oh, I think I'd know the girl with her pubes shaved into the shape of a lightning bolt if I saw her again.' Paul grinned, as Rosalie snuggled into his embrace.

She couldn't help but return his smile. Her fears that they wouldn't find a suitable swing partner over the weekend seemed to be proved groundless. The magic of Vegas had caught hold of her, and something special was going to happen at the masked ball, she knew it.

The Zephyr Hotel's ballroom resembled a scene from Rosalie's most debauched fantasies, peopled with guests in next to no clothing; bodies proudly on display and faces disguised behind all manner of sequinned, beribboned and feathered masks. Dancers in tiny, glittery bikinis gyrated on high podiums, and bubbles spewed from machines, floating

154

through the air all around her.

In keeping with the party's lingerie dress code, she'd chosen to wear a skimpy peach slip, trimmed with scalloped lace, and a matching pair of panties so small she might as well not have any on at all. Paul wore only black trunk-style underwear that outlined the firm cheeks of his arse and left no mistake as to the state of his arousal. He'd been hard before they even left their hotel room, turned on by thoughts of Rosalie being fucked by another man, or having her cunt licked by a cute blonde like the one who'd come on to them the night before.

'Hey, look, there's a stripper pole!' Paul said, pointing out a little catwalk in the corner where partygoers could try out their best moves. As they watched, a lithe redhead twirled around the pole, hair flying as she tossed her head back. 'Fancy having a go, Roz?'

Rosalie shook her head. 'I think I'll leave it to the experts, if it's all the same to you.'

They wandered over to the bar. Unlike the clubs they usually attended in London, where only soft drinks were available, the alcohol flowed freely here. Paul ordered a couple of Champagne cocktails, and they stood by the bar for a while, sipping their drinks and watching the guests at play all around them.

It seemed the etiquette was to meet here, then head to one of the designated playrooms for the serious action. Though all the light groping, kissing and partial undressing taking place close to where they stood was exciting enough.

'And how are you enjoying our beautiful city?'

Rosalie started at the voice in her ear, low and sensual, carrying the heavy Southern drawl she always associated with Elvis Presley. She turned to see a man a good head taller than her own five foot six, broad-shouldered and slim-hipped, wearing dark underwear not dissimilar to Paul's. The top half of his face was hidden behind a black domino mask, and his lips were set in a generous pout. *Hello, beautiful stranger,* she thought.

'I'm having a great time,' she admitted, 'but I have to say you don't sound like a local.'

'No, ma'am.' He grinned and brushed the back of her hand with his long fingers, sending a little thrill of lust coursing through her. 'Though neither do you.'

'Well, then, that makes us even. I'm Rosalie, this is my husband, Paul, and we're over for the convention from London.'

Paul and the stranger shook hands, each silently appraising the other. 'London, hey? Now there's a city I've always wanted to visit. Though I couldn't imagine living anywhere but here. Moved here eight years ago, and it was the best thing I ever did. I'm Riley, by the way.'

'So, is your wife partying with someone, or–?' Rosalie asked, already thinking about all the possible permutations. If Riley asked them to exchange partners, she had no intention of refusing.

Riley shook his head. 'No wife, no girlfriend. Just me. One of the few single men who's lucky enough to get a pass into this wild and wonderful event. And believe me, the organisers know just how grateful I am they allow me in year after year. But then, I know how to behave myself ...'

His finger trailed along the length of her arm. Rosalie's pussy, already plump and wet, responded with another gush of juice into her ineffectual panties.

She glanced at Paul, silently asking his permission to invite this man to join them for sex. A slight nod of his head told her he felt the same way she did.

'Riley. I was wondering ... Would you like to take this party somewhere a little quieter?'

'And just where did you have in mind?'

The playrooms would be busy, and besides, Rosalie wasn't in the mood for public sex. 'Come up to our room.'

'Why, I'd be honoured.'

With that, they left the ballroom, pushing through the

crowd of masked revellers. Rosalie couldn't believe how easily they'd found a suitable swing partner, but the fit felt right. This courteous Southern gentleman with the body of a god and what seemed to be a nice-sized cock tucked away in his clinging shorts was everything she'd hoped to find.

He kissed her for the first time in the elevator, head tilted so their masks didn't get in the way. His mouth was soft, tasting faintly of peppermint, and his hands clutched the cheeks of her arse through the slip. Paul merely watched, knowing it wouldn't be too long before he too joined in the action.

As the lift approached their floor, Riley pushed the silky slip from her shoulders. It slithered to the floor, and, when she stepped out of it, Paul snatched it up before she could. Between them, the two men had contrived for her to walk down the hallway to their room in nothing but her soaking wet panties. There was very little chance of them being seen, and in a hotel full of swingers, no one would turn a hair at the sight of her strutting along topless, but even so she fought the urge to cover her breasts with her hands. Part of her almost wished one of the men would grab her wrists, so she'd have no option. Maybe they'd even pull her panties down, stripping her completely. With two big, gorgeous men for her to play with, there were so many options …

Paul let them into the room, raiding the mini-fridge for the complimentary bottle of fizz they'd found waiting for them on arrival but been too tired to drink the night before. He opened it with a flourish while Rosalie made herself comfortable on the bed. Spreading her thighs, she beckoned Riley to join her.

He needed no more in the way of invitation, but first he removed his mask, revealing high cheekbones and deep-set brown eyes. Peeling down his shorts, he treated her to a first sight of his cock. Like most Americans, he was circumcised, an intriguing contrast to Paul, and his shaft had a distinct curve to the right. How would that feel, she wondered, pushing up inside her? What spot would it hit on the inside of her sugar walls? She couldn't wait to find out, but Riley had other pleasures in mind.

Settling between her legs, he mouthed her pussy through her panties, the thin fabric barely dulling the feel of his tongue tip on her clit. Twining her fingers in his thick, black hair, Rosalie let her own mask fall to the bed, giving herself up to the thrill of being licked. When Riley hooked the crotch of her panties to one side, allowing his mouth to make contact with her exposed sex, little ripples, the foretellers of orgasm, eddied through her belly.

Paul came over to the bed, handing her a glass of Champagne. Sipping it while Riley tongued her to the verge of climax was the most decadent thing she'd ever done. Her husband had shed his mask, and his face was a perfect study in lust as he watched Riley please her, stroking his cock through his shorts.

'I want you,' Rosalie groaned, directing her words at both men. They scrambled to obey her. Though Paul had been largely a passive spectator up to this point, he took charge now, taking a condom from the nightstand and fitting it on his erection.

Riley eased Rosalie up on to all fours, already working out the perfect position for what he had in mind. He guided his long, curved cock to her mouth, urging her to open up and swallow it. She did, relishing the faint salt taste and the way she had to stretch her jaws wide to accommodate the thickness of him.

Pulling him almost all the way out, letting her tongue flicker over the head, she fixed Paul with a look that implored him to enter her. Coming up behind her on the bed, her husband pulled down her panties, and she readied herself for the feel of his cock in her cunt. Instead, to her surprise and delight, he scooped some of her juice from the well of her pussy, smearing it over and inside her arsehole. Judging her to be ready, he entered her with a series of slow, steady

158

thrusts, lodging his condom-covered length deep in her arse.

These were the moments they lived for as swingers: joined together so intimately, yet with room for another to be part of their shared pleasure. Finding a rhythm that suited all three, Paul began a slow, thorough reaming of Rosalie's arse. He didn't often fuck her there, but she loved it when he did, and with every thrust driving her head firmly on to Riley's thick shaft, she was as full of cock as she'd ever been.

Panting, sweating, the three of them moved towards orgasm. Rosalie, already pushed so close by Riley's clever tongue tricks, was the first to peak, the muscles in her arse contracting tight around her husband's cock as she did. He couldn't fight against the gripping pressure, and with a despairing cry, he shot his come into the condom.

That left only Riley. Paul pulled out of Rosalie's arse, leaving her to concentrate on the task of bringing their new friend to climax. Taking him deeper into her throat, it only took a little sustained suction for her to accomplish that task.

'Well, thank you, ma'am,' he murmured, when he could finally speak again. 'Thank you both. It's been a real pleasure.'

'You sound like that's the end of the fun for tonight,' Paul said, handing him a glass of Champagne. 'And it isn't, is it, Roz?'

Rosalind glanced at the two limp cocks before her. Cocks that would soon recover under her expert ministrations, growing hard and ready for more. And how could she let Riley leave before she'd experienced the thrill of being fucked by him? This could never be anything but a one-night deal, and she wanted to make the most of every moment. 'Oh, no,' she replied, 'not by a long way …'

They woke late the following morning, sunlight streaming through drapes they'd neglected to pull the night before. Rosalie felt a strong pang of regret that Riley hadn't been able to stay the night, but he'd told them he had to be at work by nine, and on work days he liked to wake in his own bed. He'd left her with a long, lingering kiss and a promise to hook up again, should they ever find themselves in the same city.

Over breakfast, Paul asked, 'So, was it everything you'd hoped for?'

Rosalie nodded, thinking back to the feel of Riley's supple tongue on her clit, as Paul's cock thrust in and out of her arse. 'It was amazing. I'm so pleased we did it. So what are our plans for today? More sightseeing?'

'Better than that. When you were in the shower last night, I rang one of the wedding chapels. We're booked in for our vow renewal with Elvis at one.'

She couldn't deny her husband was full of surprises. It was another of the reasons why she loved him so much.

After breakfast, they changed into the outfits they'd brought when they'd planned such a ceremony; a sober black suit for Paul and a simple cream shift dress for Rosalie, with a feathered fascinator to fix in her dark red tresses.

The couple before them were finishing their marriage ceremony as they arrived, emerging from the low white wooden chapel in a flurry of confetti thrown by friends and family. Waiting their own turn, Rosalie felt the same rush of nerves she'd experienced ten years before, arriving at the register office in North London where she and Paul had married.

While Paul dealt discreetly with the financial arrangements, Rosalie was handed a bouquet of white roses. The doors to the chapel swung open. She took a deep breath, and together, she and Paul walked down the aisle. The Elvis impersonator who was to perform the ceremony, resplendent in a tight white jumpsuit, hair styled into an immaculate quiff, crooned *Can't Help Falling In Love*. Tacky but perfect, just as they'd hoped.

As they paused before the altar and Elvis opened his mouth to speak, Rosalie realised there was something very familiar about the man she and Paul now stood before. The voice, the pouting mouth, the beautiful brown eyes ... When Riley said he'd be working today, she'd never thought to ask where. Now she knew.

Nothing was said, but a look passed between the three of them, silent acknowledgement of this bizarre coincidence. Then Rosalie stepped forward, to reaffirm her love for her husband in front of the two witnesses the chapel had provided for them.

Only in Vegas could you find yourself renewing your marriage vows in a ceremony officiated by the man who'd shared a delicious threesome with you the night before, thought Rosalie, solemnly promising to love Paul tender, now and for the rest of her life. Only in Vegas.

Local Delicacy
by Mariella Fairhead

Even before we set eyes on her, it had been one of the best days of our married lives: breakfast overlooking the gently lapping shore, and a long leisurely 'forget-it-all' stroll along the beach, kicking through the gentle waves as they broke across our feet. Then, just when we were starting to feel a little restless, we stepped onto the boat that would take us right out to the heart of the Great Barrier Reef, where we would scuba dive together, which we'd looked forward to doing for a few years.

We'd both dived several times before we'd met, and regularly talked about how much fun we'd had – and so we booked it. *And where else in the world would you really want to go to dive!*

So here we were on a boat bobbing gently on the surface of the Coral Sea, just off the coast of Queensland in north-east Australia. We were moored at a place called Steve's Bommie, a stop off on the absolutely beautiful Ribbon Reefs, which believe me; you had to see in person to fully appreciate. However, even the wonder and majesty of Mother Nature's landscape all around us, with its exquisitely elegant forms, kaleidoscope of vibrant colours and soothing, glimmering sea, had to bow down to the beauty of what we saw next, the vision of womanhood that we saw climbing up the side of our boat.

'Everyone!' the skipper shouted to get everyone's attention, just as her head appeared above the side of the boat, 'this is Maryse, she's going to be helping with the dive today, please make her feel welcome, and please feel free to ask her any of the questions that I don't have the answers to.'

A ripple of laughter ran around the other people on the boat as they wriggled into their suits and double-checked their gear, but I wasn't laughing, not when faced with such absolute beauty. I was transfixed, soaking in her voluptuous, super-sexy curves, and her beautiful, angelic looking facial features, as she finished climbing into the boat. Water dripped and streamed from every bump of her bikini-clad body, to splatter loudly on the deck and pool around her feet, beneath a set of long, lithe legs.

'Maryse has lived on and around these reefs for nearly thirteen years,' the skipper continued, his mainland Australian accent thick and strong, 'since arriving here as a fresh faced ten-year-old, from her native France, and she knows absolutely *everything* there is to know about the environment, and the various types of wildlife you'll see once we hit the water.'

And with that, he gave a little appreciative hand gesture towards the gorgeous creature.

'Maryse!'

'Hi everyone,' she said confidently, elegantly pushing her long dark hair back from her face, as she waved around the group of divers getting ready, many of whom had also been enraptured by her stunning natural beauty.

And then she spoke quietly and informally with the skipper, just out of earshot. A few seconds in, she gestured to the right of our boat, which when I followed their gaze, I realised was to point out the tiny little motorboat she'd arrived in. They both shared another little laugh, and then he gave her a little pat on the back, a friendly, *colleague's* pat, showing there was nothing more between them.

'You can pop your eyes back in now,' my husband whispered in to my ear. I turned to him and smiled, realising only then how much I'd been staring at the beautiful diving assistant.

'She is hot though,' he added discreetly, then let out a little "phew" sound, and shook his head.

I gave him a playful slap on the thigh, which drew a feigned childish yelp from his lips.

'Keep your eyes on your beautiful wife please! OK?'

'Of course, dear,' he sighed, and smiled at me again.

As we finished readying our tanks, we both watched in wonder as she helped others with theirs. She stopped by a couple directly opposite us, who had some trouble with their apparatus. To fix it, she took hold of the offending article, leaned over the side of the boat, and stretched right down to rinse it in the sea water, which presented my husband and me with an unhindered view of her perfect upturned, upthrust bottom. Her bikini bottoms stretched wonderfully across the full round curves of her cheeks, showing off the firm, healthy, swimmer's muscle beneath. And between her legs, the thin, still sopping material was pulled tight across her crotch, moulding to every curve of her pussy, the full bulge of her puffy outer lips clearly visible. *Discreetly,* we both watched with delight as she wriggled and squirmed over the edge of the boat, doing whatever it was she was doing. At one point, her legs drifted even wider apart, showing off yet more of her bulging crotch, and the soft tender flesh of her inner thigh.

I could feel my chest heaving slightly as I imagined crouching down behind her, and licking ever so slowly up along those thighs, until my tongue reached the sticky, gooey treat at the top, which I'd lap and suck enthusiastically like a grateful little puppy dog slut, coating it in my sticky saliva, and drinking down her delicious girly cream, as she moaned and writhed against my face … At least that's what I would have liked to do at that very moment. I've never actually done anything with a girl before – bi-curious only, you see.

Luke knows about my desires, and has even tried to set up a threesome a few times, but there's just never been that instant *connection* I'd wanted with the woman, an instant and powerful attraction, that I just *had* to act on! The very same connection I was feeling right at this moment for Maryse.

And then I got a shock, when she pulled herself back to her feet, and while she shook out the unit she'd cleaned, she turned around and gave me a lovely, long dirty look, a look that said, *I know what you were looking at, and I know what you're thinking.*

'Busted!' Luke whispered out of the corner of his mouth, and then he slipped his mouthpiece in and tried his air. However I could see from the look in his eyes, that he was feeling excited by the erotic charge sparking off between Maryse, and myself, which could potentially lead to something pretty special. I knew he'd have no trouble with me bedding down with her, and would most definitely like to join in with us, if I was happy with the idea.

I blushed bright red at being discovered, but it didn't stop me from looking at her some more; soaking in her elegant hair, the full swell of her breasts, and the bulging crotch of her bikini bottoms – and more importantly, it didn't scare her away either!

Things stepped up several gears when we finally started dropping into the water to dive. She regularly swam up against me, or cupped a hand tight around my waist to turn me around to see one of the many wonders of the reef, her hand just gently cupping and rubbing across the underside of my breast through my suit as she did. And even up on the surface, maybe three or four times, she'd pushed hair from my mask, or from my pouting lips, as her knee "accidentally" rubbed and brushed between my legs, the top of a strong thigh pressing firmly against the bulge of my pussy. *Believe me, during those moments, the water wasn't the only thing making me feel wet!*

Then, after I'd not seen her for a bit, and while I was treading water with the majority of the group with our backs to the boat, mesmerised by a few whitetip reef sharks that were swimming elegantly by, I felt a tap on my shoulder.

It was Maryse, who was gesturing for me to follow, her face beaming with excitement. I did as she asked, and trailed her bubble stream, keen to see what she'd found for me to see. We ducked through a horizontal hole in the coral, which led to a wide clearing the other side, curtained all around by a shallow wall of coral.

'Privacy at last,' she gasped, as she threw off her mouthpiece.

Then before I had the chance to play coy, and ask her just what she meant, she clamped her lips to mine, and we started kissing, deeply, and passionately, as our hands roamed all over each other's bodies, fondling breasts, grabbing and groping at bottoms, and pressing firmly, deep between each other's legs.

'You like girls!' she half asked, half stated.

I didn't reply; my crotch bucking on her firmly pressing stiffened digits, my pussy lips peeling slowly open around them beneath my suit, was answer enough.

'I like girls who like girls,' she purred, as she rubbed a teasing finger across my quivering lips. 'Do you want to come to my place tonight, so we can … play?'

'Oh God yes,' I gasped, sounding more desperate than I intended, feeling mesmerised by the subtle, and super-sexy French tones escaping her lips.

'What about your boyfriend?'

'Husband,' I corrected softly.

'*Husband*,' she sighed smiling. 'Do you think he'd like to join in … or watch … or just leave us to it?'

'Definitely one of the first two,' I said with a laugh, and then I brought my lips in again to kiss her, but she held me back for a moment with a finger across my lips.

'I'll pick you up from the same jetty at nine, OK?'

'OK.'

Then our lips met again, in another dirty, sloppy, wet kiss, as the waves splashed and lapped around us.

'And this is home,' Maryse said with deserved pride, as she steered her motorboat tight to the side of a much smaller jetty, before cutting the engine, and deftly leaping out to tie it off.

It was amazing, constructed out of old wooden beams, with a ramshackled-corrugated roof, but it looked straight out over the reefs, and there was no one else for as far as we could see.

'Drinks in there if you fancy it,' she said gesturing towards a wooden case, where the jetty opened right out in front of the structure, which was illuminated by a handful of shimmering oil lamps, 'I just need to do something.'

She only disappeared for a moment before we saw her again, as she slid open a huge pair of concertina doors at the front.

'Nearly ready,' she stated, and then she disappeared into the darkness again. Seconds later she returned, pushing a king-sized bed out onto the extended jetty, under the glimmering stars, until the four wheels dropped and locked into slots in the decking.

'Very nice,' Luke beamed.

'I love it,' I gasped, pouring myself a drink.

'Shall we start?' she asked, before slipping her loose fitting dress from her shoulders, to reveal her perfect naked form beneath.

I gagged a little on my wine, as the moonlight illuminated her flesh, her bare breasts and thrusting, bulging crotch, which I could see already was glistening with wetness.

'Wine OK?' she asked as she strolled in behind me, pressed her naked body against mine, and started caressing me, running a hand across my braless breasts through my

167

sheer dress with one hand, her fingers deliciously catching my heavily erect nipples, as the other slinked down across my tummy, and started caressing my jutting mound, groping and feeling it through the thin material, before letting her fingers drift even lower, to my swollen pussy lips.

I moaned and grunted as she dug her fingers deeper through the material and started really rubbing them along my crotch. And then she moaned with delight on feeling the wetness there for herself.

'Drink up,' she sighed, her soft lips only millimetres from my ear, 'I want to taste you.'

I couldn't wait any longer! I downed my wine, let my dress slip free, revealing *my* nakedness beneath, and then clambered onto the bed, and over onto my back. Then with my eyes fixed to hers, I let my thighs fall slowly apart, offering my sex to her.

'Oh fuck,' I gasped, when straightaway she pressed her lips between my legs, locking them to my pussy lips, and then she kissed them, mashing her lips tight against them in a passionate embrace. My legs twitched and flailed as my body was overcome, from at last being eaten out by a woman. Luke went down on me, yes, but only another woman knew what I needed, knew just where to flick the tip of their tongue to truly excite me.

Maryse made my whole crotch convulse and pulse with heat, as she started quick-flicking her tongue across the entrance to my sex, just tickling across it, stimulating it, making it peel automatically further open.

'Oh God, that is … so fucking good,' I gasped.

I grabbed and pulled roughly at my nipples, as her teasing tongue pressed further forward, slowly circling around the entrance, and then further still, until she'd started properly licking around my insides.

'Yesss … that's sooo good!'

After the afternoon's teasing, and an evening of anticipation, and just these first few, exquisite, lesbian

168

touches, I was close to coming already. Sensing this, Maryse slid her lips up a touch, and started kissing softly at my clit, the warmth and wetness of her softly dabbing lips producing a powerful rolling surge of arousal, that flooded my crotch with heat.

She built up an almost relentless rhythmic action with her kisses, each one causing my crotch to buck up against her mouth, forcing it hard against her lips. And then, when she was sure I wouldn't last for much more of this treatment, she lashed my sensitive nub with the stiffened tip of her tongue, again and again, which drew powerful convulsions from my hips, and caused a rush of wetness to surge along my sex.

'I'm going to co …'

As I was about to climax on her face, and her clutching, gripping lips, she drove her tongue all the way inside me, and lashed it around my inner walls, desperately attacking my twitching flesh with it.

And then I shrieked out loud, as my body exploded with overwhelming sensation, and heat surged and fired out to every part of my body, and especially to my crotch, where Maryse's mouth remained clamped on tight, as my body arched and writhed and twisted around on the bed, as I was totally overcome with lust.

And then I felt a surge of wetness at my crotch, the like of which I'd never experienced, as my juices felt like they were flowing from my pussy, straight into her welcoming mouth, where she gulped them all down, gasping with abstract pleasure as she did so.

I bucked heavily a few more times against her face, as my body shook at the peak of my climax, and then collapsed back to the bed, completely and utterly exhausted.

Maryse's head remained between my legs for a few minutes, but only to ever so gently kiss and caress my sex with her lips, as I came down from my incredible orgasm. My legs flapped and jerked softly as she teased and sipped, licking my tender flesh clean of all my juices, as my head drifted side to side, which was when I finally saw Luke, standing to the side, grinning from ear to ear. To be brutally honest, once her wonderful mouth had started to pleasure me, I'd completely forgotten about him.

'Did you like that?' came a voice from between my legs.

'Oh fuck yes!' I gasped happily; just starting to get my breath back, as Maryse slinked up the bed and straddled me, crouched on all fours above my heaving torso. When her beautiful face hovered close to mine, she leaned down and pressed her lips to my mouth, her touch wonderfully soft and gentle. I sighed happily as her tongue licked and pressed and then pushed in through my lips, allowing me a teasing taste of myself. Then she pulled her lips from mine, and with a truly wicked look in her eye, and with a condom packet held aloft in her slender fingers, she told me what she wanted next.

'Can I have a go on that?' she asked, nodding towards my husband's cock, which he was happily wanking on, the very idea making it twitch erratically in his hand.

I hesitated for a moment, never, ever really expecting to be in this situation, before finally giving my consent.

'Just a quick go,' I warned with a smile, 'and then I want it back.'

'A quick go is all I need,' she sighed, returning my smile. And then she turned to Luke. 'I'm more than ready for you, stud.'

My darling husband looked adoringly at me as he rubbered up. Then as soon as I cast him a nod, my face flushed with excitement, he moved in on the bed behind Maryse, and positioned his cock at the entrance to her pussy.

'God, you're dripping wet,' he sighed. And then I saw him moan, as it looked like he ran the head of his cock up and down the length of her slippery slit, which made our gracious host sigh, her warm excited breaths washing across my face.

'You tell him to start,' she sighed to me, her soft, wet lips teasing around the outside of my mouth.

My lips pouted hungrily for their touch, as I did as she asked.

'Fuck her, Luke,' I moaned, just before she slipped a few fingers into my mouth for me to suck, which from the taste of them, she'd just shoved inside her creamy slit.

Maryse titled my head slightly to the side, so while she slipped her delicious fingers and her filthy tongue in and out of my mouth, I could watch, as my husband thrust inside her. I could see his chest heave as the moment approached.

'No teasing, no tenderness – just fuck me hard! I'm really close already from eating out your wife,' she gasped, half instruction, half to turn me on even more. And then she pressed her lips full to mine, and started snogging me, roughly.

She grunted lustfully into my mouth seconds later, when I felt her whole body shake, as Luke did just that, slamming his cock hard into her sopping pussy, right in up to the hilt on the first push.

'God, she's fucking hot around my cock,' he grunted to me, as he took hold of her hips and started pistoning his cock in and out of her sex, 'and dripping wet too.'

I pushed Maryse's lips from mine for a second.

'Drill her Luke!' I gasped breathlessly, 'give her the *fucking* she so desperately wants!'

I heard him gasp at my rudeness, and at my total willingness about the whole situation, and then saw him accelerate his rocking hips, smashing them hard into her upturned rear end, driving his cock deep into her sticky depths, faster and faster and faster, making her kiss and moan more passionately into my mouth.

She seemed to get massively turned on when I started sucking and kissing at her lips like a love-struck teen, her escalating moan of arousal growing louder and louder, as her actions became clumsier, as she lost more and more control to Luke's cock, which was literally pile-driving into her now.

Quickly and urgently, she slithered her wet lips from mine, so she could speak.

'Please … don't stop … don't … stop!' In her heightened state of arousal, her French accent was thick and strong.

'Keep doing her, Luke,' I gasped, as I held *her* now needy lips from mine, totally embracing everything that a threesome had to offer, to the both of us.

'Does she feel good around your cock, husband?' I asked, already knowing the answer from the wondrous look on his face.

'Fucking … good!'

He was staring down at her pussy, which was no doubt bulging obscenely around his thick shaft as it plunged in and out.

'She wet too?'

'Soaking!' he moaned, as the squelch of his cock slipping in and out of her sex grew even louder.

'And hot?

He grunted, and his actions stuttered slightly from my explicit questioning, probably still amazed that this was happening at all.

'Like a … fucking … volcano.'

Maryse's whole body was writhing and twisting above mine as Luke gave her the fucking she truly needed, *and deserved!* The nipples on her full, free hanging breasts caught mine a few times, drawing a helpless gasp from the pair of us.

'And would you like to come inside her?' I asked provocatively, even though of course he was safely rubbered up. They both let out a deep, excited grunt in reply to this, and Luke's thrusts stuttered again.

Then I looked up into Maryse's face, and after flashing my tongue sluttily across her lips, I asked *her* something too.

'OK if he finishes off inside you?'

Again they both grunted, and the gorgeous young woman

on all fours above me, let out a helpless whimper, as her expression begged for my lips on hers. But I held firm.

'Do you want to feel his cock expand inside you, as he unloads a ball-load of spunk up there?'

Despite the violent jolting of her body, I still read the desperate affirming nod of her head.

'Oh fuck … I'm close,' Luke gasped.

'Do you want to feel the tip of his cock swell right up, as he fires out jet after jet of his married seed?'

'Oh … God …' she grunted, her eyes brimming with tears of joy, as she nodded frantically.

A smile grew on my lips.

'Then kiss me, and let him do it.' And with that, I let her lips fall down to mould perfectly to mine, and we kissed again.

As we started to become completely lost in passion, I reached down with both hands and pulled her cheeks apart, giving my husband a perfect view of his deep penetration, and at the same time giving him final permission, and encouragement, to unleash his pent up spunk.

Straightaway he screamed, and then slammed his cock hard forward, locking the entirety of his shaft inside her body, as he came.

I could feel him come through her body, through the desperate gasps and sobs on her lips, through the tension in her torso, and the burning pleasure of her hugely erect nipples pressing into my flesh. I could almost feel it each time his cock swelled inside her, stretching her soft inner walls wide apart, as she convulsed helplessly around his shaft, as his hips jerked, and he kept pumping his spunk out deep inside her body. She came strong and hard on me, waves of emotions flooding through her, taking her.

And then a *total shock*, as I felt Luke lift my hips up off the mattress, press my legs apart, and then shove his pussy-juice-slicked cock in its silky smooth covering, deep inside my pussy, where he unleashed the second half of his release, which I could feel was scalding hot, and which set my insides on fire, almost instantly triggering a second orgasm in me, causing Maryse and I to writhe and squirm our lips together in sweet, helpless embrace, until finally, we were done, and we all collapsed into a huge sweating heap of bodies on the bed.

After a few minutes, Maryse finally got the strength to lift her face to mine.

'How about a midnight swim … and then we go again?'

'Definitely!' I exclaimed, gently stroking her hair from her face.

'But I'm not sure I'll be … ready,' Luke sighed, sounding exhausted still.

'Don't worry,' Maryse replied, flashing me a wink, 'for the rest of the night you are optional.'

'That's right,' I laughed back, 'optional!'

'Hey – no fair!' he moaned.

But Maryse and I were already racing along the jetty, heading for the crystal clear water, laughing all the way.

Maya Gold
by Catelyn Cash

'Are you sure you won't come?'

The Mexican sun beat down as Arya watched her friends pile into the hotel minibus. She shook her head. 'No thanks. I'll be fine.'

'What if we see someone famous?'

Arya hadn't come to Mexico to hang about in the heat for a glimpse of some big shot actor. She'd come for the ruins, the culture, and unlike her friends had been gutted when she'd found out Hollywood had taken over some of the ancient ruins and filled them with film crews and superstars.

'I'll wait and see the film when it comes out,' she assured them. 'I'm just going to take it easy. Maybe go for a walk.'

'I can stay and help you relax.' Rick, the self-declared stud of the group, wiggled his eyebrows suggestively.

'I can relax on my own,' Arya told him coolly.

'Don't stray too far,' warned Susie. 'You know the rep doesn't want us wandering off on our own.'

The tour rep had warned them repeatedly about the hassle they could expect from the locals if they left the luxury complex but to be honest from what Arya had seen of the local villagers they were friendly and politely tolerant of the tourists wandering rudely through their lives, snapping photos of their palapa houses and marvelling over their "primitive lifestyles."

'I'll be careful.'

Finally everyone who wanted to give up a precious day

of their holiday for a glimpse of a celebrity was on the bus and Arya waved them off. The moment she was alone she set out through the hotel grounds, across the golf course towards the jungle. The tip of a glorious pyramid loomed above the tree tops and she used this as a marker, as no doubt people had done for thousands of years.

But the pyramid wasn't her destination. She'd been there yesterday and was the only one of her group who had climbed to the top. The only one to walk through the huge, stone doorway carved in the shape of a snarling jaguar head, to see the King's tomb. She'd seen carvings of the King too, a regal looking Mayan with a jaguar headdress and what seemed to be an impressive looking erection jutting from between his stone thighs.

Her guide had tactfully not mentioned the royal boner and neither had Arya but she couldn't help thinking that if Rick had a willy like that, she'd be more willing to be a notch on his hotel bedpost. From the top of the pyramid she had gazed down over the tree tops trying to ignore the hotel complex in the distance and instead, appreciate the incredible history of her surroundings. She had been surprised to see the glitter of water between the trees and when her guide told her about the cenote, Arya had known she had to see it.

Finding the gate where a waiter at breakfast had told her it would be, she stepped into the jungle. Although the vegetation was dense there was a clearly defined path and she followed this till she saw a small sign to the cenote leading down another, more overgrown track. And then she saw it; a beautiful shimmering pool of clear fresh water sunk deep into the surrounding rock. The jungle grew right down to the water's edge and tangled, moss-covered vines trailed down into the water from leaning palms. Fantastically coloured parrots darted over the surface and called to each other from the trees.

Arya felt her skin prickle at the timeless beauty of the

scene. Her guide book said that these magical pools had once been the only source of fresh water in the area. Legend had it they were sacred gateways to the underworld and looking over water glittering a dozen impossible shades of blue and green, Arya could believe it.

The air was steamy and humid and strangely still, despite the teeming life in the jungle around her and Arya felt her skin tingle with awareness. Or static electricity. Or magic.

Coming prepared, she had her bikini on under her clothes and after a quick look round to check she was alone, she stripped off and waded into the cool, silent water. She swam for a while, then, floating on her back, she gazed up through the tree tops, to see a family of curious spider monkeys peering back at her. And beyond them, against the blue sky, the ageless, looming presence of the Jaguar King's pyramid.

The water was deliciously cool, a treat in the jungle heat and she swam and drifted lazily. When she was done she kicked out for a flat, high rock which overhung the water. Beneath the rock the water was almost black, suggesting it was much deeper here or maybe heralding the entrance to the underground cave system which connected many of the cenotes.

Or the entrance to the underworld as the guidebook hinted?

Smiling at the fanciful thought Arya scrambled up onto the rock and sat in the sun to dry off. It looked like even the locals were off watching the filming so after another quick look round she took of her bikini top to work on her tan. Spreading her towel she lay back and fanned her blond hair out to dry. Again her eyes were drawn to the pyramid which seemed to shimmer in the heat. Had the Jaguar King looked down from his throne to the cenote while the ancient priests made their bloodthirsty sacrifices?

Thinking of the King reminded her of his massive cock immortalised in stone and she smiled again. Hopefully he had had better things to do with any captured virgins than sacrifice them to his gods.

Keeping her face turned to the sun, Arya closed her eyes and sighed happily. This was definitely a moment to remember, to replay in her head next week when she was back at work in the midst of a Yorkshire winter.

The rock was in partial shade so the sun felt good rather than too strong and she lazily watched the world turn. Her nipples had puckered in the soft breeze and she brushed them lightly with her palms, feeling an instant, answering tingle between her legs.

Sex hadn't played a big part in Arya's holiday so far – not with Rick possessively chasing off any competition – and her pussy had been badly neglected. Now she let her hand slide inside her bikini bottom, pleasantly surprised at how wet she was. All the while she stayed on high alert, listening for the sound of anyone approaching but there was only her and the parrots. And maybe the monkeys. If they were still watching, she hoped she wasn't corrupting them. It felt wonderfully decadent lying in the sun playing with herself with nothing but the sounds of the jungle around her but the bikini was restricting her access and impatiently she lifted her hips up and tugged it off. With her now bare bum on the rock she spread her legs wide.

The feel of the sun on her cunt was a whole new sensation but Arya didn't want to have to explain sunburn down there. Reluctantly she covered herself with her hand, her fingers gliding inside her passage while the heel of her hand gently rubbed her clit. She was so wet, her pussy so neglected that she came almost immediately gasping softly at the release.

With a contented sigh she lay back, warning herself not to fall asleep in the sun. Which was when she heard a noise.

Her eyes flew open and she sat up warily, scanning the jungle, Nothing. She looked down at the water but the cenote was empty, as still and silent as before. Wishing she hadn't removed her bikini, her eyes scanned the jungle.

178

Nothing moved. Nothing stirred but her skin was covered in goosebumps despite the heat and her nerves were screaming a warning. The very air around her seemed to crackle with electricity but still she couldn't see any threat, couldn't see anything different. Except …

There! At the edge of the jungle. Oh shit. Two men watching her.

Now she was really nervous. She looked round wildly for her bikini but she must have kicked it off the rock when she was … when she was. *Shitshitshit!* Had they been watching? Had they seen her masturbating? Heat that had little to do with the sun flushed her whole body.

The men didn't move and her initial panic began to recede just a little. Both were so dark haired and golden skinned, she assumed they were locals rather than tourists. But what the hell were they wearing? In her surprise she forgot her nerves and her nakedness, forgot everything as she stared at them in amazement.

Neither man was wearing much more than she was. Soft leather belts tied around their waists, with jaguar skins covering their dangly bits. One had a beaded headband with colourful feathers stuck in it. The other though … he wore a headdress made from a jaguar head, the sharp, lethal looking teeth coming down over his forehead. Both wore necklaces of animal teeth and claws. Nothing else. Just golden skin over rippling, well muscled bodies. These men were fit, like really fit. It took Arya a moment to realise who they were and only then did her racing heart begin to return to slow.

Actors from the film. With bodies that buff, they had to be. Aware she was still naked and they were between her and her clothes, she had no choice but to try and brazen it out.

'Hi. Do you think you could toss me my clothes?' The men moved silently towards her and her nerves tingled alarmingly at the way they were looking at her. She tried again. 'Sorry, I thought I was alone. I assumed everyone

179

was off watching the filming.' Still no response. In fact, she wondered if they even understood a word she was saying. She tried to remember her Spanish but her night class hadn't really covered public nudity and masturbation.

Barefoot they made no sound as they crept forward, staring intently, but not at her boobs or pubes as she would have expected. No, their gazes flicked from her long blond hair to her green eyes then widened on the leopard skin patterned acrylic nails she had treated herself to before the holiday.

'How's the filming going anyway?' she asked a bit too brightly. Still not a word. Their silence was creeping her out. Especially as the entire jungle seemed to have gone quiet too, listening and watching. Again the hairs on the back of her neck tingled.

The men jumped effortlessly onto the rock and stopped a few feet away. Arya was incredibly aware of them towering over her, of her nakedness, and of their hard, fit bodies.

The one with the jaguar head reached out and touched her hair.

'Hey!' She jerked away and tried to stand up but she had moved too quickly in the heat and her head swam dizzily for a second until she dropped back onto the rock. Thankfully he didn't do any more, just trickled her long blond hair between his fingers like liquid silk.

'I take it you don't get many blondes around here?' she asked, trying to lighten the mood.

He cocked his head and turned his chocolate brown eyes on her. A jolt, like an electric current passed through her but this time it was sexual heat rather than nerves that brought her out in goosebumps. God, he was good looking. She hoped he had a decent part in the film and wasn't just part of the crowd. Though maybe not a speaking part; because he did strong and silent really well.

The other man crouched down, staring intently at her. Next moment he reached over and touched her nipple.

180

'Hey!' she protested again, but weakly. He ignored her, rolled the nipple between his fingers till it jumped to attention. His touch was gentle and Arya couldn't help it; she moaned softly, getting turned on despite the weirdness of the situation.

The two men looked at each other and a signal seemed to pass between them. The crouching man put his hands on her knees and gently but firmly pried her legs apart.

'Wait a minute!' Arya protested but he kept up the pressure and she had no option but to open her legs. They both gazed at her gaping pink pussy and she saw their eyes darken as her musky scent reached them. The one on his knees touched her – not her pussy but her blond curls – almost reverently and Arya shivered, getting more and more turned on.

Maybe a quickie with two hot actors in the steamy jungle was an even better memory to play back in Yorkshire.

The men were obviously thinking along the same lines. To Arya's utter shock the one with the jaguar head lifted the animal skin covering his groin and tucked it into his leather waistband. He was completely starkers underneath.

And he had the biggest cock Arya had ever seen. Really. The biggest fucking cock ever. It could have been the model for Big Dick, the outsized dildo that lived in her bedside drawer at home and Dick was *huge*. This cock was only half erect but it was growing before her very eyes, taking on enormous proportions. Arya could barely tear her eyes away to look up at him. He was still holding her hair, staring at it with the same awe with which she was staring at his cock. He felt her gaze and their eyes locked.

Arya felt lightheaded. Again she felt that strange crackling in the air around them and again her skin tingled.

Jaguar man took his cock in his hand. He said nothing but it was clear what he wanted. A blow job. He didn't force the issue, though, just held his cock and waited. Looking at it, Arya's mouth watered. This was the biggest cock she had

181

ever seen and unlike Dick it was warm and pulsing. What would it be like to suck on this?

Nervously she glanced at the second man. He was still staring at her pussy. She knew she was swollen and wet but even so, no man had ever looked at her quite so reverently and she felt a growing buzz of excitement.

It was the heat, she told herself. She also told herself she should get out of the sun but she couldn't move. Didn't want to move. Jaguar man's cock was now at full attention. Long and thick, the head was darkly purpled and aimed at her mouth. She made up her mind. Leaning forward she opened wide and wrapped her lips around him. He tasted salty, smelled of musk and man and something else, some jungle herb that filled her head and her nostrils, making her even giddier.

Even relaxing her jaw she could get little more than the tip of his cock in her mouth but she felt him shudder. Looking up she saw he had closed his eyes, saw his jaw was tensed in pleasure, the veins on his neck, corded. Huge or not, a cock was a cock and men just liked getting them sucked. Relaxing into the task. Arya wrapped her hands around his shaft. She could barely close her fingers at the base it was so thick. And even holding him hand over hand there was still plenty left over.

Sucking on a cock this big would be bliss anywhere; but here in the steamy jungle heat she knew it was an experience she would never forget.

The other man had crept forward, his dark head moving between her thighs. When his tongue found her slick opening and darted inside, Arya jerked in shock almost letting the cock slip from her lips. Almost. As a finger joined the tongue in her pussy she moaned and began to suck again with renewed vigour.

Grabbing Jaguar man's buttocks, she tried to take him deeper but he at least had enough common sense to know her limitations. But she wanted him, God how she wanted to

182

make him come in her mouth. Another finger slid into her pussy and another, stretching her wide and she squirmed, whimpering helplessly as his tongue expertly lashed her clit. She needed both her hands for balance now and she placed them on the hot rock behind her, lifting her hips, offering her pussy to his willing mouth. Jaguar man replaced her hand on his cock with his own, working it hard, jerking himself off into her mouth Arya could see his balls drawing up, hard and tight, swollen with come. His entire body tensed, she could feel his excitement building. But so was hers ... so was hers ...

Her cunt tightened around the thrusting fingers just as Jaguar man wrenched free of her mouth, and she cried out in protest. Next moment though she was crying out again in pleasure as her orgasm ripped through her. Jaguar man was looking down at her, his fist tangled in her hair, his expression avid as he watched her lose control. Their eyes locked again and her entire body was juddering, her face contorted in a pleasure she had no hope of hiding.

She sank back utterly wasted by the best orgasm she'd had in a long time. Both men were on their feet now, looking down at her. Both now sported impressive erections. Arya wished she had the energy to do something about them both. And she would, too. All she needed was a few minutes. Just a few minutes rest then she'd make them feel as good as she felt now

She wasn't getting a few minutes. Gentle but insistent hands drew her to her feet. Her legs felt rubbery, but that was OK, she had two men supporting her. In fact she could see the powerful muscles on their biceps shift and flex as they lifted her.

One of them stepped behind and wrapped his arms around her waist, nuzzling into her neck. Jaguar man was in front of her. Behind him she could see the pyramid shimmering through the heat haze and her mind jumped back to yesterday, the Jaguar King statue with the huge

183

cock.

Casting had done a hell of a job with this guy if he was playing the King.

Completely intent on what he was doing, he lifted her and realising what he wanted, she wrapped her legs around his waist, gripping him tightly. He was going to fuck her while his friend supported her, a position that was far more appealing than losing a layer of skin off her backside on the bare rock.

Excitement and trepidation shot through her in equal measures. She could take Big Dick but only after a lot of foreplay. On the other hand, her pussy was wetter than it had ever been. Could she take all of him? She had no idea. Did she want to try? Hell yes. She looked down at the cock rising up between them, its dark glory resting on her damp curls and all the way up her belly. Despite her eagerness she felt herself tense. He really was huge.

Nervously she looked at his face. He looked back, as though awaiting permission. Still not a word.

Breathlessly, she nodded.

He slid his fingers into her pussy and released a flood of moisture, slicking his cock with her juices, before pushing against the entrance to her body. There was resistance and Arya wriggled, panicking slightly. But next minute the smooth, satiny head slipped in. Pleasure burst through her and they both watched as inch by inch, his cock disappeared inside her.

Her panic receding, Arya began to relax. Wrapping her arms around his neck, she shifted her balance to him and he supported her easily. Slowly, unbelievably slowly she began to take even more of his cock. Only her bodyweight and gravity controlled the delicious slide as he stretched and plundered her. Down, and down she slid, biting her bottom lip against a pleasure that was almost painful in its intensity.

He felt huge inside her; she had never been so stretched. Her head lolled on his shoulder and she was panting hard but she had done it. She had taken him all!

Left to her own devices, Arya would have stayed right there. In fact she could have stayed there for the rest off her life but she had forgotten all about the other man. Or she had until she felt something pressing against her bottom. Her head whipped up but Jaguar man held her gaze. He nodded soothingly, as though telling her it was OK to let his friend explore her backside.

Slowly Arya begun to relax again, to enjoy the new sensation as a finger gathered her own juice from her pussy and stroked it over her puckered opening. And then she felt his cock press against her …

Excitement spiralled through her as she realised what he was going to do. And then there was nothing but sensation, as the second cock pushed past her resistance and eased inside her.

Arya had felt stretched before, but that was nothing to what it felt like to have two cocks invade her. As Jaguar man thrust forward, he pushed her back onto the second cock. As the second man drove forward in turn, he impaled her on the first cock. Gently at first they rocked her between them, back and forth. As her moans grew louder they thrust harder and faster, always in rhythm, keeping the beat until the only sounds were Arya's increasingly loud cries.

It was beyond anything she had ever imagined. Two cocks, two men fucking her, their movements no longer gentle but out of control, frenzied and primal while the jungle birds drowned out her cries. And then she was coming, her body splintering apart, coming back together and dissolving again instantly as they fucked her and she was screaming, crying like an animal, writhing uncontrollably on the twin cocks that hammered her.

Jaguar man gasped, his mouth opened and his cries joined hers as she felt his huge cock pulse deep inside her, filling her with his come, jet after jet of hot liquid filling her cunt. And then the second man was coming too and his cries joined theirs. The parrots in the trees above rose in one protesting flock, adding their squawking complaints.

Arya must have slept. Or maybe she lost consciousness. But when she next opened her eyes she was alone on the rock. The pyramid still towered over everything: the animals and birds had returned to their chatter, voices shrill and agitated at the disturbance. Slowly she sat up but there was no sign of the two men.

Her skin was pink and she knew she had been in the sun too long but she didn't regret a moment. Sliding off the rock she eased into the water, swimming naked, cooling her skin, washing away the signs of sex. Hearing a splash she turned quickly. Under the overhang of the rock the cenote was black and deep but ripples disturbed the surface of the water. Arya waited, staring at the black depths for a long time but saw nothing that could have caused the disturbance. Finally she waded to the edge and climbed out.

The minibus was just arriving as she reached the hotel and she waited to greet her friends.

'How was the film set? See anybody famous?'

'No. It was crap. It was all a decoy. The filming was at another ruin near Mexico City. They wanted to keep the crowds away so they let on it was here.'

Arya felt the hairs on the back of her neck stand up. 'So, no actors?'

'No actors, no extras, nobody. Just a lot of disgruntled press and tourists. What about you? You obviously weren't sunbathing. In fact you look like you've seen a ghost ...'

The Liberation of Paris
by Sylvia Lowry

Paris is freedom, I imagined as I tossed John's final correspondence into the Seine. I expected that it wasn't the first breakup letter to be discarded into the waters off the Île Saint-Louis, and as the envelope vanished beneath the Pont Louis-Philippe, I thought of the graves of star-crossed Abelard and Heloise in the Père Lachaise cemetery, a mile away from where I stood. Of course, Abelard had been castrated – if only John had met such a dishonourable fate.

Now I proclaimed my emancipation, striding along the Quai d'Orléans as my liberation became absolute. I had left John behind in Minneapolis, and had been living in a tiny apartment on the Rue Orlotan in a state of world-weary boredom for three months, desperately attempting to write, and now a new and delectable phase of my life had begun; I imagined blissful fireworks detonating over the Eiffel tower as I navigated the grand Boulevard Saint-Michel before finally crossing from the Luxembourg Gardens to the Place Odéon. The windows of the alleyways seemed to tremble with excitement, poised to release an uncontainable secret realm, a subterranean current of yearning and subversion.

I decided to seat myself by the Théâtre de l'Odéon to rest, and I noticed that a performance of Moliere's "Tartuffe" had ended. The audience dispersed and the entire plaza descended into calm as I lit a Gauloise, taking an exhilarating drag.

'You should light a strong cigarette with confidence!' I

heard a man's capricious voice, accented in French, followed by a slowly emerging silhouette.

'*Bonsoir*!' I awkwardly exhaled, briefly coughing. 'But you're speaking English – how could you tell I'm American?' He wore a light gray jacket over an open shirt and I could view his face as it emerged from shadow, finely lined but young; I estimated that he was in his early thirties, but I always questioned my ability to draw firm truths from fleeting details.

'You have a certain aura – the North American in Paris with artistic aspirations. I can't really explain it. *Possiblement* it's your beret?' His voice registered a note of hilarity and concern.

'I love to embrace clichés …' I smiled as I removed the hat, defiantly tossing it to the ground. 'And believe it or not, I *am* trying to be a writer – you've read me well. I'm a newly single woman in pursuit of a timeless formula.' I idly kicked the discarded hat. 'But I have a little problem.'

'*Un problème*?'

'My work is going nowhere – I have writer's block.'

The man placed his hands in his pockets. 'I understand. I'm also an artist. Perhaps I can assist you.'

'Assist?' I laughed inwardly, instinctively skeptical.

'Assist with your writer's block, of course. I have a suggestion. We exchange our arts. You tell me the story you are trying to tell and I sketch you at the same time.' He smiled. 'Consider it an exchange of … aesthetic gratification.'

'How charming …' I smiled, contemplating the situation with mischievous irony. 'I should warn you, the story is maybe a little … indecent.'

He laughed. 'Well, as Picasso says, where it is chaste, it is not art.'

'Why the hell not?' I smiled and stood readily. 'Lead on, *ami*.' I smiled and stood, intrigued by this sudden and enigmatic request, my hands trembling as we walked across the plaza. The bell on the clock tower in the Luxembourg Gardens rang, startling me as my cell phone vibrated in tandem; glancing furtively, I noticed a text from my roommate, Maggie: *"Amelia, will you be late"*. Smiling, I turned off the device.

He opened an ornate door and we ascended an iron stairway, progressing further down a hall and into a small apartment, the space dominated by two large chairs, one positioned before a bed. On a table, a series of drawings lay arranged in a scattered pattern, surrounded by paper, pens and brushes. One caught my eye as I admired the contours of a female nude, sketched in a vaporous style, reclining suggestively.

'*Voilà – le studio.*' We remained silent for a moment; the austerity of the space invoked the stasis of a dream.

He gestured to the chair. 'Perhaps we can begin.' I seated myself as he reached for a blank sheet of paper and began to sketch, executing an outline composed of ethereal lines. 'Now tell me the story you are trying to write.'

I cleared my throat, summoning my courage. 'The story is about a woman who is lonely and is seeking new lovers.' I paused. 'I'm alone …' I coughed inelegantly. 'Excuse me, I mean *she* is alone for the first time in years and wants new experiences. She imagines embracing life in a new city. Paris, of course. And she wants to, if I may be so indecent …'

'Yes, go on.' He continued to sketch diffidently.

'She wants to … fuck new men.' I spoke in a soft decrescendo, my voice trembling. 'And she finds herself on an evening like this … with a promising conquest … She imagines teasing a cock, licking it, salivating on it, slowly embracing its contours before fucking …' I swallowed nervously. 'She becomes so excited by the thought that she compulsively begins to …' I inhaled deeply. 'She begins touch her clit gently, then …'

'Please demonstrate.'

I became more aroused as I focused my eyes on the drawing suspended near the door, its volatile contours exploding from the wall in ecstatic release. I moved my panties downward, releasing the garment from my waist and pulling it to my knees and started to finger my pussy in a circular motion; I stroked harder and my cunt contracted reflexively around my finger. 'Shit … it feels fucking amazing. God, I love … I mean s*he* loves playing with her pussy.' I raised my dress further, extending my finger more deeply into my snatch, sensing my clit and labia swelling, consumed by a blush that spread into my inner thighs.

'Continue. Tell me more.' He continued to sketch with startling discipline and concentration, looking downward.

'God, her finger almost feels like a nice hard cock. Not that she can remember what it's like to have a cock inside her.' I closed my eyes, imagining my creative impasse vanishing. A new emboldened sensibility had emerged, a potent artistic impulse materializing as my pussy shuddered, an unendurable craving forming itself in my nipples; I felt the shadow of an orgasm emerge and retreat and I grasped my neck impulsively, tendons rising.

'And next?'

'Hmm …' Glancing at my neckline, sunburned and covered with a patina of sweat, I contemplated my breasts, still clothed, nipples plump and erect; I felt a distant regret for my vulnerability and legacy of unconsummated efforts. But as I turned my eyes to the artist, I became further emboldened.

I beckoned insistently. 'She summons her consort … she wants to fuck and needs immediate attention.' I extended my lips, first striking tentatively at the intersection of his cheek and neck line, then greeting his mouth in a more confident assault, first absorbing the lower lip as I inserted my tongue, then compulsively licked his neck, biting gently, tracing light stubble as I raised my dress and cast it to the floor, my tongue plumbing his ear in a circular motion.

190

'Let's accelerate this little tale, shall we?' I had become impatient with the leisurely intellectual pretence of our game and unceremoniously unzipped his trousers, voraciously grabbing his pulsing erection. 'Let's release your French cock. Lovely, *ami*.' I insistently grasped the base of his shaft, stroking its length, relishing its palpitations as I guided him to the edge of the bed, where I leaned onto my shoulders and removed my bra.

'I have a confession – I've never had a Frenchman suck on my nipples.' He paused, briefly uncomprehending. 'Let's see if you can do it.' I could feel the night air cross my tits, imagining a release from a rigid containment as he bent and sucked on them, licking my swollen aureoles, I could imagine a classical symmetry emerge, an image of ancient beauty honored by the intensity of his tribute, envisioning myself as the emboldened statue of Nike of Samothrace at the Louvre, brazenly propelling my tits into his face.

'Suck harder on those ripe American tits – don't be afraid.' He responded, lightly compressing my left nipple between his teeth, a sensation of uncontainable energy rising from the back of my throat as I grasped his hair insistently, pulling him towards me as he extended his attention to my thighs, flicking his tongue in rapid horizontal motions, slowly rising towards my pussy as I anticipated his entry.

'Don't tease me. Fuck me with your tongue. Stick it inside me.' I leaned back and whispered inarticulately as his tongue, rigid and extended, fully entered my snatch, gyrating as it probed the wet opening, then retreating as he licked slowly from bottom to top, pausing to encircle my entire vulva in a whispering caress. 'Fuck, that feels good. Spit on that fucking pussy.' He generously salivated on command, drenching my clit as he deposited a delectable stream of moisture onto my pussy before licking feverishly in a repeated, vertical assault.

'Goddamn ... I'm coming all over your fucking tongue.' As he fellated me, I could feel the beginning of an orgasm rising from the depths of my pussy, my lower body trembling ardently before the sensation faded as it neared its apex; in the following moment, newly inspired, I grasped his cock again.

'I have a little request. *Une petite service …*'

'*Quoi*? What is it?'

'May I please …' I winked, trembling. '*S'il vous plaît* …wrap my lips around that nice French cock?' Rather than wait for an answer, I impishly inhaled his shaft into my mouth, relishing his erection as it slid gracefully across my lips and tongue. He appeared to be lost in a state of diverted concentration and as he clenched his eyes in determined pleasure, I saw an intense, communicative sympathy emerge, a sensation expressible only in a filthy tête-à-tête of the flesh.

He gasped and uttered '*Merde*,' his ass shuddering as I salivated on his cock, compelling me to imagine that I was devouring the energies of Paris while inhaling his shaft, consuming the filthy essence of the City of Light. My tongue sensed the powerful, sanguine pulse of the *parisien* as I returned to his trembling head and wrapped it in my tongue. But I felt that I could not sustain the motion; an overwhelming sensation, a relentless craving shuddered through my pussy, assaulting my nipples and throat.

'Another request, *ami*.'

'*Quoi*?'

'I want to feel that lovely cock slide into my pussy. *Baise-moi!*' Spreading my legs, I observed the shadow of a wayward cat flicker against the wall and playfully uttered, 'Meow,' as I sensed the first thrilling contact of his cock, the head grazing my engorged clit as my ass convulsed in pleasure, puckering ecstatically as his shaft made its rousing entrance into my pussy. I'd always loved the first moment of penetration, the instant when all the niceties of foreplay are done and an energetic fuck can finally commence. But as the distant cat yawned and twitched its tail, I could feel that only the minutest length of his cock had begun its sublime journey inwards. Wrinkling my brow in impish protest, I whispered, 'Mmm, let's have a little more, shall we?'

'*C'est bon*?' I could hear him panting urgently and he thrust to a slightly greater depth, unleashing a delicate, sloppy sound as his shaft caressed my sodden clit.

'Shit. Slide it all the way in, *homme*.' Following my command, he dutifully thrust his hips and ass forward and penetrated me to his full length. I could sense his swollen head probing inquisitively, releasing a deluge of stimuli, my nipples engorging as he grabbed them ferociously. 'Well, well … your cock fits me perfectly.'

'*Mon dieu*,' he muttered, aspirating, arching his head backward, exhaling ferociously.

'*Mon dieu* is right …' I can tell you're fucking turned on.' He paused as I felt his cock convulse rapidly inside my pussy, already nearing orgasm as he whispered imperceptibly in French, closing his eyes as he licked my ear, as if to avert an impending detonation. 'Every stroke feels like you're about to explode inside me.' I could feel his erect nipples unite with my own engorged tits, and as he resumed his thrusts, I watched the shaft as it entered into my pussy, relishing the vision of his pulsating cock disappearing into the trim hair of my cunt. I closed my eyes as he fucked me, imagining a virile and intrepid presence, a Victor Hugo character come to life, a filthy Jean Val Jean of the boudoir.

'Oh, shit.' Abruptly, my pussy contracted forcefully as the frottage of his shaft against my clit intensified. 'Your cock is making me come. Damn … damn …' My unfinished story, my failed literary endeavor, flickered again into life as I thrust my hips upwards to enhance the pressure of his cock against my pussy, my body contracting and trembling as I propelled myself roughly against him, complementing the angular friction of his body, the sensation inundating my mind like a descending wave. In literary cliché, wasn't an orgasm always described as a wave?

'Fuck, fuck, fuck.' I abandoned the polite world of thoughts, phrases and sentences, reflexively collapsing my thighs together as I came, inspiring him to thrust harder and more rapidly, watching his erection as it plumbed my contracting pussy, transfixed by its insistent motion, yielding to the gratification of his anonymous cock. I imagined a hallowed state of complete vulnerability and exposure; his head, still engorged, invaded the full interior of my sodden cunt as the shutters of the room moved in the wind, as if they were connected sympathetically to the trembling movement of the bed. I could hear a delirious, rhythmic soggy sound, the delectable, accelerating friction of flesh striking flesh.

I saw the dim lights of apartments outside and wondered how many in the expanse of nocturnal Paris were fucking. Were any fortunate *parisiennes* savouring a hard cock with my same sense of renewal and discovery? But then my thoughts were interrupted by the deliciously dirty sight of the artist's glistening, convulsing ass, reflected in a mirror, propelling itself into me, tensing and relaxing in a ferocious cadence, perspiring frantically – the whole vision excited me, making my clit swell further as I constricted my legs around his back.

'Damn I love your cock … your cock in my pussy … your fucking French cock.' I muttered dirty banalities, imagining that I had prepared years for this event, my life's disappointments finally allowing me to consummate a vigorous fuck in confidence. And as he inserted the full length of cock into me, I reached downward to caress his contracting scrotum as he thrust forward, relishing the contours of his balls and the exclusivity of its shape, the small variations that distinguished it from my few conquests of the past. Small rivulets of moisture descended my thighs and ass as I thrust upwards to meet him.

'Keep fucking my pussy. *N'arrêtez pas!*' First biting his neck in affection, I proceeded downwards, sucking his

194

nipples, drawing the hardened teats fully into my mouth, looking into the exposed purity of his eyes as he fucked me in hard ripostes, his face radiating a feral benevolence in the midst of the feverish moment.

'Damn. *Qui c'est*? Who are you?' He glanced away and I realized I didn't know him, but he embodied real life, a carnal world outside writing and abstract thought, an image of action and impulse. As we fucked, I surrendered to pure fancy, savouring the delicious friction inside me, grinding my hips against him, my clit responding to the insistent movement, a crescendo stirring as he cried out and withdrew, his entire shaft quivering.

'I want to see you shoot your load – it fucking turns me on to watch a man come. Let's see the payoff of your labours, *mon homme*!' As if in response to my utterance, I witnessed a surge of moonlight cascading through the shutters as a magnificent arc of spunk erupted from his trembling cock; he jacked off to hasten his climax, buckling forward to match the force of his orgasm, a warm spray of semen travelling in a sloppy crescent as his load crossed my nipples, tracing my midriff to my clit, still distended and aroused. I placed my index finger inside my pussy, still soaking, caressing myself until another violent upsurge returned, the climactic tremor engulfing my torso as I maniacally clutched the sheets.

'Let me sample that come, *chéri*. It looks fabulous.' I leaned downwards, extending my tongue, tasting the fine rivulet of spunk that lingered on the head of his cock, gently absorbing a droplet into my mouth as I closed my eyes. A new, ineffable sensation had arrived, my inhibitions evaporating, my writer's block escaping to the window and ascending to the sky beyond the Place Vendôme.

I looked towards his sketch, deposited on the floor, my startlingly detailed and nude figure appearing as a network of ecstatic lines. In the drawing my eyes lay closed, an image of serene meditation. Outside the window, I could see the three colours of the French flag illuminated and flapping in the breeze, evoking the motto of my new home: *Liberté, égalité, fraternité* ...the timeless values of liberty, equality and fraternity.

I leaned back, watching his cock as it regained its quivering erect state, filling with ardent new blood. I imagined a flag unfurling in my honor.

À la liberté!

Après-Ski Adventure
by Peter Baltensperger

When Ursula asked Anthony if he would like to see her exercise room, he naturally pictured a small home gym with the usual equipment of the kind many people have. He wasn't one for exercise equipment and gyms himself, so the idea didn't excite him to any great extent. Yet it was obviously the invitation he had been looking for, especially as he had been fantasising about her ever since he saw her the first time.

Little did he know that her idea of exercise was completely different from his and that he was much closer to fulfilling his fantasy than he realized. Never in his wildest dreams would he have imagined her in connection with the kind of sex she was about to introduce to him.

Anthony was vacationing in one of the luxurious ski resorts in the Swiss Alps for a couple of weeks, and Ursula was one of the receptionists in the alpine hotel where he was staying. She was a beautiful young woman with an amicable smile, an engaging personality, and a tantalizing body. Her attire was always very chic with skin-tight pants and revealing tops accentuating her full breasts. Her auburn hair was tastefully streaked and fell in soft waves down to her shoulders. She was a true woman of the mountains he admired so much, firmly rooted in her environment yet also enigmatic and alluring. And she always found time to chat with him when he passed through the lobby.

After three days of gorgeous weather and excellent

skiing, a storm front moved through the mountains and pretty much closed all the slopes. In the afternoon, after spending the morning in his room reading, Anthony went down to the lobby to find something to do. He was very pleased to find Ursula sitting behind the front desk, so he went up to her and they started chatting. Her replacement arrived at the end of her shift and she started packing up her things. Anthony decided it was time to do something.

'Could I interest you in going out for supper with me?' he asked, wondering how seriously she had been taking their casual encounters in the lobby.

'I would like that very much,' Ursula agreed with a big smile on her face.

They went to one of the elegant restaurants on the main strip of the town next to the hotel and had one of those incredible dinners the Swiss know so well how to prepare and serve. They ordered the house specialty of the restaurant's famous and absolutely delicious potato rosti covered with a generous amount of tender veal strips in a delectable wine and cream sauce. Anthony ordered a plate of escargots in herbal butter and a bottle of Riesling from the Valais wine-growing region and they resumed their pleasant conversation until their dinner arrived. It was then that she asked him if he would like to see her exercise room, and of course he readily agreed.

Once they completed their dinner with an excellent cup of coffee and some delicious pastry, they braved the weather outside and hurried through the thickly falling snow and the bitter wind, laughing as they braced themselves against the driving storm. Ursula lived in a pretty little chalet on the outskirts of town overlooking one of the slopes, a small treasure in a blistering day. They brushed the snow off each other on the porch and took off their boots on the dry mat in front of the door. Then she took him into her cozy home, her face flushed from their brisk walk, her bright eyes sparkling with excitement.

'Downstairs,' she said. 'Come, I'll show you.'

She took his hand and led him down the stairs where she opened a door and flicked on the light. The room was bathed in a soft glow from some invisible sources and he peered inside. He couldn't believe his eyes. There were no exercise machines or weights or anything like that. Instead, one wall was equipped with metal rings and leather straps. The wall across the room was completely covered in mirror tiles making the room look twice as large and reflecting everything inside. One of the short walls was full of shelves with all kinds of leather gadgets and implements neatly arranged. A large wooden table with a padded top stood near the fourth wall, leather straps hanging from the top all around.

'Well,' Ursula said. 'What do you think?'

'Interesting,' was all he could say. He didn't know what to think. The whole thing was so totally unexpected and seemed to be so completely out of character for her, yet there they were, in a complete dungeon all her own. He had never seen anything like it in his life.

Ursula laughed, gleefully. 'You don't sound very convinced. Just come in. You'll get used to it in no time.'

'Do you use this often?' Anthony wanted to know.

'Quite regularly,' Ursula said lightly. 'Mostly on weekends. I have some friends.'

She shut the door and started to take off her clothes. He could only stare at her as she quickly uncovered her body, completely at ease with herself. She was even more beautiful naked, with a slender, well-proportioned body and deliciously firm breasts topped with big, light brown nipples. She had long, shapely legs crowned by a carefully trimmed dark triangle, and a tight little behind. He couldn't take his eyes off her.

She knew very well he couldn't, but she just laughed again, teasingly this time. 'Come on,' she chuckled. 'Stop staring and take off your clothes already!'

He tore himself from his reverie and began to undress, still staring at her in wonder and admiration. She was staring at him just as much as he was staring at her, although she probably wouldn't have admitted it. Her face was serious as she watched him take off his clothes, but her eyes kept sparkling delightedly. By the time he pulled down his briefs, his penis was erect and hard from seeing her naked like that. Everything was so much better than any of his fantasies.

She chuckled again, took a step towards him, and reached for his penis, tugging at it a couple of times and smiling her bewitching smile. 'I see you're ready,' she said. 'That's good, and I'm glad. So let's get started, shall we?'

He just wanted to grab her breasts and put her down on the carpeted floor right there and then. She was so hot and tempting in her sleek nudity; he ached to have her wrapped in his arms and feel all that beauty against his body, but she obviously had other plans.

To his utter disappointment, she took him by the hand again and led him through the room to the wooden table. 'Lie down,' she directed him.

'Really?' he asked. 'On here?' He wasn't at all sure where this was going to lead and just what exactly she had in mind. All he knew was that she was incredibly sexy and he was alone with her in her chalet.

'Yes, really,' she said.

Somewhat reluctantly but also rather curious and strangely excited and aroused by her commanding demeanor, he climbed up on the table and stretched out. The padding was very comfortable, making him feel somewhat more at ease.

'Now what?' he asked expectantly yet also dreading what she was going to say.

'Now I'll tie you up,' she said, lightly but firmly, her pretty smile spreading across her face.

'You're kidding!' he burst out. His whole body tensed.

He could feel his jaw tightening, his arms and legs stiffening on the padded surface. What was he getting himself into?

She obviously sensed his unease, for she put her soft hands on his chest and started to rub him lightly, gently. 'Just relax,' she said quietly in her melodious voice, her words soothing, very calm. 'Don't worry, I won't hurt you.'

'Are you sure?' he said, still wondering what this whole evening was all about.

'Promise,' she said. 'Just lie still and let me do this. Please?'

'Oh, all right,' he concurred. 'Just tell me what you're going to do before you do it so I can prepare myself.'

'No problem,' she said. 'I'm going to strap you to the table with the leather straps. If you lie still, you won't feel a thing. Just don't make any sudden movements.'

With that, she reached for one of the straps fastened to the side of the table and tied it around his wrist to secure his arm, then another one around his ankle to put his leg in place. She walked around the table and tied his other wrist and ankle. He flexed his arms and legs only to find that he couldn't move them, although the straps didn't hurt, just as she had said.

'Don't move,' she warned him, rather unnecessarily. 'You'll only hurt yourself.'

She placed a long leather strap across his chest, another one across his hips, and a third across his thighs. Then she walked back over to the other side and tied up the three straps expertly against the opposite edge of the table. He couldn't move at all any more. He almost panicked. He had never been immobilized like that by anyone. A fly at the mercy of a spider? He shuddered.

'Are you sure you know what you're doing?' he gasped. 'This is getting rather scary, you know.'

'Don't worry,' she said, still very quietly, soothingly, very sure of herself in everything she did and said. 'If you really don't like this or you get too scared, just tell me and

I'll untie you right away. But I would really like it if you'd let me do this, all right? We'll get to the good stuff in a minute.'

'All right, all right,' he muttered. He didn't want to look like a coward. Besides, it was very arousing, he had to admit, seeing her move around him in her nakedness and doing things to him while he could just lie there and watch her beautiful body float around the table. His penis was twitching quite lustily by then, so he decided to wait and see what other things she was planning to do.

Just as he was wondering about the next step in the unusual procedure, Ursula walked across the room to the shelves and came walking back with a cat o' nine tails in her hand. Anthony couldn't believe his eyes. This was definitely going too far.

'Oh, no, you don't!' he exclaimed. 'I really don't want to do this any more.'

'Please?' Ursula said. 'I told you I won't hurt you. Just let me start and you'll see how good it feels.'

Anthony gave up. She was obviously determined and there didn't seem to be any stopping her. He tried to relax, but his body refused. He felt stiff as a board on the table. His teeth were grinding a mile a minute and his fists were clenched so tightly he was digging his fingernails into his palms. Why was he letting her do this to him? She was a beautiful creature with beautiful breasts and he had been fantasizing about her, that was why. He couldn't help himself. He was completely under her spell.

Then he felt the leather strands of the cat on his body and she was moving them around slowly, over his chest and his belly, again and again, and he finally found himself able to relax. It did feel wonderful, being stroked like that, very sensuous and arousing. He looked up at her and she smiled, contentedly.

'Doesn't it feel good?'

'It does,' he admitted, despite himself. 'What else?'

She didn't answer, just smiled her beautiful smile, let her enticing breasts and her tight body sail past his eyes, and continued running the leather strands over his body. She moved them down to his thighs, and then up to his penis, and he just about cried out with the incredibly exciting sensation. She kept brushing her implement over his erection, over his balls, back down to his thighs, back up to his penis, teasing him, stimulating him, driving him to distraction. She was really good at what she was doing and he was definitely enjoying himself.

She moved her strands back up to his chest, lifted them up in the air, and let them come down on him. He tensed again, involuntarily, but it didn't hurt. She lifted the cat up again and brought the strands back down, a bit harder this time, and then again, still a bit harder and still he didn't mind. Her strokes were beginning to hurt, but only slightly and in a very pleasant and arousing kind of way. She still had the same contented smile on her face and was obviously enjoying herself.

The more she hit him, the more excited he felt. There was something very sensuous about a beautiful woman wielding a whip, about the slapping noise of the leather on his bare skin, about the whole sensation that became more stimulating and pleasurable than painful with every stroke. He definitely hadn't expected this, and he realized that he was enjoying himself more and more. As was she, quite obviously, judging from the delighted look on her face and the sparkle in her eyes. He hadn't known that any kind of pain could feel this good, so luxurious, so arousing and invigorating.

The whip began to move downward from his chest, over his belly again, down to his thighs and his shins and his feet until his whole body was tingling, burning, vibrating from the unusual treatment. His mind was filled with images of her naked body, with the rush of her stimulation, the pleasure of the sensuous pain. What he had dreaded so much he now didn't want to stop, she was making him feel that good with her skilful manipulation of his body, his senses, his mind.

Then it did stop. Ursula put the whip down and came back to stand beside him. She put both hands on his chest again and stroked him lightly as she had done at the start of the session, cooing soothing words, brushing away the pain, slowly returning him to himself. He wanted so badly to take her into his arms, feel her body against his, make them one, complete his fantasy.

Just as he was imagining her lying on the floor with him on top of her, she took the initiative again and climbed up on the table. Straddling him and balancing herself with her arms, she slowly impaled herself on his aching, hungry penis, sliding her swollen lips over his pulsing glans. She pressed her pelvis down on him until he was completely inside her. There she stayed, bearing down on him, flexing her interior muscles. For the longest time, she skilfully played with his erection, smiling down on him with a deeply sensuous look in her eyes.

He was getting more and more aroused, his whole body tingling with the incredible pleasure she provided. He still felt rather strange, being firmly tied down as she had made sure he was, and not being able to react, to touch her, fondle her, dominate her. His entire being wanted her in his arms, yet there was the titillation of the strangeness and the newness of his situation that sent shudders of deep pleasure through his immobilized limbs and up and down his spine, from his stimulated penis to his excited mind.

He pushed his pelvis against hers as best as he could to show her how much he enjoyed her ministrations. She, in turn, started to bounce up and down on him, faster and faster, her breasts swaying above him, so close yet so completely out of reach it hurt. But it felt incredibly good, finally being inside of her, feeling her wet cave sucking him, rubbing him, bringing them closer and closer to the apex of their passion. It wasn't what he had imagined at all, but it was definitely good.

She reached down to put her hand on her pussy and started rubbing her clit as she was bouncing up and down, moaning with pleasure, her eyes closed, her face transformed, glowing with the excitement of the final stage. Her body began to tremble and she rocked through her first orgasm, crying out her satisfaction. She put her free hand on his shoulder and dug her fingers into him in the throes of her release. Continuing to finger herself rapidly, she brought herself to another powerful orgasm and finally collapsed on top of him.

She was breathing heavily, her body shuddering deliciously against his as she rocked through the aftershocks of her orgasms, satiated and content. After a while, she pushed herself up, climbed off him, and untied him from the table. He flexed his limbs until he could move again after the lengthy restraint, then climbed off the table and, finally, took her luscious body into his hands. They sank down on the carpet and wrapped their arms around each other, he finding her beautiful, firm breasts with one hand, her dripping pussy with the other, stroking her and rubbing her with his eager hands until she shivered through yet another screaming orgasm, clinging to him as if she were drowning in her own passion.

He let her lie there for a while until she caught her breath and relaxed her body, then climbed on top of her as she spread her willing legs for him. Finally arriving at the core of all his fantasies about her, he took her breasts into his hands and penetrated her slowly, savoring every moment of the impalement. He gradually pushed himself into her until he filled her completely, then began his long ride home.

Ursula wrapped her arms around his neck and her legs around his hips and pulled him against her as tightly as she could. He lay on top of her with his penis buried deep inside her, twitching against her tight muscles. Holding her trembling breasts in his hands and teasing her nipples with his fingers, he rocked himself to his own orgasm until he was empty and spent, gasping for air and groaning his own pleasure into the room.

After a while, he rolled off her and stretched out beside her to catch his breath and relax his own body from the strenuous encounter. Then they wrapped their arms around each other and fell asleep among the majestic snow-covered peaks of the Alps, totally content and satisfied with each other and themselves.

Reunion
by Kate J Cameron

I walked into the lobby of the Emirates Palace Hotel and stopped, gazing up at the interior of the massive dome that crowned the hotel. As many times as I had seen it, it never failed to take my breath away. At a cost of more than $3 billion dollars, it was the most expensive hotel ever built, and it was amazing. The sun filtered through the stained glass of the dome and cast a golden glow over the ornate décor. As I approached the front desk, I noticed many of the men in the lobby glancing surreptitiously at me. I realised that a bit of my auburn hair was peeking out around the edges of my *khimār*, which I wore as a courtesy to my Arabic hosts. It was difficult enough for some of them to consider me as an equal during the contract negotiations in Dubai, and if wearing a modest silk scarf over my hair made a difference, then I was willing to be accommodating.

But the next round of meetings was not due to start for another week, so I had decided to make the short trip to Abu Dhabi for some downtime. A room at one of the world's most expensive hotels, and its close proximity to some incredible shopping, made this an ideal place to relax and let my mind drift away to something other than indemnities and liquidated damages. I deliberately left the other members of my group in the dark as to my plans, letting only my assistant back in Houston know my destination, and she was sworn to secrecy. I needed some time to myself, away from the same faces I had been huddled with, day after day, for two weeks.

The gentleman behind the front desk greeted me with a smile. In flawless English, he said, 'Good afternoon, Ms Wallace, your room is ready.' He handed me a key and a small envelope bearing the hotel crest and the name *Ms Emily Wallace*. 'You also have a message. Welcome back, and please let me know if I can be of further assistance.'

'Thank you, Samir.' I smiled at him, and then turned, opening the envelope as I walked away from the desk. Suddenly, I stopped short as my brain processed the single word written on the fine linen paper in a masculine hand.

Surprise!

My head snapped up and my gaze swept the room. As I began to turn towards the front desk again, strong arms encircled my waist from behind, and in my ear, a voice whispered, 'Hi, beautiful.'

'Steven!' I whirled around to see him standing there, in the flesh. I was so stunned I could barely breathe. 'Where …? How …?' I tried to take in the sight of him all at once – the face with its strong jaw, tanned and windburned, with white circles around his eyes where his sunglasses rested; the short cropped hair, the lean, muscled chest, the trim waist. His time in Iraq was taking a toll on him – this much I could see also. There were lines around his eyes that had not been there when he left the States six months ago, and a tiredness in his face that spoke of stress and worry. Still, he was here, and though I had yet to figure out how he had managed it, I was not about to complain.

I met Lieutenant Commander Steven Carlisle in Houston during a political fundraiser. He and several other officers from the Naval Air Station in Corpus Christi had come into town to serve as part of the honor guard for the President that night. At one point during the evening, I had stepped out of the ballroom onto a balcony in an effort to dodge a local businessman who, through a haze of alcohol, was determined that he and I were destined to spend our lives together, notwithstanding the fact that he was not yet divorced from his third wife. I had managed to give him the slip as he staggered in the direction of the nearest bar for a refill. With any luck, he would pass out on the way back.

As I rounded the corner of the terrace, I ran directly into a hard chest, which, as it turned out, belonged to Commander Carlisle. Having had enough of the hot crowded ballroom for a while, he, too, had stepped out to clear his head. He kept me from falling, I apologised, we began to talk, and before we knew it, the evening was at an end. His group from Corpus was leaving and as he said his goodbyes, Steven had asked if he could see me again. He had looked so handsome in his dress whites. Having always been a sucker for a man in uniform, I could not refuse, and gave him my card. A large bouquet of flowers arrived at my office the next day, followed by phone calls, emails, and dinner one evening when he *just happened* to be in Houston. Pretty soon, we were finding ways to spend nearly every weekend together, schedules permitting. Steven was kind, intelligent, witty, and at the right moment, he also proved to be a skilled and thoughtful lover.

We talked endlessly about everything and laughed often about nothing, simply enjoying each other. Life – and love – with Steven was *fun*, something that had been in short supply in my ambitious, career-oriented life. His frequent military physicals and my cautious nature had removed the need for condoms, which was a good thing considering how spontaneous some of our lovemaking turned out to be. Never before had a man been able to turn me on with just a look. And once he gave me that look, I wanted him then and there, damn the torpedoes.

Then one weekend, as we lay in bed, in a quiet voice, he told me that he had received orders. In six weeks, he was being sent to join an onshore command in Iraq. I hardly knew what to say. I could tell the connection between us was growing stronger, and this threatened to change everything. The days passed by quickly before he left, and we said our goodbyes without knowing what our futures held. We agreed to keep in touch, and see if this was a relationship that was meant to be.

And now here he was, in front of me. I began to step forward, but I hesitated, mindful of the cultural restrictions. I wanted nothing more than to throw myself into his arms, and kiss him senseless, but although Abu Dhabi was one of the more liberal cities in the Middle East, it was still the capital of a Muslim nation. Steven must have read my mind, because he gave me a grin and looked down at my hand, still clutching the white plastic card key to my room.

'Is that a room key, or have you melted all the colour off your VISA card?'

I was still so surprised to see him that I had to think hard to answer him. 'Yes, it's my room key. I was just going up to my room where this key fits the door to my room …' I stammered, and then finally stopped speaking, realising how ridiculous I sounded. Steven laughed that low, husky laugh that sent tingles down my back.

'Why don't we go upstairs so you can say hello to me in a more … appropriate way?' he said softly, and took the key card from my hand. 'What room are you in?'

I managed to regain some semblance of dignity. 'I am in the East Wing … a Khaleej Suite. Do you have a bag?'

'My bag is with the bellman – I'll let him know to bring it up.' Steven walked over to the front desk, and after a short conversation, he rejoined me. Placing a hand on the small of my back in a possessive manner I had grown to love, he and I walked over to a discreet bank of elevators. He presented my key to the plainclothes security officer standing near the elevator doors, and with a swipe of the card, the man summoned a car to take us to the suite level.

The butler, Massien, was waiting as the doors opened on the 21st floor. 'Ms Wallace, welcome back. Your bags have been transported to your room, and you have an 8:00 p.m. dinner reservation at Sayad.' He paused as Steven stepped off the elevator behind me. 'Aaah, I see you have a companion. Should I make that a reservation for two?'

'Yes, thank you, Massien. Commander Carlisle will be joining me for the duration of my stay, as my guest. Please see that his belongings are brought to my room.'

Massien gave a short bow, and said 'Of course, madam. It will be my extreme pleasure to extend the Commander every courtesy the Palace has to offer. Now, may I show you your suite?'

Massien was his typical thorough self in making sure that every detail of our room met with my approval. Usually I appreciated his kindness, but for once, I found myself wishing he would just shut up and go. Finally, the door closed behind Massien as he took his leave, and I was finally able to do what I had been longing to do since the lobby.

My feet literally seemed to skim the ground as I ran across the room into Steven's arms. I crushed my lips to his, and threw my arms around his neck as he picked me up and spun me around, never breaking our kiss. Finally, we came up for air, and he laughed.

'Now that is a much more appropriate welcome. God, I missed you …' He leaned in for another kiss, but I stopped him.

'Oh, no. Your lips will just keep on missing me until you tell me just how you knew I was here and how you got here and what you are doing here … everything!' I led him over to one of the plush couches in the suite's lounge area, and we sat close, holding hands. I think I was afraid that if I wasn't touching him, he would disappear.

Steven smiled and said, 'I was sitting around, missing you, and hating the fact that you were so close to me, relatively speaking, but not close enough. Before I realised what I was doing, I was headed over to my CO's office, and the next thing I knew, I had a four day pass. I didn't even stop to change out of my work clothes – just threw some stuff in a bag and scrammed. A transport to Doha, a flight across to Abu Dhabi, a cab from the airport and here I am. I called your assistant en route and she told me where you were staying.' He gestured at the opulent room around us and grinned. 'I should have known – only the best and most expensive for my girl.'

Steven pulled his shirt away from his chest and sniffed, making a face. 'And right now I smell like one of the camels I saw on the way in. I need a shower.' He stood, and held his hand out to me, a mischievous look in his eye.

'Care to join me?'

In response, I stood up, facing him. I removed the *khimār*, dropping it carelessly on the floor, and seductively ran my fingers through my shoulder length auburn hair. Steven stood there watching, entranced. Slowly, deliberately, I unbuttoned my blouse, and let the silk slide down off my shoulders, revealing my black lace bra. I heard him take a quick breath, and then he stepped forward, gently placing his hands on my breasts.

'My God,' he said in a ragged voice, 'it's been a long six months.' He leaned over and placed a single kiss on the top of each mound. My skin seemed to burn where his lips touched.

He then proceeded to make quick work of the rest of my clothes, as well as his own. Once he stood naked and magnificent in front of me, and our clothes lay in a pile on the floor, he scooped me up in his strong arms and carried me off to the enormous bathroom, its spacious shower having more than enough room for two.

The water beating down on our bodies from every angle was at the perfect temperature, but we noticed little more than the feel of each other's lips as we kissed with the pent up emotion of a six month separation. Steven slid his fingers down my body, caressing my breasts, before taking my face in his hands and pulling me closer to him for another deep kiss. His fingers ran through my hair like my own had just moments before. He held my head in a firm but gentle grip, while his kisses, which were anything *but* gentle, intensified even more, giving me the first hint of the depth of his need.

My own hands were exploring his body as well, relearning the curves of his arms and back, cupping the firmness of his ass, tracing the path of the hair that ran from his chest down to his maleness. Steven was thinner than I remembered, and leaner as well, but his muscles were more defined. They rippled as he broke off the kiss and pulled me against him for a strong hug, so that my breasts were pressed against that wonderful chest that I loved so much. His erection brushed against the curls between my legs and an erotic shiver ran through me.

We fumbled with the soap, laughing and giggling like children as we lathered up each other's body, taking care to make sure every part, especially the "naughty bits", were adequately cleaned. His hand kept straying to the cleft between my legs, lightly sliding in and out of the wetness there that was not all from the shower. With every touch of his hand, my desire increased even more.

Finally, I sat down on the shower bench and told him to sit down on the floor in front of me, facing away. With a handful of rich smelling shampoo, I began to wash his short cropped hair, kneading his scalp with my fingers. He groaned and his shoulders slumped as I began working out the kinks in his neck and back with my soapy hands. I could feel his tension start to slide away as I continued my ministrations. I used the handheld sprayer to rinse the shampoo away, leaving behind a strong, virile, and, finally, clean man, sitting between my legs.

Apparently he had the same idea I did, because he turned around to face me with a decidedly wicked grin on his face. 'That was wonderful … incredible even …' he said as he leaned up to kiss me deeply. 'But I'll bet you could use some relaxation too …' Without another word, he buried his

213

face between my legs.

The effect on my body of his tongue on my clit was the same as a direct hit of lightning. I immediately tensed, arching my back, and gasping his name, as he slid each of my knees over a broad shoulder and settled me back more firmly against the bench and the shower wall. I rested my hands on his head and luxuriated at the feeling of having a man between my thighs once more. It had been a long six months for me too.

The water beat down on my breasts as he spread me apart and began to use his tongue in the most incredible ways. He licked and nibbled and stroked my most sensitive spots. The heat inside me was so great that I felt like my pussy was about to melt away. My whole body shook as he eased a finger, then two, inside of me. His lips teased my clit while his fingers were sliding in and out of my sex. The sensations of water and heat and his tongue and his fingers were nearly overwhelming. Before I knew what was happening, I gasped out, 'Oh, Steven!' and exploded into a maddening, pulsing, mind-blowing orgasm. I shuddered as my pussy spasmed, gripping his fingers tightly with each convulsion.

Steven drew me down onto the floor of the shower with him, and I lay there in his arms, heart racing, as the water continued to rain down on our bodies. It had been so long since I had climaxed that hard, and my head was spinning.

'I have been tasting your body in my dreams,' he whispered in my ear as he softly kissed my neck. 'I had almost forgotten the deep emerald green of your eyes. You are more beautiful than I remembered.'

'And you are as talented as I remembered,' I murmured, as my fingers drifted down the side of his neck, across his chest, and down into his lap. What I found there was a clear reminder that our business was not yet finished. I'd had my fun – now it was his turn.

I stood up and turned off the shower. Tossing him one of the oversized bath towels, I smiled and said 'I know you are tired from your long trip, sailor. I think you need to go to bed.' Eschewing the plush cotton robes that hung by the shower, we walked naked, hand in hand, to the massive bed just outside the bathroom door.

I turned down the covers, and slid onto the bed, suggestively patting the sheets beside me. He had just started towards me with a wicked gleam in his eye when there was a quiet bell indicating someone at the door.

'Must be my bag', Steven said with a wry grin. 'Hold that thought, I'll be right back.' Grabbing one of the robes from the bathroom, he walked out of the bedroom and across the suite to the front door.

I decided to make the most of his absence, and scrambled off the bed to where my luggage lay. Retrieving several objects from my accessories case, I got back on the bed just as he returned, his garment bag slung over his shoulder. He hung his bag in the oversized closet, and then strode determinedly back across the room to where I reclined on the bed, watching him. He dropped his robe and I admired for the thousandth time the lean body that was now, miraculously, just inches from my hungry eyes.

He paused for a moment and looked down at me, lying naked before him, waiting for him to reclaim my body as his own. His erection was enormous. As if that weren't indication enough of what he was feeling, he made no effort to hide the desire in either his expression or in his voice as he said 'To think that this time yesterday I was living in a modified shipping container at some airbase in the desert, wishing I could hold you for just a single moment. And now this …' He took a deep breath as he lay down on the bed and reached for me. 'God, Em, all I can think about is how much I want to be inside of you …'

I sat up and pressed him back onto the bed. 'Not so fast, Commander. I plan to make this moment last for a while.' I threw my leg across his waist and straddled his chest, my pussy in his direct line of sight. He reached up and stroked

215

my still sensitive clit, and I gasped. But it wasn't my turn any more. Leaning forward until my breasts brushed lightly against his chest, I asked, 'Feeling adventurous?' and I teasingly held up the silk scarves I had retrieved from my bag.

Steven grinned. 'If the adventure involves you naked, then sign me up.' He obediently raised his arms over his head as I loosely tied each of his hands to the bed with the silk scarves, leaving him with limited range of motion but relying on his willing participation to keep him secured.

Then I had him at my mercy.

Straddling Steven's naked body again, I leaned down until my lips were millimeters from his. With my tongue, I traced his lips, nibbling on each one in turn. I nuzzled his neck with my nose, placing small, light kisses along the sides of his jaw and down his neck. I nipped his earlobe playfully, and whispered, 'I am going to drive you mad before I let you fuck me ...' His only response was a soft inhale. Steven's eyes were closed, his lips slightly parted. He seemed to be relaxed but I could see the pulse pounding in his neck.

I left his ear and moved slowly down his chest. I sucked his nipples, first the left, then the right, not hard, but enough to provoke a reaction. They immediately grew rigid. I blew across them and watched the skin goose pimple up around them. He shivered a little, and the hairs on his arms stood up.

'Poor baby ...' I whispered, my lips placing random kisses on his taut belly. 'Are you cold? Do I need to warm you up?' I slid lower down his body, closer to his rock hard cock. I buried my nose in the thick hair that surrounded the base of his shaft, and I felt more than heard another quick intake of breath as my lips brushed the sides of his penis. My fingernails traced a path from the head of his straining cock to the base, up and down. This time, the noise I heard was definitely a groan.

'Em … baby … please …' He pulled against his bonds but could not reach out for me. 'God, I need you … please …'

I laughed and leaned forward, taking the entire length of his rock hard dick in my mouth. Steven's neck arched, his muscles tensed and he gasped. My tongue ran the length of his shaft as I began to tighten my mouth around him. I took his balls gently in my hand and licked them lightly with my tongue, then started in on his cock again from the bottom up, using the warmth of my mouth to drive him wild. I focused my attention again on the sensitive head, tasting the sweet drops of fluid that were starting to form, and that elicited yet another muffled groan from the head of the bed.

With every stroke of my mouth up and down his cock, his body responded. I could feel his dick getting harder and harder as I continued to work every inch of him with my tongue, lips and fingers. He was ready to come, and I was going to oblige him … but not yet.

As soon as I felt he couldn't be far from the edge, I stopped, abruptly. An anguished cry came from Steven's lips and he struggled against the scarves.

I slid up his body and shushed him with a finger to his lips.

'Do you want me, Steven?' I asked.

'Oh, God, yes, Em, yes …'

'Then fuck me, Steven. Fuck me hard. Now.'

With a roar, he slid his hands free of the scarves. Throwing me over on my back, he rose up above me and impaled me, slamming his hardness deep within me. I was wet and ready for him, and I lifted my hips to meet his every thrust, urging him on, nails running up and down his back. The strength of his erection was incredible, as he pounded into me again and again, filling me completely. Steven looked down at me and our eyes met. The raw passion in his beautiful brown eyes was intense. My gentle lover was gone – this man was a warrior and he was going to fuck me until

217

one of us surrendered.

And all of a sudden, the person surrendering was me. Steven shifted ever so slightly and his throbbing dick immediately started stroking directly on my G-spot. My clit was still sensitive from his attentions in the shower, and the combination of the two sensations was more than I could stand. The orgasm washed over me almost without warning, and once more I was spinning, body quivering with the intense climax. My pussy contracted hard around his cock with each wave of pleasure. I knew he could not hold on much longer.

Finally, with a shuddering cry, Steven came too, and came hard, filling me with his semen. He collapsed on top of me, still shaking and breathing hard. I wrapped my arms and legs around him, holding him as close as I could, savouring every moment.

Finally, he rolled over next to me, and lay facing me, his fingers tracing the contours of my face. He smiled at me with sleepy eyes.

'Amazing.'

He kissed me, gently, and pulled my body to his. My head found its familiar spot in the bend of his neck, and I inhaled deeply of his scent, a raw blend of maleness that was uniquely his own. His strong arms wrapped around me and held me close.

And then we slept, bodies entwined, as the evening call to prayer sounded outside our window.